FRANCIS DU[RBRIDGE]

Design for Murder

PLUS

Paul Temple's White Christmas

WITH AN INTRODUCTION BY MELVYN BARNES

COLLINS
CRIME
CLUB

COLLINS CRIME CLUB

An imprint of HarperCollins*Publishers*
1 London Bridge Street
London SE1 9GF
www.harpercollins.co.uk

This paperback edition 2017

First published in Great Britain by John Long 1951
'Paul Temple's White Christmas' first published in *Radio Times* 1946

Copyright © Francis Durbridge 1946, 1951
Introduction © Melvyn Barnes 2017

Francis Durbridge has asserted his right under the Copyright,
Designs and Patents Act, 1988 to be identified as the author of this work

A catalogue record for this book is
available from the British Library

ISBN 978-0-00-824207-7

Typeset in Sabon LT Std by Palimpsest Book Production Ltd, Falkirk, Stirlingshire

Printed and bound by CPI Group (UK) Ltd, Croydon, CR0 4YY

MIX
Paper from
responsible sources
FSC™ FSC™ C007454

FSC™ is a non-profit international organisation established to promote
the responsible management of the world's forests. Products carrying the
FSC label are independently certified to assure consumers that they come
from forests that are managed to meet the social, economic and
ecological needs of present and future generations,
and other controlled sources.

Find out more about HarperCollins and the environment at
www.harpercollins.co.uk/green

Introduction

In November 1951, when John Long published *Design for Murder*, Francis Durbridge (1912–1998) had for many years been the most popular writer of mystery thrillers for BBC radio and was soon to make his mark on television and in the theatre. He remains best known as the creator of the novelist-detective Paul Temple, who first appeared in the 1938 BBC radio serial *Send for Paul Temple*. This was an immediate hit, and led to Paul and his wife Steve rapidly becoming cult figures of the airwaves in the sequels *Paul Temple and the Front Page Men* (1938), *News of Paul Temple* (1939), *Paul Temple Intervenes* (1942), *Send for Paul Temple Again* (1945) and many more. These first five radio serials were all novelised, published by John Long between 1938 and 1948, and most recently reissued in 2015 by Collins Crime Club.

In 1950 there was an interesting development in Durbridge's career with the publication of *Back Room Girl*, a novel that was not based on any of his radio serials. He followed this in April 1951 with *Beware of Johnny Washington*, a rewrite of his first novel *Send for Paul Temple* with various plot changes and a new set of characters, including replacements for Paul and Steve.

From this it appears that in the early 1950s Durbridge was trying to widen his appeal to the reading public, and although his radio serials had made him a household name his books gave him the opportunity to be recognised as more than the creator of Paul Temple. This might also have been insurance against the slim possibility that after five novels some readers might have begun to tire of the Temples, which was a factor that shortly afterwards influenced Durbridge to create a brand of record-breaking television serials that deliberately excluded them.

Design for Murder, his next book, was the novelisation of his radio serial *Paul Temple and the Gregory Affair*. Originally broadcast from 17 October to 19 December 1946, its ten episodes made it the longest Temple serial. The plot was vintage Durbridge, with Sir Graham Forbes of Scotland Yard enlisting Temple's help in investigating the murder of a young woman found in the sea off the Yorkshire coast. As always Temple is reluctant to become involved, until he finds the body of another young woman in his garage and the two murders are linked by the message 'With the compliments of Mr Gregory'.

Given the passion for Durbridge on the continent, several European countries produced their own radio versions. In Holland it was broadcast as *Paul Vlaanderen en het Gregory mysterie*, in Germany it was *Paul Temple und die affäre Gregory*, in Denmark it was *Gregory-mysteriet* and in Italy it was *Paul Temple e il caso Gregory*. The BBC maintained for many years that the original UK ten-episode scripts had been lost, but several decades later a full set was recovered and used to re-create the serial for broadcast in 2013.

In respect of his books, however, Durbridge was keen to continue demonstrating his non-Temple credentials to his readers. So *Design for Murder*, instead of the Temples, features Detective Inspector Lionel Wyatt and his wife Sally who have retired to a smallholding in Kent. Wyatt has left the force with the nagging regret that he never succeeded in identifying and arresting the one person who merited the description 'master criminal', but soon his former chief convinces him that his arch-enemy is again terrorising Londoners with kidnappings and murders. The latest victim is Barbara Willis, found strangled in the sea off the Devon coast, and this has been linked with the disappearance of a policewoman whose body Wyatt later finds in his garage. As with the radio serial, in both cases there are cryptic messages – but this time it is 'With the compliments of Mr Rossiter'. Although almost every character name is changed, the book follows the plot and dialogue of the radio serial very closely and Durbridge's trademark cliffhangers make effective chapter endings.

Rather strangely, there have been two versions of this novel published in Germany. *Schöne Grüße von Mister Brix* appeared in 1961–62 as a serial in the magazine *Bild und Funk*, with yet another change of names as Inspector Richard Grant and his wife Margaret pursue Mr Brix! The slightly later version, *Mr Rossiter empfiehlt sich*, was a direct translation of *Design for Murder* with the Wyatts pursuing Mr Rossiter.

After *Design for Murder* Durbridge went on to produce many more novels. Apart from his standalone title *The Pig-Tail Murder* (1969), they consisted of two series that could always be assured of a devoted readership: the Paul Temple mysteries and novelisations of his phenomenally popular television serials. Paul Temple books continued to appear from 1957 to 1988, of which three were original novels and five were based on his radio serials, and sixteen of his television serials were also novelised between 1958 and 1982. There were two more books that showed Durbridge to have retained the art of recycling long after the 1950s, because *Another Woman's Shoes* (1965) and *Dead to the World* (1967) were both originally Paul Temple radio serials (*Paul Temple and the Gilbert Case* and *Paul Temple and the Jonathan Mystery* respectively) that became non-Temple novels with new characters.

So there can be no doubt that this reprint of *Design for Murder*, a title that like *Back Room Girl* and *Beware of Johnny Washington* has been out of print for more than sixty-five years, is something of an event for Durbridge fans. Similarly, the bonus short story 'Paul Temple's White Christmas' has not been reprinted since its publication in *Radio Times* on 20 December 1946 – the day after the final broadcast episode of *Paul Temple and the Gregory Affair*, which is mentioned in the story.

MELVYN BARNES
June 2017

CHAPTER I

Death of a Policewoman

Ex-Detective Inspector Lionel Mandeville Wyatt sat back and mopped his forehead. It was a warm July afternoon, and he was sitting at his roll-top desk, wrestling with the intricacies of a Ministry of Agriculture and Fisheries form.

Even in his palmiest days at the Yard, Wyatt had been notoriously averse to what was known as desk work, and his hectic life during the war years had not helped him to concentrate his energies upon comparatively minor details.

His gaze strayed to the window and beyond, where the Kent orchards stirred gently in the hot wind, and there was a shimmery heat haze over the corrugated iron roofs of the sheds in a distant meadow. Away to the right he could see the ample figure of Fred Porter in the midst of a field of beans, hoeing slowly and methodically between the rows as if he had been doing it all his life. It seemed hard to believe that only a year ago Fred had been one of the most reliable drivers in Scotland Yard's famous Flying Squad.

Wyatt had been quite surprised at the time when Fred Porter had asked him if he required any help on the small-holding he had bought. The Inspector proposed to retire there at the end of the war, following a series of operations on his right leg that had been badly burnt in a flying accident. Wyatt still limped quite noticeably, and at times leaned rather heavily on the walking-stick he took with him when he went out, but his general health had improved steadily ever since Sally had kept a careful eye on him in this pleasant little house.

He wished Sally were within call now, but she had gone to Faversham on her weekly shopping expedition, and would not be back until about tea-time. She understood more about the poultry on the holding than he would ever begin to learn. With a sigh, he tore a scrap of paper off a scribbling block and tried to work out how many ducks under six months old they had now.

Somehow he could never summon up much interest in poultry; on the other hand, bees had fascinated him right from the start. Sally said he seemed to enjoy getting stung, and he was always ready to spend an hour peering into the hive and watching its thousands of inmates minding their own business as avidly as any respectable citizen.

'It wouldn't surprise me if the little beggars hadn't their own CID,' he told Fred Porter.

'Aye, and MI5, too, I shouldn't wonder,' added Fred, with one of his rare grins.

Wyatt flung down his pencil and crumpled the bit of paper into a ball. He was sure they had more ducklings than that. Maybe Fred would know. Anyhow, it was a reasonable excuse for a little stroll on this very pleasant summery afternoon. He was always restless when Sally was out of the house, and if he didn't have some active occupation he would be positively irritable by the time she returned.

Yes, he reflected, Fred often fed the ducks when Sally was

away; he would have a rough idea. And if the worst came to the worst, they would have to wait until Sally came back, for they certainly couldn't count them at this time of day, when they were foraging round the orchards.

Still frowning at the buff form in front of him, Wyatt reached for his favourite cherrywood pipe and slowly eased tobacco into its charred bowl, trying vainly to recall how many ducklings they had had at the last two hatchings ... and then there was that box of seven-day-olds they had bought at the market ... it was no use. When the pipe was burning smoothly he reached for his stick. At that moment, there was the sound of a car stopping in the short drive at the front of the house. Wyatt stood listening. Surely Sally couldn't be back already ...

Suddenly the old-fashioned front-door bell jangled imperiously. Perhaps it was Sally after all, and she'd forgotten her key ...

Wyatt limped across the room and into the hall. Before he could reach the front door, the bell rang again even more noisily.

'All right, damn you,' he muttered under his breath. Little irritations like this upset him more than most people. He flung open the door, expecting to see one of the ladies of the village collecting for some charity.

But there were two men standing there, and one was a very familiar figure.

'Good lord! Sir James!' murmured Wyatt, blinking in the strong sunlight. For the Assistant Commissioner of New Scotland Yard was one of the last visitors he had expected to see there. Apart from the prompt payment of his pension, Wyatt had received no communication from his former employers for over two years. One after another, several suspicions surged through Wyatt's mind as to why his former chief was visiting him, but Sir James offered no immediate solution to the problem.

He stood there smiling, looking as distinguished as ever in his well-cut medium-grey suit, neat black tie and white shirt. His hair was a shade more sparse around the temples, but he looked much the same as ever to Wyatt.

Sir James introduced his somewhat saturnine companion as Chief Inspector Lathom, who was new to Wyatt, but seemed to have heard quite a lot about him. They gossiped for a few minutes, with Sir James explaining that he and Lathom had been to Sittingbourne and had decided to make a detour on their way back to look up Sir James' former colleague.

'You're just in time for a cup of tea,' said Wyatt, after they had accepted his invitation to come inside. 'Unless you'd prefer a whisky and soda.'

'Just a small one, if you can run to it,' said Perivale. Wyatt looked across at Lathom, who nodded his agreement, and he took three glasses from the sideboard.

Wyatt poured a generous three fingers for each of his visitors, and a smaller measure for himself.

Perivale took a gulp of whisky with obvious satisfaction and leaned back in the large armchair he had taken. 'I could do with that, Wyatt,' he murmured. 'We happen to be on rather a tough job at the moment.'

Wyatt sipped his whisky somewhat cautiously, and ventured no comment, except to say that Sir James was looking quite fit.

'I feel pretty tired,' murmured the Assistant Commissioner. 'I don't mind admitting that this Willis case is taking it out of me.'

Wyatt looked thoughtful.

'Wasn't there something about it in the papers?' he enquired politely.

'There certainly was!' put in Lathom. 'Barbára Willis was quite a well-known Society girl – they don't disappear without trace every day.'

Wyatt shrugged.

'Yes, of course. She disappeared,' he said casually. 'Women are always doing it; they often turn up again.'

'You certainly haven't been reading your papers lately,' said Lathom.

'No, I haven't, as a matter of fact, we're pretty busy here this time of year, and I don't seem to get a chance in the mornings ... what happened about the Willis girl?'

Perivale placed his glass on a small table beside him and leaned forward in his chair.

'On the day Barbara Willis disappeared,' he began slowly, 'she had been to the theatre with her fiancé, a young fellow named Maurice Knight. Afterwards, they went on to the Alpine Club in the Haymarket, leaving there about eleven-thirty. Knight apparently had some trouble with his car, so he put the girl into a taxi. The next time he saw her was four weeks later – when he was called in to identify the body.'

Wyatt whistled softly under his breath, and rammed his thumb hard into the bowl of his pipe, which he had picked up while his former chief was talking.

'Sounds like a cosy little case,' he commented in a non-committal tone.

'Wait a minute,' said Perivale. 'There's plenty more to come. Two days after the Willis girl had vanished, her fiancé received a diamond brooch by registered post. She had been wearing that brooch the night she disappeared; he was quite positive about it. In that registered packet with the brooch was a slip of paper, and on it was scrawled in red ink: "With the compliments of Mr Rossiter".'

'Well, it's a fairly well-known name,' ruminated Wyatt, sipping the last of his whisky. 'Another of these exhibitionist crooks, eh?'

Sir James flicked the ash off the end of his cigarette.

'The point is,' he added deliberately. 'The man who wrote it wasn't named Rossiter. I had a couple of handwriting experts checking that writing for the better part of a week, and they are pretty certain it's the work of your old friend who used to call himself Ariman. That was your last case before you joined up, wasn't it?'

Wyatt nodded shortly. The man who called himself Ariman had been the toughest customer he had encountered, a blackmailer of the most unscrupulous type, two of whose victims had committed suicide. Though the Yard had been very close on the heels of the master criminal, he had used his gang unscrupulously to cover his retreat, and had managed to get out of the country at a time when most of the police resources had suddenly to be diverted to tracing a black market in forged coupons. The police had never seen him, they had no photograph, and his associates had either been sacrificed when he made his getaway, or had contrived to disappear on their own account when there was a depleted staff at the Yard, where they had been secretly relieved to discover that Ariman himself had flown. All he had left them by way of souvenir was a torn scrap of a letter addressed to one of his victims in what was presumed to be Ariman's own handwriting.

Wyatt sat for a few moments deep in thought.

'So that customer's back,' he murmured at last. 'I always

thought he'd be here again one day. I suppose he's run through the packet of money he's said to have taken out of the country with him. Tough luck, Sir James.'

The Assistant Commissioner held up his hand.

'I still haven't finished,' he said. 'What do you think brought us to Sittingbourne, Wyatt?'

Wyatt frowned.

'I haven't the least idea,' he said.

Sir James puffed out a stream of smoke.

'You remember Mildred Gillow,' he said quietly.

'Of course,' nodded Wyatt. 'She worked with me on the Ariman job – smart little blonde – one of the best women police I ever came across when it came to tailing a suspect – next to Sally, of course!'

Sir James could not repress a smile, for the romance between Lionel Wyatt and policewoman Sally Spender had been the talk of the Yard for weeks. Sally had been very temperamental, and it had taken a lot of persistence on Wyatt's part to persuade her to abandon her career for the less exciting duties of the home. In fact, he never ceased to marvel secretly at the manner in which she had settled down to life on the small-holding.

'Sally used to know Mildred Gillow quite well, too,' went on Wyatt. 'Nothing wrong with her, I hope?'

Sir James shook his head.

'She hasn't been too well, lately. Hasn't been sleeping – generally off colour. She was given a few days special sick leave, and was due back on duty two days ago. She spent the leave with an aunt in Sittingbourne, and left there in good time to catch a train to report for duty ... but she never arrived. This morning, her father received a bracelet of hers, with a small slip of paper wrapped round it. Here it is.'

Sir James took out his wallet, extracted a piece of paper and passed it over to Wyatt, who examined it carefully, then handed it back.

'Why pick on this "Mr Rossiter" stunt?' he mused with a puzzled frown.

'He's probably trying to confuse us,' said Lathom. 'When he was over here before, he was known as Ariman – that was a touch of vanity all right, but he left no messages lying around. He's out to keep us guessing, and this "Mr Rossiter" business is one way of sidetracking us. As a matter of fact, there was a petty blackmailer named Rossiter operating when Ariman was last over here, but we know for certain he's been going straight ever since he came out of Wandsworth two years ago. And he was never the type to go through with murder and then advertise the fact!'

Wyatt carefully knocked the ashes out of his pipe.

'So you've been down to Sittingbourne to check up with Mildred Gillow's aunt, I take it,' he said. 'Did you have any luck?' Almost as soon as he had spoken, he felt himself blushing.

'I'm sorry, sir,' he said to Perivale. 'It's no business of mine, of course. But I wouldn't like to think anything had happened to Mildred and—'

'It's all right, Wyatt,' interrupted Sir James, waving aside the apology. 'This matter may well concern you very closely indeed. In fact, you may be able to help us more than anyone – you know this customer better than any of us. It was you who chased him out of the country.' He hesitated a moment, then asked: 'Wyatt, d'you think Ariman knew Mildred Gillow was helping you?'

'Certainly,' replied Wyatt at once. 'He made at least one attempt to get her out of the way.'

Sir James and Chief Inspector Lathom exchanged a significant glance which did not escape Wyatt.

'You think "Mr Rossiter", alias Ariman, has been gunning for Mildred, and that maybe he'll try and settle a few old scores with me?' he demanded with a faint grin.

'That would be yet another confirmation that Ariman and Mr Rossiter are one and the same person,' Sir James reminded him.

'Yes,' agreed Wyatt thoughtfully, 'I suppose it would. But what am I supposed to do about it?'

Sir James shifted rather uneasily in his chair.

'You can listen to the rest of my story, and then give us the benefit of your advice, if nothing else,' he suggested in a tone that carried a hint of mild reproof.

'Of course, Sir James,' said Wyatt at once. 'I'm only too willing to help, but I'm rather out of touch these days. Smoking out bees is more in my line.'

'All the same, something might occur to you ...' Wyatt took Sir James' glass and refilled it. Lathom, however, refused a second glass. When he had returned to his chair, Wyatt demanded with obvious interest:

'Is there anything else about Mildred Gillow, Sir James? Did you find anything at her aunt's place?'

'Nothing of any importance except an empty medicine bottle on the shelf in her bedroom. We took it down to the local chemist, who had made up the prescription, and got him to look up the doctor's name in his book. It was a Doctor G. H. Fraser, in Wimpole Street.'

'Do you know the doctor?'

Sir James shook his head.

'And the prescription?'

'Just a sedative.'

'Then why was the bottle so important?'

'Because,' explained Sir James deliberately, 'a prescription was found on the dead body of Barbara Willis, made out by the same doctor.'

Wyatt thoughtfully smoothed the bowl of his pipe against, the palm of his hand.

'That's certainly a point,' he agreed. 'Have you interviewed this doctor yet?'

It was Lathom's turn to speak.

'I did telephone the doctor as a matter of routine, before we found the bottle, but there was no reply. It'll be my first port of call when we get back to Town.'

'I hope nothing's happened to Mildred,' said Wyatt with a thoughtful frown. 'Sally would be upset; they were great chums in the old days. It's a nasty business all round – isn't there any sign of a motive in the other girl's death?'

Sir James shrugged.

'All I can tell you is that Barbara Willis' body was found at a little Devonshire fishing village called Shorecombe, not far from Dawlish. A Norwegian named Hugo Linder was out fishing with one of the locals, an old chap called Bill Tyson. Linder was on holiday there – I believe he still is.'

'Have you questioned him?'

'Yes, he seems reasonable enough. Both he and the old boy got rather a nasty shock, and I think it genuinely upset them.'

Wyatt nodded absently, picturing the two men hauling at their nets and suddenly revealing the ghastly sight of the dead girl's body.

'Was it death by drowning?' he asked.

'No, the girl had been strangled. The body had been in the water somewhere between five and eight hours, as far as we could judge.'

Wyatt picked up his pencil and began doodling on his scribbling pad. The Ariman case had worried him more than any of his others, and the memories of it disturbed him uneasily. He felt he needed another drink, but dismissed the idea, for he realized it would only upset him on this hot afternoon.

'What about this Norwegian, Linder?' he queried. 'Have you checked up on him?'

'He's all right as far as we can trace,' replied Lathom. 'He's been over here since 1933 – quite respectable.'

Wyatt leaned back against his desk and looked at his visitors speculatively.

'I can see I shall have to start reading the papers more closely again,' he murmured. 'I'll be very interested to follow this case, and I'm sure I wish you luck. Now, if you'd like a basket of strawberries to take back with you ...'

'Just a minute, Wyatt,' interposed Sir James. 'You don't seriously think we've delayed getting back to Town by two hours just to come down here and talk over old times.'

Wyatt could not repress a smile.

'It was good of you to look in and warn me that my old friend Ariman's on the warpath again,' he said pleasantly. 'But I don't think he'll have any time to worry about me now I'm no longer getting under his feet. He never bothered very much about small fry. All the same, I'll be on my guard, and I'll give Fred Porter the tip – you know he's working here?'

He got to his feet.

'I won't detain you any longer, Sir James, if you want to get moving. I can see the inspector is bursting to get back on the scent.'

Sir James made no move to go.

'Sit down a minute, Wyatt,' he said somewhat brusquely. 'I didn't come down here to warn you; I know you are quite capable of looking after yourself. I came here to make a suggestion.'

'I beg your pardon, sir,' apologized Wyatt. 'If I can help in any way to trace Mildred Gillow ... though I'm a bit out of touch lately. She writes to Sally at Christmas I think ...'

Sir James stubbed out his cigarette.

'Mildred Gillow is only one aspect of this case,' he replied abruptly. 'If it's really this fellow Ariman back on the job, we'll need all our biggest guns. And that includes you, Wyatt. I'd like you to come back on the strength as long as Ariman is at large.'

Wyatt shook his head slowly.

'That wants thinking over, Sir James. I appreciate your offer, but I'd have to discuss it with Sally.'

'Where is she?' demanded Perivale impatiently. 'I'll talk to her. We can use her, too – she'll be very useful ...'

'I'd sooner put it to her myself, if you don't mind, Sir James,' replied Wyatt, who was more than a little impressed by the note of urgency in his superior's tone. 'She's out shopping in Faversham, but I'll put it to her the minute she gets back. Of course, we can't really leave this place, but perhaps I could get some help from the Agricultural Committee.'

'I might be able to pull some weight there,' nodded Sir James thoughtfully. 'How d'you feel about getting back into harness?'

Wyatt gave a slight shrug.

'Maybe you won't want me when you've got me. I'm a bit of a crock these days, you know, sir.'

'It's your brain we need; not your legs,' Sir James told him.

'And what about Chief Inspector Lathom?' queried Wyatt. 'How would he feel about having a stranger barging in on his case?'

Lathom's inscrutable features gave no hint as to how he felt, and before he could reply Sir James said:

'You can play a lone hand as much as you like, Wyatt. Or ask for help whenever you feel you need it. It won't be a case of your butting in; Lathom will remain in charge and look after the desk work and keep you *au fait* with the latest developments. We'd like to think we've got you up our sleeve as a master card when things get hot.'

'I'll telephone you as soon as I've had a talk with Sally,' promised Wyatt, and Sir James levered himself somewhat reluctantly out of his armchair.

'Are you sure you won't stay to tea?' asked Wyatt. 'It won't take Fred ten minutes to lay everything on …'

'No, thanks, Wyatt. We must get back at once. There are a lot of things to follow up at that end. I'll expect you to telephone me before this time tomorrow, then we can decide on some plans for you if you care to take on this job. I'm relying on you to talk Sally into it.'

Wyatt accompanied his visitors out to their car, enquiring after one or two of his former colleagues at the Yard, and welcoming this rare opportunity to talk shop, which was not often vouchsafed to him nowadays, for Sally hardly ever referred to the old days. She always believed in living in the present, and all her energies seemed to be absorbed in running the smallholding.

When he had waved goodbye to them, he limped back to the front porch and sank into a deck-chair. He had forgotten all about the form that was waiting to be filled up; instead, his brain was awhirl with the recollections of the Ariman

13

case. He was still sitting there when their ancient but solid coupé drew up outside, and Sally flung open the door.

'Hi there!' she called. 'Wake up and give me a hand with the parcels!'

He got up and went slowly towards the car, taking in her trim figure, with neat blue shirt open at the neck, which somehow made her look amazingly cool even after a six-mile drive and two hours' shopping on a warm afternoon.

'Hallo, Sally ... you're back,' he murmured lamely. 'Have a good time?'

'Nothing special.' She smiled at him ... it was a frank, welcoming smile that shone from the depths of her unusual grey eyes, and was reserved only for her husband.

'What have you been up to?' she wanted to know. 'I hope you filled in that form, and wrote that letter to the poultry food people ...'

'I've had visitors,' he interposed. 'An old friend of yours.'

'So you've done nothing except snooze in a deck-chair. Didn't they stay for tea? And who was this old friend?'

'Sir James Perivale, no less. He had to get back to Town in a hurry.'

Sally puckered her shapely lips into a low whistle of surprise. 'Whatever brought him here?' she wanted to know.

'He was down at Sittingbourne, and thought he'd like to see how we're getting on,' replied her husband evasively, as he gathered up an armful of parcels.

'I'd like to have seen the Chief again,' said Sally. 'How was he?'

'He looked quite fit. Said he was very sorry to miss you, but he had to rush off. The old boy's absolutely tireless. He's busy on a case that Mildred's mixed up in.'

Sally paused in the act of collecting her shopping basket from the back of the car.

'Mildred? I haven't heard from her for some time. What's she up to nowadays?'

'Nobody seems to know,' replied Wyatt. 'You see, she happens to have disappeared. Let's go in and have some tea, and I'll tell you all about it.'

In the kitchen they found Fred Porter, with a face like the rising sun, just pouring out some tea. He stayed long enough to drink one large cup, then went back to hoeing his beans. Fred was a man of few words when his mind was intent upon a job of work, so Sally quickly prepared a tray and carried it into the sitting-room, where her husband had returned to his desk in the corner.

'I suppose you wouldn't have any idea how many ducklings we have under six months?' he enquired.

'Thirty-four,' she replied without a moment's hesitation, pulling up a small table and starting to pour out the tea. 'Now, what's all this about Mildred?'

He told her all about the strange disappearances of the two girls, and of the death of Barbara Willis. But he did not mention the Chief's invitation, for he wanted to clarify the situation a litttle more in his own mind. After tea, he returned to his form-filling, while Sally fed the livestock and did a dozen other odd jobs that had accumulated during her shopping expedition.

Fred came in, washed himself, and cooked his own supper. He had a little room of his own, where he presently retired, and Wyatt suggested to Sally that they might go to the pictures in Faversham, as there was just time to catch the last house.

The main feature was one of those fast-moving American crime epics, concerning the adventures of a tough 'private eye', who found himself embroiled in a chain of bizarre situations of growing intensity, and remaining as tough as ever even when the girl practically threw herself into his arms for the final fade-out.

Wyatt found it quite stimulating, and as they walked to the car park he determined to tell Sally about Sir James' proposition on the way home. But it was not until they had left the outskirts of the town behind, and he was cautiously steering the car through the dusky country lanes, that he came really to the point.

'So that's what was in the wind this afternoon,' said Sally after he had finished. She made no further comment for two or three minutes. The car's headlights picked up a young rabbit which scurried ahead of them for a hundred yards, then suddenly swerved into the hedgerow.

'What d'you make of it, Sally?' he asked. 'The Chief wants you in on it, too – and I told him I wouldn't do anything without consulting you.'

'I'm glad of that,' she replied. 'Because you're certainly not going to do anything. We're not breaking up our happy home for the Home Secretary himself!'

'But wait a minute, Sally,' he began to protest, but she shook her head quite decisively.

'You know perfectly well the doctors said you weren't to go taking chances with that leg of yours,' she reminded him.

'He says he only needs my brains,' he reminded her.

'I dare say he says that,' sniffed Sally, 'but you know as well as I do that if you started in on a case, you'd always be pushing your nose into the most dangerous corners. It isn't fair, Lionel ... just as we've settled down so nicely here.'

Lionel Wyatt sighed. He supposed Sally would have her way, as usual. Not that there wasn't something to be said for her point of view. A woman hankered after a settled sort of home and a husband around, not a man who was gadding all over the country and getting mixed up with unpleasant customers at every turn.

'Well, I won't phone the Chief till tomorrow anyhow. I reckon it won't do any harm to sleep on it,' he said presently, as they came to the familiar turning that led to their little farm.

'Fred's closed the yard gate again, damn him!' muttered Wyatt under his breath. 'He might have left it for me.' He opened the car door and got out to open the gate. After he had done so, Sally saw him leave the glaring cone of the headlights and pick up something from the grass verge beside the road.

He came back to the car and switched on the dashboard light to examine his find. It was a neat lady's leather handbag.

'Is this yours?' he asked.

Sally shook her head.

'I don't make a habit of leaving my handbags at the side of the road,' she replied rather pertly.

'You've left them in all sorts of places,' he grinned. 'Remember that time you left one in the witness box at the Old Bailey?' He fumbled with the clasp of the bag and carefully opened it. The contents gave no indication of the owner; there was a lipstick, mirror, powder compact, a handkerchief, a stub of pencil and a book of stamps. He was about to replace the stamps when something caught his eye and he held the buff-coloured book closer to the light.

'What is it?' asked Sally.

'There's a name scribbled here rather faintly ... "Doctor Fraser".'

'That's the name Sir James mentioned, isn't it? The one they found on the prescription belonging to Barbara Willis.'

Wyatt nodded thoughtfully and snapped the bag shut, pushing it into the cubbyhole at the end of the dashboard. He flicked off the light and drove slowly into the yard towards the disused stable they had converted into a garage. Neither of them spoke again until they were facing the garage doors, when Sally said: 'My turn this time. I can manage the doors now since Fred put the new catch on them.'

He nodded absently and watched her pull open the heavy left-hand door. As the car's headlights penetrated into the garage, he saw her stiffen suddenly. Then she turned, with a look of horror which seemed more ghastly in the strong glare.

'Lionel! There's somebody in there!' she cried.

He leapt out of the car and rushed over to her.

'All right, Sally – all right.' His hand gripped her shoulder and he followed her gaze. Just within the circle of light was a woman's foot. He could see the shape of the girl dimly; she was slumped in a far corner against a large oil drum, just beyond the range of the headlights.

'Stay here, Sally,' he ordered, and went over to the other end of the garage. Five minutes later, he was back.

'She's been strangled,' he said quietly.

Sally caught her breath.

'Who is she?'

Even as she asked, something seemed to tell her what he would answer.

'This will be a bit of a shock,' he said slowly.

'You know her?'

'Yes – it's Mildred Gillow.'

His hand on her shoulder felt her recoil physically as if from a blow.

'Poor Mildred,' she whispered. 'Then Sir James was right – it must be ... Ariman ...'

Wyatt left the car where it was, switched off the lights and closed the garage door. Immediately on entering the house they went to Fred's room, and found him in bed, snoring heavily. With some difficulty, Wyatt woke him and asked if he had seen any strangers about during the evening.

Fred rubbed his eyes and ruffled his sandy hair thoughtfully.

'I've been down in the far orchard most of the time since supper,' he recalled sleepily. 'Didn't see anybody except old Ted Woolley shooting wild pigeons. Why, what's the matter?'

'You're sure you didn't see anybody else?'

'Not a soul,' yawned Fred. 'But there was a phone call for you – not that I could make much sense of it. Some feller said he'd got an important message for you, so I said I'd give it you when you came in. But you couldn't call it much of a message, at least, not to my way of thinking.'

'What did he say, Fred?'

Fred yawned again.

'As far as I could make out, all this cove said was: "Present my compliments to Mr Wyatt. The name is Mr Rossiter".'

It was well after midnight before Wyatt and Sally were able to get to bed. They had had to contact the local police, who had removed the body of Mildred Gillow to the mortuary. Fortunately, Wyatt had been on friendly terms with the constable at the village police station for some considerable time, but even so, the sergeant who came over from Faversham was inclined to query some of his statements. Quite understandably, he found it difficult to believe that Mr and Mrs Wyatt could discover the body of an old friend in their garage without having at least a clue as to how it had got there.

In the end it was Sally who suggested that her husband

should ring up Sir James. The sergeant pricked up his ears, and Wyatt was bound to explain to him:

'She means my old chief at the Yard – the Assistant Commissioner.'

The sergeant was obviously impressed as Wyatt picked up the receiver and gave the familiar number. As he had expected, Sir James had left his office, but Wyatt eventually managed to get his home telephone number from one of the inspectors on night duty, whom he had known slightly some years previously.

When Wyatt broke the news to Sir James, the familiar voice positively crackled, so they could hear it all over the room.

'You've got to come in on this case, Wyatt … you've simply *got* to … and there's no time to lose.'

Wyatt looked across at Sally questioningly. She reached over and took the receiver from him.

'All right, Sir James,' she said quietly. 'You can count us in.'

CHAPTER II

A Lift from Doctor Fraser

At ten o'clock next morning Wyatt and Sally were heading west, bound for the fishing village of Shorecombe. Wyatt had persuaded Sir James that a trip up there was a very necessary item in their plan of campaign.

They found there was no hotel in the place; the best accommodation they could get was at a not unattractive inn called the Silver Fleet, which catered for a certain number of visitors during the summer months. Their room was rather cramped, but very clean, and they both rather enjoyed the friendly atmosphere of the saloon bar down below, where the fishermen mingled with local shopkeepers and a sprinkling of visitors. Wyatt got on well with Fred Johnson, the landlord, a jovial type of Yorkshireman in the early fifties, who was quite ready to discuss the recent tragedy, though he could throw no light on it. He did, however, vouch for the character of Bill Tyson, the fisherman who was with Hugo Linder when they discovered the body.

'I've known old Bill best part of thirty years,' he informed

Wyatt. 'Straight as a line – asks favours of no man. I'd trust 'im wi' me last bottle of Napoleon brandy.'

Wyatt smiled. He intended to see Bill Tyson himself sometime, but he felt now that perhaps he would not learn very much. However, it would be interesting to hear his version of the discovery of Barbara Willis. They were in their room the morning after their arrival, when Fred Johnson suddenly appeared in his shirt-sleeves to announce that Hugo Linder was down below, asking if he could have a word with them.

'You could see him in the back parlour if you like,' volunteered the landlord.

'Thanks,' nodded Wyatt, 'will you tell him we'll be down almost at once?'

They found that Hugo Linder was a typical Scandinavian, with fair hair and Nordic profile, a profile marred only by a slightly twisted nose, which, they learned later, was the result of amateur boxing activities in his college days.

'I got your message, Mr Wyatt,' he began, after introducing himself, 'so I thought I'd come round right away. I've just been reading this morning's paper about the other girl being found, and it seems to me there's no time to be lost.'

Wyatt nodded, and went on to ask him a series of questions about the discovery of the body of Barbara Willis. These revealed nothing new, but they helped Wyatt to get all the details firmly fixed in his mind.

'And what about Mr Tyson?' he asked at length. 'Was he upset when he saw the body in the water?'

'We were both upset. One moment we were laughing and joking, and the next we were struggling to get that girl out of the net.'

Linder spoke perfect English, but there was just the faintest trace of his Norwegian origins in his intonation.

22

'Did you know it was Barbara Willis?' asked Sally.

'No, I hadn't the slightest idea who it was. But Tyson recognized her at once. He had been reading all about her, and her photo had been in his paper for several days.'

Wyatt put his empty glass on the mantelpiece, and said: 'How long are you staying here, Mr Linder?'

The young Norwegian frowned thoughtfully.

'Perhaps another two or three weeks. I am usually here for a month at this time of year – it's my annual holiday. I rent a small, furnished cottage over on Fallow Cliff, not far from Bill Tyson's place. My home, of course, is in London.'

'What part of London?' idly queried Sally.

'St John's Wood.'

Wyatt continued pleasantly:

'I was hoping that Tyson could have come along with you. Maybe I'll walk over and see him later on.'

Linder smiled.

'I'm afraid poor old Tyson does not like answering questions, and he's had rather a lot just lately. You may find him a little difficult to handle, Mr Wyatt. He was quite rude to that other fellow.'

'What other fellow?' demanded Wyatt at once.

'Why the man who came over from Teignmouth. I think his name was Knight.'

'Knight?' repeated Sally. 'Wasn't that the man who was engaged to Barbara Willis?'

'That's right,' nodded Wyatt.

'Then I suppose it was understandable that he should be curious about his fiancée's death,' said Linder. 'He drove over from Teignmouth yesterday morning. He seemed most anxious to know what actually happened when we discovered the body.'

'You say Bill Tyson lives near you at Fallow Cliff?' persisted Wyatt. Linder nodded.

'Yes, just the other side of the bay – about four miles by road. The best time to catch him would be in the evening, I should think.'

'Right. Will you tell him we'll be along about eight-thirty tonight?'

'I'll tell him,' promised Linder, making a move towards the door. With his hand on the knob, he hesitated uncertainly for some moments, then said:

'Mr Wyatt, I read in the paper about your finding the girl in your garage. Do you think she was murdered by the same person who killed Barbara Willis?'

'Yes,' said Wyatt after a moment's pause.

'But it is so horrible!' exclaimed Linder incredulously. 'Two girls strangled in a few weeks! Who would do a terrible thing like that?'

'A man called "Mr Rossiter",' replied Wyatt simply, eyeing Linder shrewdly.

'Mr Rossiter? But who is this Mr Rossiter?'

'That,' said Wyatt confidently, 'is what I'm going to find out, Mr Linder.'

Sally and her husband spent the afternoon in Teignmouth, and after tea they drove slowly round the lanes encircling the coast, with the idea of eventually ending up at Tyson's cottage. Sally tried to follow their route on a road map, but very soon lost herself. Her husband offered neither help nor criticism: he sat without speaking for minutes at a time. Having discovered her bearings at last, she was almost startled when he suddenly asked:

'What did you make of Hugo Linder?'

'He seemed rather a pleasant sort of person, I thought. Though I should say he's on the nervy side. Almost neurotic in some respects. He was pretty het-up about everything, wasn't he?'

'He was.'

Sally switched on the headlights.

'What does he do for a living?' she asked.

'He's supposed to be an architect, I believe. Though I should imagine he has private means.'

They had just passed a small waterfall when Sally imagined she caught a glimpse of a car overtaking them. They rounded a bend and she lost the car in her driving mirror, but on the next level stretch the oncoming car began to overhaul them rapidly. Suddenly, its headlamps snapped on, and Wyatt half-turned in his seat. The car crept up until it was fifteen yards behind them, then seemed content to remain at the distance.

'Why doesn't he go ahead if he's in a hurry?' murmured Sally, who was vaguely annoyed by the headlights in her mirror. 'In any case I wish he'd put those lights out ...'

'Sally you'd better slow down – we're coming to one of those hump-back bridges and the road narrows,' said Wyatt, who had caught a fleeting glimpse of it about two hundred yards ahead. Sally took her foot off the accelerator, but the car behind made no attempt to pass them.

'Why doesn't he go ahead?' demanded Sally once more. It was not until they were about seventy yards away from the bridge that the car behind suddenly put on a spurt.

'Sally, for God's sake, look out! He's trying to pass you!' cried Wyatt.

'But we're nearly on the bridge!' exclaimed Sally desperately.

'Pull over ...'

'I can't! There's no room ...'

They were forced into the side of the road, and as they came to the steep little bridge, the overtaking car suddenly shot in front, leaving Sally no alternative but to steer right into the parapet. The car shot clean through the low wall as if it had been matchwood and took a neat somersault right into the river below. The driver of the other car straightened out expertly, stepped hard on his accelerator and disappeared into the night.

Wyatt was never quite sure whether he completely lost consciousness after feeling the terrific impact of the car meeting the water. He was aware that the car was lying on its side, and that he could feel the steering wheel in the middle of his back. He tried to open the door tilted above him, but the fall had jammed it. The window, too, was stuck. For a few frantic moments he fumbled in the back of the car and eventually found the starting handle.

The water was swirling into the bottom of the car, and Sally lay motionless, with her head against the side window. Desperately Wyatt raised the handle and struck at the glass in the window nearest him. It took him some seconds to dispose of all the jagged edges. Then he lifted Sally as high as he could and tried to gain a footing on the floor of the car.

The sharp sound of breaking glass seemed to restore Sally to consciousness. She opened her eyes and then clutched Wyatt's arm.

'Sally! Can you hold on a minute?' he gasped, trying to steady her. She nodded and took a grip on the handle of the sunshine roof, which had also jammed. In a few seconds Wyatt managed to clamber out of the window. It was not easy, however, to stand with water well above his waist and

26

help Sally to follow suit. After this was accomplished they had to cling to the car for some minutes to recover.

Meanwhile, Wyatt surveyed their position. It was lucky that the river was running low, and was no more than five feet deep in the centre of its channel. Nevertheless, the current was strong under the narrow bridge, and he had considerable difficulty in getting Sally on to the bank. They lay there exhausted for quite a while; then Wyatt became conscious of his saturated clothes, for the night was appreciably cooler.

It was starlight now, and they could just discern the outline of the car in the middle of the stream, with the fast-flowing waters surging around it.

'What time is it?' asked Wyatt at last.

'No idea. My wrist-watch has stopped.'

There was no sound of life, apart from the gurgling waters and the occasional rustle of some animal or bird in the bushes that grew thickly on the bank.

'This is a very quiet road,' mused Wyatt. 'No one has been along here for nearly half-an-hour.'

'Lionel, did you see who was driving that other car?' asked Sally nervously.

'No,' he replied quickly. 'Did you?'

'I couldn't see anything – what with the glare of those headlights, and being so scared. Oh, it was horrible!'

She covered her face with her hands.

'Don't upset yourself, darling,' said Wyatt. 'At least, we're sound in wind and limb.' But he was wondering how they were going to get back to the inn from this isolated spot.

'I think we'd better make for the nearest village,' he decided at last. 'We'll never find Tyson's place now.'

He stopped speaking and sat up straight, his head turned

towards the road. After a couple of seconds, he could hear a car approaching.

'Wait here, Sally,' he said, getting to his feet, and hobbling a few steps towards the road.

'Lionel! Don't leave me!' she begged.

'We must try to get a lift, darling,' he urged, 'and this might be our only opportunity. I won't take any chances.'

He squelched his way up the steep incline towards the road and peered anxiously at the oncoming car. There was nothing for it but to take a chance, so he stepped cautiously a couple of yards into the roadway and waved his arm with an air of urgency. With a sense of relief, he heard the car slow down, and he was even more pleased to note that the driver was a woman.

'Hello, there! What goes on?' called an attractive feminine voice with just the trace of a Canadian accent. Wyatt stepped up to the car and got a closer view of the woman at the wheel. As far as he could judge in the half-light, she was about thirty years old, with a considerable amount of self-assurance. From her shadowy outline, he somehow sensed that she was well dressed.

'I'm most awfully sorry to stop you like this,' he began to apologize, 'but we've had an accident.'

She took in his bedraggled appearance with a swift glance.

'You look kind of wet and miserable,' she nodded. 'Did you say an accident?'

'Yes, my car went over the bridge here.'

'Over the bridge! Say, is anybody hurt?'

'No, no, we had rather a lucky escape. My wife is rather badly shaken, but I think she'll be OK.'

'Over the bridge!' she repeated in quiet amazement. 'I didn't think they did that sort of thing, except on the movies.'

'Well, apparently they do,' said Wyatt with a little laugh. 'Could you please give us both a lift into Shorecombe? I assure you we'll replace your upholstery if these wet clothes do it any harm. By the way, my name is Wyatt ...'

'Wyatt?' she echoed quickly. 'Not Lionel Wyatt?'

'That's right,' he nodded.

The girl said:

'But I was on the way to see you, Mr Wyatt.'

'To see me?'

'Yes,' she nodded. 'It's quite a coincidence our meeting like this.'

'It's certainly rather unconventional – I'm afraid I don't know your name or—'

'That's soon settled. Allow me to introduce myself, Mr Wyatt. My name is Fraser. Doctor Gail Fraser.'

CHAPTER III

The Cottage on the Cliff

Wyatt said quietly:
  'Doctor Fraser!'
She turned sharply.
  'Anything wrong? You seem very surprised.'
  'That's putting it mildly,' he assured her.
  'Don't I look like a doctor?'
  'I wouldn't like to say. Anyhow, that's not what I was thinking.'
  'What were you thinking, Mr Wyatt?' There was a note of challenge in the slightly husky voice. Actually, Wyatt was wondering if she was the driver and this was the car which had forced them over the bridge.
  'Why did you want to see me?'
  She leaned back in her seat and eyed him shrewdly
  'Well, now,' she said, 'that's quite a story. Much too long to tell at the moment. Let's pick up your wife and go back to Shorecombe, then we could all have a drink together at the pub after you've changed into some dry clothes.'
  'Yes, that's a good idea,' agreed Wyatt at once.

'Will you need any help?'

'No, no, Sally will be able to walk all right,' said Wyatt, descending the sharp incline beside the bridge. He found Sally had already walked somewhat painfully up to the parapet, and had been listening to odd snatches of the conversation.

'It's all right,' he whispered encouragingly. 'She'll take us back to Shorecombe.'

He gave Sally his arm, and they moved slowly towards the car. Doctor Fraser had already opened the back door and they climbed in rather painfully.

'This is my wife – Doctor Fraser,' Wyatt introduced them. Sally gave a tiny exclamation, but Wyatt squeezed her hand quickly, and she contrived to turn it into a polite greeting.

'We are very grateful to you for giving us a lift,' said Sally. 'We seem to have been waiting hours, and there hasn't been a soul passing by.'

Doctor Fraser expertly engaged the gears and they moved smoothly towards Shorecombe.

After they had proceeded in silence for almost a mile, the doctor said suddenly:

'I know it's no business of mine, but would you say that affair of yours was an accident?'

'Certainly not,' replied Wyatt promptly. 'We were quite deliberately forced off the road.'

Doctor Fraser nodded thoughtfully.

'Now who,' she mused, 'would want to do a thing like that?'

'Your guess is as good as mine, Doctor,' replied Wyatt. 'Are you surprised to hear of all this?'

A tiny smile played around the shapely mouth.

'I don't surprise very easily, Mr Wyatt,' she assured him.

She did not offer to pursue the matter, but switched the conversation to the subject of avoiding chills.

'I've got some tablets in my case, Mrs Wyatt. You must take a couple and get your husband to do the same when you go to bed. And a glass of hot whisky might help.'

'Are you staying at Shorecombe?' asked Sally.

'No, I booked a room at the North Royal Hotel in Teignmouth – it's only twenty minutes away by road. You can phone me there if you get any after-effects of this little adventure.'

When they arrived at the Silver Fleet, Doctor Fraser insisted on helping to put Sally to bed and examining her bruises, which she pronounced to be superficial and in no way serious. Then she went downstairs while Wyatt changed into a more presentable suit. He found her waiting for him in the back parlour.

'You look a different man now,' she greeted him.

'I feel like two different men. I was glad to get out of that suit. I hope you'll excuse my wife, Doctor. I think it will do her good to stay in bed now she's there.'

'Of course. Playing leap-frog over bridges isn't exactly good for the constitution.'

Wyatt went over and switched on the small electric fire and at that moment Fred Johnson appeared with a tray.

'I've taken the liberty of ordering you a whisky and soda,' said Doctor Fraser. 'I hope that's OK.'

'It's perfect!'

Fred set the glasses down on a small table.

'Two whiskies and sodas – is that right?' he asked.

'Just what the doctor ordered,' replied Wyatt without realizing the significance of the phrase until he caught a twinkle in his companion's eye. 'Oh, I beg your pardon,' he smiled, handing Fred a ten shilling note.

After Fred had gone they chose the most comfortable chairs and sat facing each other on either side of the fire. Wyatt swallowed half his whisky at a gulp, and felt better almost immediately.

'Well, Doctor Fraser,' he said presently. 'I think you mentioned that you wanted to see me.'

She nodded.

'When I told you my name, Mr Wyatt, I got the impression that it came as a surprise to you – as if you'd heard it in some connection before. Had you?'

Wyatt refused to be drawn.

'You still haven't answered my question,' he reminded her. 'Why did you want to see me?'

She gripped the arms of her chair, and her attitude became noticeably more rigid.

'Because I'm puzzled about something, Mr Wyatt. I'm worried and bewildered, and I need your help.'

'Better tell me the whole story,' he suggested.

She took a sip of her whisky and set down the glass. He offered her a cigarette and lit it for her. She leaned back in the chair and blew out a stream of smoke.

'About six weeks ago I had a phone call from a girl who called herself Barbara Willis, who said she had been recommended to me by a certain Doctor Grayson. I'd never heard of him, but I made an appointment to see her at my flat in Wimpole Street. She was rather a highly strung, sensitive type of girl, but as far as I could make out from a routine examination, there didn't seem to be much wrong with her.'

'What did she say was wrong?' asked Wyatt.

'Miss Willis told me she was suffering from severe headaches and fits of depression. I had a suspicion that she had been drinking rather heavily, and when I questioned her as to her occupation – she didn't seem to have any – and general background, I became sure of it. In fact, I told her that before I could start to treat her, she must cut down on liquor and go on the wagon for at least a month. I put this to her in quite a friendly way, but her reaction to the suggestion quite startled me.'

'She felt insulted, perhaps,' Wyatt put in.

'She must have done. She simply got up, looked me straight in the eye, and said: "I get that sort of advice from my fiancé Maurice Knight, and it doesn't cost me three guineas." With that, she slapped down my fee on the desk and marched right out.'

She flicked the ash from her cigarette into the fireplace, and went on:

'Of course, I'm pretty used to awkward patients – sick folk are inclined to be fractious at times, but that little incident rattled me a bit. But that was nothing to what came later.'

'Well?' said Wyatt.

'It must have been three weeks after that interview that I read in the newspapers about the mysterious disappearance of Barbara Willis. There was a picture of her, with her fiancé, Maurice Knight. I could hardly believe my eyes.'

'You mean she'd changed?'

'Beyond all recognition. The girl I interviewed at my flat was not the girl in the newspaper ... not the real Barbara Willis. I'm quite positive about that.'

'Newspaper photos can be misleading at times,' he reminded her.

'I went out and got all the papers I could buy. There were pictures in four others – just the same. There can't be any doubt about it, Mr Wyatt.'

Wyatt rubbed his chin thoughtfully.

'But why on earth should anyone impersonate Barbara Willis and make an appointment with you?' he murmured.

'I don't know, Mr Wyatt. But that isn't all. About ten days ago I received an urgent telephone message, asking me to go to an address in St John's Wood. When I got there I found a girl who seemed to be on the verge of a complete nervous breakdown. She told me that her name was Mildred Gillow.'

Wyatt whistled softly.

'I gave her a sedative,' continued Doctor Fraser, 'and promised to look in again and see what I could do. Yet, when I went back there the next morning the house was completely deserted. There wasn't a sign of life anywhere! I've never seen that girl again, from that day to this. But I saw the photo of Mildred Gillow which appeared after the body was found in your garage.'

'And how did that compare with the original?'

'It was not the girl I saw at St John's Wood, Mr Wyatt,' she asserted with quiet emphasis. 'I am absolutely sure of that.'

Wyatt took a couple of sips of whisky without speaking, then asked:

'Did you see anyone else at the house the first time you went there?'

'Only the girl – she answered the door herself.'

'Didn't that strike you as rather odd?'

'Well no, I don't think so. It didn't occur to me at the time, anyway.'

Wyatt stubbed out his cigarette and leaned back in his chair.

'You certainly seem to have been running into a chain of amazing coincidences, Doctor,' he mused, trying hard to fathom what might lie behind the woman's story. 'Though I can't quite see at the moment how I can be of any help ...'

'Wait,' said Doctor Fraser. 'There's more to come. Yesterday morning a girl came to see me – she said that her name was Lauren Beaumont. Does that name ring a bell?'

Wyatt shook his head.

'Anyhow,' Doctor Fraser resumed, 'this girl said she was worried about being a little overweight, and that she had been recommended by a friend of mine, Doctor Clayburn.'

'Is there a Doctor Clayburn?'

'Oh, yes – he really is a friend of mine. I happened to bump into him at the clinic that same afternoon, and thanked him for sending Miss Beaumont along. To my amazement he didn't seem to know what I was talking about. Said he'd never set eyes on the girl.'

'I should have thought he would have remembered an unusual name like that. Did you describe her to him?'

'Oh, yes, I told him what I'd prescribed for her – everything. But he insisted that he knew nothing about it.'

'It's certainly very odd,' said Wyatt in a guarded tone.

'I don't know who that girl was, or the real reason why she came to see me, Mr Wyatt. But I've a premonition – an awful feeling – that the girl was an impostor, and that what happened to the genuine Barbara Willis and Mildred Gillow will sooner or later happen to Lauren Beaumont.'

'What was she like – your visitor, I mean?'

'Rather a well-built brunette. Nicely spoken and quite well dressed.'

'H'm ... and did you go to the police?'

'No, I was bewildered and rather confused about things, but I didn't want to go to the police. Then, this morning, I switched on the early news bulletin and heard about your discovery in your garage last night. I telephoned your home and your man said you'd just left. I decided I must see you at all costs, so I got in my car and came straight away ... got here soon after tea, and traced you to the Silver Fleet. They told me you were out, so I fixed somewhere in Teignmouth, then went scouting around ... and that's how I found you at the bridge.'

'Well, you certainly turned up at an opportune moment,' he commented. 'Now, about Barbara Willis – had you heard of her before that girl who impersonated her telephoned you?'

She shook her head.

'And Maurice Knight – her fiancé, did you know him?'

'Never heard of him until the girl mentioned the name. The same goes for Mildred Gillow. I didn't know there was such a person until I had that call asking me to go to St John's Wood.'

Wyatt finished his drink, set down his glass, yawned heartily and then apologized.

'I'm afraid I haven't had much sleep just lately,' he said. 'What with last night's affair, then driving up here, then the accident—'

'Mr Wyatt,' she interrupted, 'don't you believe my story?'

'Would you like another drink, Doctor?'

'No, thanks. What I do want is to get to the bottom of this affair. I've an idea there are several things I should be told, Mr Wyatt. Don't hold out on me. I'm used to giving out bad news, and I guess I can take it myself.'

Wyatt offered her another cigarette, but she waved it aside.

'Come on now, Mr Wyatt – I want the truth.'

Wyatt shrugged.

'I don't know if Scotland Yard would approve of my telling you this, but I'll take a chance. You asked me some time back if I'd heard your name before this evening. As a matter of fact, I had. It was found on a prescription that belonged to the real Barbara Willis. It was also established that you supplied the real Mildred Gillow with a prescription for a bottle of medicine. It was made up for her by a chemist who—'

'I don't believe it!' interrupted Doctor Fraser, her eyes ablaze. 'How could I prescribe for them? I never set eyes on either of those girls.'

Wyatt shrugged again.

'That's your story, Doctor; now I'm telling you the one the police are working on.'

'But what does it mean, Mr Wyatt?' she demanded in some apprehension.

'I don't know,' he admitted with a thoughtful frown. 'The whole affair seems to be getting rather involved. But I don't think there's anything for you to worry about. If I were you I should go back to Town and just carry on normally. I shall be up there myself very soon, and I'll contact you if there's anything important.'

She stared broodingly into the fire for a few moments, then rose and picked up her handbag.

'All right, I'll do that,' she agreed. 'But what if the police—?'

'If it becomes necessary I'll tell your story to the police,' he assured her.

'You're very kind,' she said in a relieved tone. 'Is there anything else I can do for Mrs Wyatt?'

'Sally will be OK when she's had a night's rest,' he replied. 'She's pretty tough really, you know – she used to be in the police force!'

Doctor Fraser smiled appreciatively, and moved over to the door.

'I shall leave first thing in the morning – here is my London address and phone number.'

She opened her bag and gave him a small card, which he slipped into his waistcoat pocket.

As he held the door for her, Wyatt asked quite casually:

'By the way, do you happen to know a young man called Hugo Linder?'

She hesitated, as if trying to recall the name.

'No,' she said eventually.

'You've never heard of him?' insisted Wyatt, noticing her hesitation.

'I'm afraid I haven't. Of course, I get a lot of patients, and I don't remember all their names ...'

'Yes, he might have been a patient,' said Wyatt. 'He looks a nervy type.' He went on to give her a brief description of Linder, but again she shook her head.

'Have you any particular reason for asking, Mr Wyatt?'

'No,' he replied blandly. 'I just wondered – that's all.' He walked out with her to her car, and as he was returning, Fred Johnson beckoned to him.

'You're wanted on the telephone, sir. It's in the sitting-room behind the bar. There's nobody there.'

'Thanks, Fred,' said Wyatt, following his host's directing finger.

If Wyatt was a little surprised to hear the voice of Hugo Linder at the other end, he gave no sign of it.

'Mr Wyatt, I've just heard about your accident,' he began in an anxious voice. 'Are you all right?'

'Perfectly all right, thanks,' replied Wyatt somewhat mechanically, for his mind was busy with a dozen conjectures. Had Linder telephoned to find out if there had been any fatalities? Had he, in fact, been the driver of the overtaking car?

'What about Mrs Wyatt?' went on Linder.

'She's a bit shaken up, but I think she will be all right in the morning.' Wyatt paused a moment, then added as casually as possible: 'How did you find out about the accident?'

'I drove over the bridge about ten minutes ago,' was the immediate reply. 'I saw the breach in the parapet, so I stopped to investigate. It gave me quite a turn when I recognized your car.'

'How did you recognize it?'

'It was standing in front of the Silver Fleet when I came to see you. I knew it again at once. My word, you must have had a narrow squeak! It's quite a relief to hear that neither of you was badly hurt.'

'Thank you, Mr Linder,' replied Wyatt politely. 'It was very nice of you to telephone.'

'Not at all. By the way, did you see Mr Tyson?'

'No, we were actually on our way there when the accident happened.'

'How very unfortunate. I had told him to expect you.'

'Never mind. We'll probably pop over in the morning if I can get a car. I should imagine that ought not to be too difficult.'

'I'd lend you mine, but I'm going back to Town tomorrow.'

'That's rather sudden, isn't it?' said Wyatt, still trying to suppress any note of curiosity in his voice.

'Yes, there's something rather important come up, and I have to attend to it right away. If you want to get hold of me in Town, my number's in the book.'

Just as Linder was about to ring off, Wyatt said suddenly:

'I almost forgot to tell you, Mr Linder ... I saw a friend of yours tonight. She sends her kind regards.'

'Oh? Who was it?'

'Doctor Fraser,' replied Wyatt without a moment's hesitation, wishing he were face to face with Linder so as to be able to note his true reaction.

'Oh ... Doctor Fraser,' said the voice on the wire, in a tone which defied analysis. 'How is she?'

'She's fine.'

'Is she staying down here?' Wyatt imagined he detected a note of caution in the inquiry.

'Just for the night. Apparently, some special business brought her down here.'

'I see. Well, goodbye, Mr Wyatt. I expect we shall meet in Town.'

'I expect so, Mr Linder. Goodbye.'

Wyatt thoughtfully replaced the receiver and slowly made his way back to the bar, where he drank a final whisky by way of a nightcap.

Next morning he was very glad to find Sally showing no after-effects of the accident. He was also relieved to find that his leg was none the worse. It was a fine sunny morning, and they sat by the window where they had a glimpse of the sea between two ancient cottages. Sally ate an enormous breakfast, and seemed quite anxious to discuss the events of the previous day. Wyatt told her that he had been making some inquiries about Barbara Willis, but that no one had seen her if she had stayed in Shorecombe prior to the tragedy. He had called at the local police station to report the accident, and had made further inquiries there about the elusive Miss Willis, but without success.

'And what did you make of Doctor Fraser when you had me safely out of the way?' smiled Sally.

'She seemed quite an affable sort of person,' said Wyatt in a non-committal tone. 'What did you make of her?'

'I rather liked her. Did she have much to say?'

'Yes, quite a lot.'

He gave her a brief outline of Doctor Fraser's experience.

'Do you believe all that?' asked Sally when he had finished.

'Do you?' he countered. 'You're the woman; you're supposed to work by intuition.'

She shook her head thoughtfully.

'I don't know,' she had to confess. 'She doesn't look the type who would make up an involved story like that.'

'On the other hand,' he reminded her, 'we have to remember that she is a doctor; a woman with a brain well above the average. I shouldn't think concocting a story like that would be beyond her powers.'

'Is there no way of checking it?'

'Not till we get back to Town. I think it can wait till then.'

Sally left the table and stood by the window, watching a cart move slowly along the narrow street outside.

'What are we going to do today?' she inquired eagerly.

Wyatt slowly tipped all the remaining sugar into his last cup of coffee, then said:

'I thought we'd go out and see Tyson this morning, then probably catch the 3.45 back to London.'

'Must we go to London?' asked Sally rather wistfully.

'I'm afraid so,' said Wyatt. 'I've got to see Sir James as soon as possible.' He lit a cigarette and sipped his coffee. When the door opened to admit a handsome young man, they both had the idea that he was another guest at the inn. He was well dressed; his hair was smoothly plastered and he had a neat toothbrush moustache which distracted attention from his slightly receding chin.

'I must apologize for interrupting you,' he began, 'but if you could spare me a few minutes ...'

Sally turned and eyed the intruder curiously, while Wyatt rose.

'It's Mr Maurice Knight, isn't it?' he inquired.

'Why yes, how did you—'

'Your picture's been in the papers rather a lot,' Wyatt reminded him.

'Oh, yes, I was forgetting that wretched business for the moment – at least, that aspect of it.'

He smiled at Sally.

'I am sorry to barge in like this, Mrs Wyatt, but I'm on my way back to Town, and I did rather want to see Mr Wyatt for a few minutes, if he can spare the time.'

'I'll ring for some fresh coffee,' said Sally. 'I'm sure we could drink another cup – if you'll join us.'

Wyatt pulled up a chair for their guest, and when the landlord had taken their order, he looked a trifle apprehensive.

'I suppose it's all right to talk here,' he began in a low voice.

'As good as anywhere, I should imagine,' replied Wyatt. 'I don't think we can possibly be overheard.'

Maurice Knight sat on the edge of his chair and leaned forward; he spoke in a confidential tone.

'Mr Wyatt, you know why I came to Shorecombe?'

'I could probably guess,' said Wyatt.

'I wanted to find out what had brought my fiancée, Barbara Willis, down here.' He suddenly became tense. 'I wanted to find out the swine who deliberately, brutally, and sadistically strangled her.'

Sally gave a little shudder.

'I'm sorry – please forgive me, Mrs Wyatt … you understand I've been very upset …'

43

'Did you satisfy your curiosity, Mr Knight?' inquired Wyatt evenly.

Knight shook his head somewhat wistfully.

'Even as an amateur detective I'm afraid I'm a complete washout,' he had to admit. 'But I did stumble across one rather interesting point, Mr Wyatt. That's why I wanted to see you.'

At that moment Fred Johnson returned with the coffee. After he had left Wyatt said:

'Well, Mr Knight? What was it you discovered?'

Knight leaned forward again, and said:

'Last night, Mr Wyatt, when I heard about your accident, I began to put two and two together. You were on your way to see Mr Tyson last night, weren't you?'

'How did you know that?'

'I went to see Tyson myself a couple of days back.' He stirred his coffee, then added significantly: 'Do you know what happened, Mr Wyatt?'

'I haven't an idea.'

Knight dropped his voice to an even more confidential level.

'I went to see Tyson in my car. When I reached the bridge, the one where you had your accident, I heard another car coming behind me. He was blowing his horn, and I pulled over to let him pass. Suddenly, and quite deliberately, he attempted to force my car off the road.'

'But that's exactly what happened to us!' cried Sally excitedly.

'Go on, Mr Knight,' said Wyatt.

'Fortunately for me,' continued Knight, 'I went into a skid, or he'd have forced me right over the bridge. He was off like the devil, of course.'

'Didn't you follow him?' asked Wyatt.

'Well, I was a bit shaken,' Knight admitted. 'And there was really not much point in my chasing him.'

'Why not?'

'Because,' explained Knight impressively, 'I managed to get his number.'

Sally sat up straight in her chair.

'You got his number!' she repeated.

Knight slowly took a small, black notebook from his waistcoat pocket and read out:

'GKC 973. Perhaps you'll take a note of it, Mr Wyatt.'

Wyatt did so.

'It looks as if someone was trying to prevent you from seeing Mr Tyson,' said Sally shrewdly.

'Exactly, Mrs Wyatt. And I think the attempt on your life was for precisely the same reason.'

Wyatt balanced on the two rear legs of his chair and considered this.

'It's quite a theory, Mr Knight,' he said at last.

Sally was looking puzzled now.

'But surely Tyson can't know anything about this business,' she put in. 'After all, he's just an old fisherman who happened to discover the body.'

'I wouldn't be too sure about that, Mrs Wyatt, if I were you,' said Knight. Wyatt gave him a quick glance.

'You saw Tyson?' he demanded.

'Yes,' said Knight, 'I saw him. He was annoyed and rather bad tempered.'

'I expect he's had quite a lot of people questioning him lately,' suggested Sally.

'I have an idea he's holding something back,' persisted Knight, turning to Wyatt. 'I wish you'd go and see him,

Mr Wyatt. I think a dose of third degree might not do any harm.'

Wyatt shrugged.

'I'm afraid third degree is hardly in my line,' he said slowly. 'But I certainly propose to see Mr Tyson.'

Knight rose at once.

'Good – I can't tell you how relieved I am to hear you say that,' he declared. 'When do you think you'll go?'

'Some time this morning, I dare say.'

'That's fine. I hope you'll catch him in a better temper – and if he isn't, don't hesitate to throw a scare into him.'

'I rather gather that you don't much care for Mr Tyson,' said Wyatt with a faint smile.

'I think he knows more than he's told anyone so far.' He finished his coffee and picked up his hat.

'I must rush off now. Perhaps I'll see you in London?'

'It's quite possible,' nodded Wyatt, taking his stick and crossing to the door with him.

When he returned a minute later, he found Sally standing at the window watching their departing visitor.

'Well?' said Wyatt.

'He's much too good-looking,' she murmured. 'I don't like it.'

'I thought he had a singularly weak face,' said Wyatt.

'He's a typical playboy, of course.'

'Do you think he was telling the truth about that car?'

'I can easily get it checked when we're in Town.'

'If he was telling the truth,' continued Sally, 'it rather looks as if there is some sort of plot to prevent people going to see Mr Tyson.'

'I suppose that's one way of looking at it,' he conceded. 'All the same, we are going to see Tyson – this very morning, just as soon as I can get a car.'

Sally turned from the window.

'Darling, why don't we walk over there? It's only four miles, and it's a lovely morning.'

'All right,' he agreed, 'if you're quite sure you feel up to it.'

'I feel fine.'

Two hours later they were slowly climbing the cliff road on which Bill Tyson's cottage stood. They had enjoyed their walk, but Sally was feeling a little tired and was holding on to her husband's arm. Occasionally they stopped to admire the view across the bay, or to watch a seagull as it swooped overhead.

There was a sudden sound of footsteps descending the rough road, and round a corner came Hugo Linder, whistling to himself. He greeted them warmly.

'I thought you were going back to Town this morning,' said Wyatt casually.

'In half an hour,' replied Linder. 'I've just been to say goodbye to Tyson.'

'As a matter of fact, that's where we're going. Is the old boy in?'

'Yes, he's in all right,' said Linder, with a certain amount of hesitation, 'but I'm afraid you won't find him in a very good humour. He seems quite morose just lately.'

'How far is the cottage?' asked Sally.

'Only just round the next bend, Mrs Wyatt. It's quite a climb up here, but I always think it's worth it.'

Linder bade them a cheerful farewell, and went swinging down the road.

'Come on, darling, put your best foot forward,' urged Wyatt, whose leg was beginning to ache for the first time since their arrival.

They toiled on up the hill, and sure enough there was a

very small cottage standing well back from the road just round the next bend. They stopped to admire the neatly kept front garden, then Wyatt pushed open the gate and went up the stone-flagged path. He knocked at the front door and waited for some time.

Sally followed him up the path, stooping to smell the old-fashioned stocks and wallflowers.

'The old boy doesn't seem to be in after all,' said Wyatt, knocking again.

'He may have gone down to the shore,' said Sally.

'It can't be more than a few minutes since Linder was here.'

Wyatt knocked again and stood listening intently. He imagined he heard a slight movement inside, but could not be certain.

'What are we going to do now?' asked Sally.

'I don't know. I should like to have seen Tyson before we leave Shorecombe and—'

The unmistakable sound of a revolver shot cut him short.

'Lionel!' Sally clutched his arm.

'It came from inside the cottage – the room at the back,' he said quickly. 'You stay here, Sally. Stand clear of the door, just in case ...'

Sally moved along to the corner of the cottage, and Wyatt vanished round the back.

He was not very surprised to find the back door half-open. He stopped for a moment and listened, but all seemed to be quiet inside. He moved up to the door and slowly put his head inside.

The back room was a kitchen-scullery, with a sink under the window. A door opposite led into the front room; this was closed, but across the table near it lay the shirt-sleeved figure of an elderly man. Wyatt walked over to the table and saw that the man had been shot through the forehead. Wyatt picked up his left hand, felt the pulse, then let it fall again. The man was dead.

A revolver lay on the floor, and Wyatt carefully picked it up with his handkerchief. One cartridge had been fired. He replaced the weapon in the exact spot where he had found it, and looked round the room. There was nothing that looked in any way unusual, and he went through into the front room and opened the door, having carefully closed the connecting door behind him.

'You'd better come inside, Sally,' he called, and she came running along the front of the cottage.

'What was it?' she demanded rather breathlessly.

'It's a nasty business,' he replied tersely. 'I'm afraid Tyson's dead.'

'Dead!' repeated Sally wonderingly, gazing at the scullery door.

'I'd rather you didn't see him,' said Wyatt, interpreting her thoughts. 'He isn't exactly a pleasant spectacle.'

'What happened?'

'He's been shot through the head; he must have committed suicide.'

'Are you sure?'

'Everything seems to point to it.'

'Was that the shot we heard?'

'Yes. And if it was fired by anyone but Tyson, then he made a very quick getaway.'

'He might still be in the house,' she reminded him.

'Yes … there's just a chance. Wait here, Sally …'

He opened a third door beside the fireplace, which led upstairs, and mounted the narrow stairs as silently as possible.

But both the bedrooms were empty, and showed no trace of an intruder. He came down slowly, to find Sally sitting on a rocking-chair and staring at the scullery door.

'Is he in there?' she asked.

'Yes, he's sprawled across the table. Don't go in, darling; it'll only upset you.'

'You're quite sure it's suicide?' she insisted in a pensive tone.

Wyatt walked slowly to the window.

'You're thinking of Linder?'

'I can't help it. We'd only just met him; I'll admit he didn't look like a man who's out to commit a murder, but one can't be absolutely certain ...' Her voice trailed away.

'But we heard the shot, Sally, as we stood at the front door. There's no one else in the place, and no one came out.'

'All right, darling,' she agreed, with a little sigh. 'It must be suicide. We'd better get the police, hadn't we?'

'I'd just like to take a last look round in there. You stay where you are; I won't be five minutes.'

He went into the scullery and closed the door.

After methodically examining the room for some minutes his eye suddenly caught a scrap of white paper which was partly hidden by the dead man's sleeve. Wyatt moved the arm slightly so that he could see the paper. The red ink was a trifle smudged, but he had no difficulty in deciphering the sentence:

'With the compliments of Mr Rossiter.'

CHAPTER IV

Sir Donald Angus is Perturbed

The subsequent police inquiries detained Wyatt and Sally until the late afternoon, so they were unable to catch the 3.45 from Whitby. Wyatt stayed to see that fingerprint impressions were taken in every likely place inside the cottage, and arranged for the photos to be sent to Scotland Yard by express delivery. The local police apparently had no suspicion of foul play, particularly when the only prints on the revolver proved to be Tyson's own.

Having caught a train in the early evening, it was just after one a.m. when Wyatt and Sally arrived at Paddington. Luckily they were able to get a room at the station hotel and enjoyed the seven hours' sound sleep they badly needed. Sally refused to accompany her husband to the Yard that morning, pleading that she had some shopping to do, and would meet him for lunch.

When Wyatt arrived at the Yard soon after ten that morning, Perivale and Lathom were busily engaged in reading the reports and examining the fingerprint impressions which had already reached them from Shorecombe. Perivale was

51

looking more worried than ever, but Wyatt could see from the gleam in Lathom's eye that he had already made up his mind about the Tyson affair.

After Wyatt had given them a brief account of his trip to Shorecombe, Perivale paced up and down, then went over to the window and gazed unseeingly at the tugs ploughing past on the Thames below him.

'I'm damned if I can make head or tail of it, Wyatt,' he said at last.

'I don't understand it myself,' declared Wyatt quite equably. 'Maybe the inspector here has a theory.' He could see that Lathom was bursting to expound.

The inspector swung round towards his chief.

'If you'll forgive my saying so, Sir James, there's quite obviously only one possible explanation,' he announced. The Assistant Commissioner's bushy eyebrows shot up.

'Let's have it, Lathom.'

'When Mr and Mrs Wyatt went to the cottage, they saw no one leave after the shot had been fired.'

'Of course no one escaped,' snapped Perivale.

'Exactly, sir. No one escaped for the very good reason that there was no one in the cottage except Tyson.'

'In other words, you're telling us that Tyson committed suicide.'

'Of course,' nodded Lathom confidently. Perivale was more irritated than ever.

'My dear Inspector, I'm quite ready to believe that Tyson committed suicide; in fact, so far as I can see, there is no other possible explanation, but the point is, if Tyson killed himself, who put that note on the table? Who wrote the note? And why, in God's name, did they take the trouble to write it immediately after Tyson died?'

'Well, there's only one possible explanation,' began Lathom once more in his somewhat superior tone. 'Tyson made up his mind to commit suicide, so he wrote the note first and then—'

'You sit there and try to tell me he wrote that note himself!' exclaimed Perivale, obviously quite staggered at the idea.

'That's what I said,' maintained Lathom doggedly.

'But, look here, Lathom,' said Perivale, obviously trying to be patient. 'We've proved quite conclusively that the note was written by the same person who sent notes to Maurice Knight and—'

'Just a minute,' put in Wyatt, who was beginning to see daylight. 'You think, Inspector, that Tyson not only wrote that particular note, but that he wrote the others as well.'

'That's about it, Wyatt,' nodded Lathom. 'I think that Tyson was crazy, most probably a schizophrenia case. He murdered Barbara Willis and Mildred Gillow—'

'Here, steady on, old man,' said Sir James. 'You don't really think that Tyson and this "Mr Rossiter" ...'

He was interrupted by a knock at the door, and a sergeant came in to tell Lathom that he had a caller waiting below.

'I can't see anyone at the moment,' said Lathom, with some annoyance.

'If you'll excuse me, sir, I think it's important.'

Lathom looked annoyed.

'Who is it?' he asked.

'A gentleman named Sir Donald Angus, sir. He particularly wanted to know if you were in charge of the Willis case.'

'Sir Donald Angus?' echoed Perivale. 'Do you know him, Lathom?'

'No, sir. But I've heard of him, of course. He's the millionaire shipowner. His company bought up the East

African shipping combine about six weeks ago. You must remember, sir; it was in all the papers.'

'I remember,' nodded Perivale. 'Bring Sir Donald in here, Sergeant.'

The sergeant went out and presently returned with Sir Donald Angus, a bullet-headed little man of fifty, with piercing pale blue eyes and noticeable Scottish accent. He seemed somewhat nervous, but Wyatt could not decide whether this was due to his strange surroundings or to something that had upset him.

Perivale manœuvred the visitor into a chair facing the window, then introduced Wyatt and Lathom.

Sir Donald turned to Perivale and said: 'Sir James, I want you to realize that this matter is confidential. It would spell absolute disaster to a man in my position if this leaked out.'

'You can rely on us, Sir Donald,' said Perivale, with the merest suggestion of irony in his tone.

'I hope so – I'm sure I hope so.'

The little man looked from one to the other.

'Well, now, I don't quite know where to begin. I don't want ye to get hold of the wrong end of the stick, as ye might say.'

'The beginning is usually the safest,' suggested Wyatt gravely.

'Verra well, then. Last Sunday I came down to London from Glasgow and booked a room – that is to say a couple of rooms – at the Royal Astoria Hotel. I had a friend with me, a young lady, and we were due to stay at the hotel until the end of this week.'

He noticed Wyatt and Sir James exchange a glance, and immediately said: 'Now, gentlemen, ye mustn't get the wrong impression. She is an awfully nice girl, and she was merely acting as my secretary on a little business deal I'd come to see through while I was up here.'

No one else spoke, so he went on rapidly.

'We had breakfast this morning – downstairs in the dining-room, of course ... and after that my friend decided to go out and do some shopping. As a matter of fact, she told me that she had a fitting at a shop in Bond Street, so I arranged to meet her for lunch at the Ritz – it's handy ye know – at a quarter to one. When I arrived, there was no sign of her.'

'You were there on time?' queried Wyatt.

'Right on time,' he replied somewhat severely. 'I'm a man who believes in punctuality. My time is fairly precious and I keep to a schedule. My programme was badly thrown out today because the lady had not arrived at a quarter to three.'

'I take it you were there all the time,' said Perivale.

'Oh, yes, I left a message with the commissionaire, the head porter and another with the head waiter – and I should certainly have seen her if she had turned up. At a quarter to three I began to get a bit worried – thought she might have been in an accident – so I walked up Bond Street and went to the dress shop she'd mentioned. To my utter astonishment, they said she had never been near the place.'

'I shouldn't worry too much, Sir Donald,' said Wyatt. 'She may have met an old school friend or—'

'Wait, Mr Wyatt,' said Sir Donald, with a note of desperation in his voice. 'I thought of all those things. Finally, I decided I had better go back to the Royal Astoria, and see if they'd seen anything of her there. I asked quite a number of the staff, but they hadn't seen her since she went out after breakfast. I went up to our – to my bedroom to try and fathom things out, and there on the dressing-table was a small parcel that had been delivered by special messenger.'

He fumbled in his coat pocket and took out a small leather-covered box. He passed this to Sir James Perivale who opened it. Inside, lying on a layer of black velvet-like padding, was a single pearl ear-ring.

'You recognize this?' asked Perivale.

'Of course. It was one of the ear-rings my friend was wearing when she went out this morning.'

'You're certain of that?'

'Quite certain. As a matter of fact, I gave them to her myself – a birthday present,' he added hastily. 'You see, she's an old friend of the family and—'

Perivale nodded. 'I see.'

He passed the box to Wyatt. 'Was there anything else in this box?' he asked.

'Oh, yes, there was this card.'

Angus took out his wallet and extracted a piece of pasteboard about two inches square.

On it was written in red ink the word: "Wait", followed by the signature, "Mr Rossiter".

They all looked at the card, recognizing the now familiar writing. At length, Lathom laid the card on the desk.

'I'd like you to describe this girl as fully as possible,' he said.

Sir Donald considered for a few moments.

'She's about five feet two … her hair is sort of honey-coloured; she has brown eyes … nice teeth … she's attractive I suppose in a sort of way …'

'Her age?' asked Lathom.

'That I can't tell ye.'

'I thought you said she was an old friend of the family.'

'Of course – but it was on my wife's side ye see … I could guess her age … I should think about twenty-eight …'

He licked his lips nervously.

'Inspector, I want ye to understand that this affair must be treated with the greatest secrecy.'

'Don't worry, Sir Donald,' said Lathom somewhat curtly, 'we'll look after that. Now, can you tell me what the young lady was wearing?'

Sir Donald twisted uneasily in his chair.

'Yes ... she had on a brown costume and rather a fancy sort of hat with a coloured little feather stuck at the side ... she had brown shoes and ...' He broke off again, and said in an anxious tone: 'Inspector, I hope ye realize that a man in my position can't afford to be mixed up in any sort of scandal. It's very important that this should be handled with discretion and—'

'Exactly, Sir Donald. That's why it is equally important that we should know the whole truth,' replied Lathom imperturbably. 'Now, Sir Donald, how long have you really known this girl?'

'I've told ye, she's a very old friend of the family. My wife has known her since she—'

'I said the whole truth,' interrupted Lathom with surprising force. They glared at each other for some seconds. Then Sir Donald sank back in his chair.

'Just over a fortnight,' he admitted in a lifeless tone.

'That's better,' said Lathom. 'Now we're beginning to get down to facts. And the next fact I want from you is the young lady's name – or at least the name you know her by.'

Sir Donald Angus looked at his questioners for a moment, hesitated, licked his lips again, then said quietly:

'Her name is Beaumont – Lauren Beaumont.'

CHAPTER V

The Girl Who Knew too Much

Lathom was about to continue with another question, but Wyatt suddenly stepped forward and said quietly:

'That's rather an unusual name, Sir Donald.'

'Yes ...' nodded the little man. 'Have you ever heard it before, Mr Wyatt?' he demanded somewhat anxiously.

'If you're wondering whether Miss Beaumont has a police record, the inspector will get that looked up for you in a few minutes. What I'm concerned with is her appearance. You say she was a blonde ... about five feet two?'

'She might have been a shade more.'

'Would you say she was well spoken?'

'Well, she had a sort of slight American accent – like you hear on the films.'

Wyatt frowned thoughtfully. This description of Lauren Beaumont tallied in no respect with that of the woman giving that name who had seen Doctor Fraser. In view of what had happened to Barbara Willis and Mildred Gillow, it certainly looked as if she was in considerable danger. Wyatt decided to try a new line of questioning.

'I take it you and the lady have been around quite a bit this week, Sir Donald. Shows and night clubs and all that.'

Angus hesitated.

'Well, we went to one or two places in a modest, quiet sort of way,' he replied uneasily. 'I don't want anybody to get the impression that we've been painting the town red.'

'Where did you go last night, for instance?'

Sir Donald plainly did not relish the question.

'It wasn't much of a place,' he said deprecatingly. 'Quite respectable, of course. I was told they give you a good meal there, so we went on from the theatre ...'

'Can't you remember the name?' said Wyatt pointedly.

'Aye, let me see now, it was called the Madrid.'

'The Madrid!' repeated Lathom in some surprise.

'Do you know it, Inspector?' asked Angus cautiously.

Lathom grunted. He had a plain-clothes man visiting there most nights, but he saw no reason to inform Sir Donald of the fact.

'It was Lauren's idea,' went on Angus, as if to justify himself. 'I had never been there before, and of course I'd no idea what sort of place it was. I think she goes there occasionally – she assured me it was all above board. Though I must say I didn't think much of the food.'

'What time did you get there?'

'Just about ten – and we left soon after midnight.'

'Did you see anyone you knew?'

'Of course not. I told you I'd never been there before.'

'What about Miss Beaumont?'

'She seemed to know one or two people – sort of casual acquaintances. There was the fellow who owns the place ...'

'Charles Luigi?' prompted Lathom.

'That's the man. He came over to our table once or twice and had a little chat.'

'What about?'

'Oh, the usual nonsense,' said Angus, somewhat irritated. 'I couldn't stand the fellow. He seemed to be laughing at me all the time, as if he had some private joke.'

The recollection obviously stirred up a considerable amount of annoyance, and Angus went on abruptly: 'What the devil's the good of talking about last night? It's today that worries me.'

Perivale, who had been jotting down one or two notes on his pad, looked up and said quietly:

'At the moment we should be glad if you would confine yourself to answering our questions, Sir Donald.'

But Angus, obviously a man of action, was chafing with impatience at this delay. He had expected that as soon as Sir James had heard his story, there would be a spate of brusque orders, radio messages and Flying Squad cars rushing in all directions. All Sir James was doing at the moment was tracing an elaborate design on his blotter.

'What am I going to do, man? You must understand my position, Sir James!' insisted Angus with some heat.

Perivale shrugged his broad shoulders and flung down his pencil.

'There's only one thing you can do, Sir Donald – and that is wait. Go back to your hotel and wait till this "Mr Rossiter" gets in touch with you again, and the moment he does so, telephone us immediately.'

'Is that all ye've got to say?' demanded Angus heatedly. 'Is that the only advice the head of New Scotland Yard can offer?'

'I don't happen to be the head of the Yard, Sir Donald,'

retorted Sir James, faintly amused, 'but I'm sure he'd give you exactly the same instructions. If you don't follow them I won't answer for the consequences. The moment you hear from "Mr Rossiter", get in touch with Inspector Lathom. Meanwhile, we'll circulate a description of the girl. Perhaps you'll be able to recollect a few more details if you go down to Inspector Lathom's office and talk it over quietly with him.'

Perivale nodded to Lathom, who went over and opened the door for Sir Donald. When they had gone, Sir James turned to Wyatt.

'Well, what do you make of that?'

Wyatt put down the card he had been examining through a small pocket magnifying glass.

'If Sir Donald was telling the truth,' he murmured, 'then it's obvious that our friend "Mr Rossiter" isn't a mental case after all. He's in it for what he can get out of it.'

'You think he's going to blackmail Angus ... yes, I suppose he must be,' mused Perivale. 'He knows Angus is a wealthy man, apparently with a weakness for the opposite sex, and he's going to cash in on it. But I still think there must be more to it than that, Wyatt. After all, we still have to explain Barbara Willis and Mildred Gillow.'

'I haven't forgotten,' said Wyatt. 'You are trying to tell me that this "Mr Rossiter" is a gentleman with quite a number of interests.'

'It's my opinion,' averred Perivale slowly, 'that he is the leader of a highly developed organization. I should imagine he has a hold over quite a number of influential persons, and he uses it without scruple.'

He was about to develop his theory further, but was interrupted by the buzz of the telephone. The call apparently came from one of his colleagues, but Wyatt could not gather exactly what it concerned until Perivale cradled the receiver and said:

'This is a curious coincidence, Wyatt. You remember asking us to trace the number of the car that tried to force that fellow over the bridge at Shorecombe?'

Wyatt nodded.

'I put the boys on to it right away,' said Perivale, 'and it seems that the car belongs to the man Sir Donald just mentioned – Charles Luigi, of the Madrid Club.'

'Very interesting,' said Wyatt thoughtfully. 'I've often wondered if Mr Luigi was on the level ...'

'You know him?'

'Not very well.'

'What sort of place is the Madrid?' asked Perivale curiously.

'Oh, the usual night club-cum-restaurant. Perhaps a little more elaborate and expensive than the majority. They often put on quite a good floor show, and their dance hostesses are not quite so friendly as some!'

'And what do you know about Luigi?'

'He's rather a curious mixture. Foreign, of course – half Rumanian I believe. A pretty shrewd bird, taken all round.'

'Is he likely to be mixed up in this business?'

'It wouldn't surprise me.'

'You don't think he's "Mr Rossiter"?'

'I don't know,' smiled Wyatt, 'but I'll make a point of asking him.'

Sir James grunted and opened a drawer in his desk, from which he extracted a small bunch of keys.

'We'd like to have you handy on this job,' he explained as he passed them over.

Wyatt looked at the ivory tag on the ring; it had 17 Cumnor

Mansions printed on it in block lettering. He knew this was one of the three flats reserved by the Yard for special visitors of all classes, varying from foreign police chiefs to men in fear of their lives, who had to be kept under special observation.

'It's going to make things a bit difficult down at the farm,' he said with a worried frown. 'I'll have to see if we can get help there.'

'The sooner you're through with this case, the sooner you can get back to your turnips,' grinned Sir James.

Wyatt smiled, picked up his stick, and went off to meet Sally for lunch, over which they planned for Fred to run the holding in their absence, with occasional voluntary help when available from the Agricultural Committee.

After lunch Wyatt went back to the Yard to see if there had been any further developments. The photos of the fingerprints in Tyson's cottage had arrived, and were almost entirely those of the dead man, the exception being those on a tumbler in the living-room cupboard. These were not in the Yard records. He was discussing the various angles of the case and possible lines of investigation with Lathom, and did not notice how quickly the time was passing, until he suddenly realized it was seven o'clock. He remembered that he had arranged to meet Sally for dinner, and it suddenly occurred to him that here was an opportunity to take a quick survey of the Madrid Club. So he telephoned Sally, arranging to meet her there at eight.

Sally had been having a busy time settling in at the flat and had to take a taxi, as she was late for dinner. She found a cab waiting just along the road, and gave the driver the address of the Madrid Club, then rather anxiously opened her bag to see if she had any small change, for she hated having to ask taxi-drivers to change a pound note.

When she looked up again, she was suddenly aware that the cab was not moving in the right direction, but was proceeding at a lively pace through the back streets of Soho. She pulled back the partition at once and called to the driver, noticing for the first time that he was a shabby young man in the late twenties, with a cloth cap and scarf.

'This isn't the way to the Madrid Club!' cried Sally. 'You must have taken the wrong turn out of—'

'I know what I'm doin', lady!' he snarled. 'You keep that ruddy window shut!' And he slammed the glass partition. Sally pulled it open immediately.

'How dare you speak to me like that! Stop this cab at once!' she ordered.

'Sit down!' he snapped.

'Where are you taking me?' she demanded in complete bewilderment.

'You'll find out. Now, keep that ruddy window closed and your trap shut, or there'll be trouble.'

Sally fumbled in her bag.

'All right, driver, if you want trouble,' she said, 'here it is.' As she spoke the end of the barrel of a neat little .22 pressed into the back of his neck.

'Sit still and keep driving,' she ordered, her voice much steadier now. 'It's only a small revolver, but it's deadly at this range.'

He half-turned in his seat, and saw she was not joking.

'What do you want me to do?'

'Stop acting like Humphrey Bogart, and take me to the Madrid!' she said, pressing the revolver more firmly into his none-too-clean scarf.

As luck would have it, when they got there, Wyatt was standing in the vestibule talking to Inspector Lathom. Sally flung open the taxi door and beckoned to them frantically, so that they came running up. She explained the situation in a couple of terse sentences, and Lathom took command at once.

'Leave this to me, Mrs Wyatt,' he said, then turned to the driver.

'All right, you – drive round to Savile Row station,' he ordered, jumping into the cab. 'I'll tell you more later, Wyatt,' he promised as they moved off.

Wyatt placed a protective arm on Sally's shoulder, and noticed that she was still trembling a little.

'Why should he want to kidnap me?' she said in a puzzled tone.

'It may not have been you 'specially – he may have been on the look-out for any well-dressed woman,' Wyatt reminded her, 'Anyhow, we can leave it to Lathom for the time being. They'll hold the man overnight, and if he hasn't talked, I'll go and see him myself in the morning. I'm damned glad you had that gun with you, Sally. You don't usually carry one round. What made you?'

'I don't quite know. I think maybe it was something in your voice when you mentioned the Madrid on the telephone. I got the impression you were up to something, and I knew you weren't carrying your own gun, so I thought ...'

'Come and have a drink,' he said, patting her shoulder. 'You've certainly earned it.'

He led the way through a small alcove and into a circular bar with ebony-black walls and chairs upholstered in vermilion.

'You seem to know your way around this establishment,' she commented, after he had given the order.

'Some people never forget a face: I never forget a night club.'

'There's no accounting for tastes – or talents,' said Sally with a tiny shrug.

As they were sipping their drinks, Sally suddenly nudged her husband.

'Darling – here's Maurice Knight,' she whispered.

Knight was advancing on them, a half-smile on his handsome features.

'I didn't expect to find you two here,' he said after they had exchanged greetings.

'If it comes to that, I didn't expect to see you either, Mr Knight.' The young man laughed, then became rather more serious.

'I wonder if, by any chance, we are both here for the same reason,' he murmured.

'I should rather doubt that,' said Wyatt, 'because I'm here simply on account of my wife. I'd promised her an evening out on our first day back in Town.'

Knight looked round cautiously to make sure that they were not overheard.

'I came here because I found out about the car, Mr Wyatt,' he confided in low tones. 'You remember the car that tried to force me over that bridge?'

'Of course ... you got the number, didn't you?'

'Yes – and what's more, I've traced it!' announced Knight with considerable satisfaction.

'Did you, by Jove,' exclaimed Wyatt.

'You're improving as an amateur detective, Mr Knight,' smiled Sally.

'Yes, I've got results this time, Mrs Wyatt. That car belongs to Charles Luigi, the man who owns this club.'

'That's very interesting,' murmured Wyatt. 'Have you seen Luigi?'

'Yes, I've just had a chat to him. He's got some story about the car being laid up for over a fortnight at the garage.'

'You don't believe him?'

'Of course not. It's his word against the evidence of my own eyes. I saw a car answering to the description of Luigi's, with the same number, trying to force me off the road. If he had anything to do with that affair, is it likely that he would admit it?'

'You seem to have the main qualification for a detective, Mr Knight – a suspicious nature,' said Sally pleasantly. 'In the first place you insisted that Tyson was mixed up in this business ...'

'And I still think so,' interrupted Knight. 'If you want my frank opinion, I think that Tyson was well paid to—'

'Tyson happens to be dead,' said Wyatt somewhat abruptly.

'Dead!' repeated Knight in amazement.

'He was shot yesterday morning, soon after Mrs Wyatt and I arrived at the cottage.'

'Then you saw who shot him?'

'We did not. The police seem fairly certain that it's suicide. But for the fact that "Mr Rossiter" left his compliments, I might be inclined to that view myself.'

'You mean "Mr Rossiter" left a card?'

'The usual message in red ink.'

Knight looked bewildered.

'Are you quite sure there was no one in the cottage when you got there?'

'I searched it myself.'

The young man shook his head helplessly.

'This affair seems to get more and more involved,' he said rather sadly. 'I think I'll go and have some food; I haven't eaten much today. I'll be in there if there's anything else to discuss.' He indicated the room at the far end of the bar. Wyatt and Sally slowly finished their drinks, and were just debating whether to indulge in another when a dapper little man wearing evening dress came in and snapped his fingers to attract the barman's attention.

He was moving away again when he caught sight of Wyatt. He came over to them at once.

'Well, well, Mr Wyatt. It's a long time since you visited the Madrid.' The little man had a foreign accent.

'I was beginning to think you had forgotten all about us,' he went on, flashing an artificial smile at Sally.

'Night clubs aren't much in my line, Luigi,' said Wyatt.

'Then why do you come this evening?'

'Just to see you,' said Wyatt coolly.

Luigi favoured him with a little bow.

'I am honoured! I did not think I could attract the attention of Mr, Wyatt, the famous flying ace. Am I to be introduced to your friend?'

Wyatt smiled.

'Ex-flying ace,' he said, 'and this happens to be my wife – Sally, this is Charles Luigi.'

'I am so sorry,' Luigi apologized, 'but gentlemen do not always bring their wives to the Madrid. If I had known you were paying us a visit, Mrs Wyatt, I would have had a little present for you ... maybe some pure silk stockings.'

'Is that another of your sidelines, Luigi?' smiled Wyatt. But Luigi refused to be drawn.

'I hear you've been having a chat to Maurice Knight,' went on Wyatt, watching Luigi shrewdly.

At first he did not appear to know the name, then he nodded: 'Ah, yes, you mean that young fellow who was asking me a lot of silly questions about my car. A very inquisitive type, Mr Wyatt. I hope he isn't a friend of yours.'

'Not exactly.'

'He wouldn't be from Scotland Yard, by any chance?' persisted Luigi.

'Not to my knowledge,' grinned Wyatt. 'I should have thought you'd have known him well. He looks the type who would spend a lot of time in night clubs. He was engaged to Barbara Willis.'

'That was the girl who disappeared, Mr Luigi,' put in Sally.

'Ah yes, I have been reading about that. Something to do with this mysterious "Mr Rossiter", eh, Mr Wyatt?'

'I suppose you wouldn't know anything about that,' said Wyatt casually. The little man shrugged.

'Was that what you came specially to ask me, Mr Wyatt?'

'Not entirely,' said Wyatt. 'I looked in because I thought you might be able to tip me off about a girl named Lauren Beaumont.'

Luigi repeated the name thoughtfully, then slowly shook his head.

'I know of no one with that name,' he replied.

'That's rather strange,' said Wyatt quietly. 'She had dinner here last night, Luigi, and you spoke to her.'

'I speak to all my guests,' replied Luigi imperturbably, 'but I do not necessarily know their names. What was she like?'

'She was a blonde, about five feet two. She was here with Sir Donald Angus, the millionaire.'

'Would you say she was attractive?'

'I should imagine so – or she wouldn't be here alone with a married man.'

Luigi hesitated a moment, then shook his head.

'I am sorry,' he said firmly, 'I don't remember the girl.'

There was rather an awkward pause, then Wyatt said lightly: 'Oh, well, if that's your story, Luigi, I hope you'll be able to stick to it when Inspector Lathom looks in.'

'What has Lathom to do with Lauren Beaumont?' asked Luigi sharply.

'We happen to be looking for her, that's all.'

'You mean she has disappeared?'

'We wouldn't be looking for her otherwise.'

'But I read in the papers that Inspector Lathom was in charge of the "Mr Rossiter" case,' said Luigi with a little frown puckering his smooth forehead.

'The papers were quite correct,' said Wyatt. 'This *is* the "Rossiter" case.'

Luigi nodded his head several times, as if he were slowly taking in this information.

At last he leaned over and spoke confidentially to Wyatt.

'Tell me, my friend, are you investigating this "Rossiter" affair?'

'Why do you ask?'

'Because if you are, then as an old friend I should like to give you a word of advice.'

Luigi was smiling expansively.

'Well?' said Wyatt.

'Don't stick your neck out, my friend! Don't get involved in matters which do not concern you. It might be dangerous.'

Wyatt leaned back in his seat and regarded Luigi thoughtfully.

'Is that a warning, Luigi?' he asked.

'I told you what it is – just a nice piece of friendly advice.'

Wyatt took out his cigarette-case, and offered one to Sally and then to Luigi, who refused. Wyatt lighted Sally's cigarette, then said in an even tone:

'Luigi, I suppose *you* wouldn't be "Mr Rossiter", by any chance?'

He watched Luigi carefully as he spoke, to see if he showed the slightest reaction. But the little man only seemed amused at the idea.

'Why do you waste your time at Scotland Yard, my friend, when you have such an exquisite sense of humour?' He turned to Sally. 'I envy you your married life – there must be very few dull moments when Mr Wyatt is around.'

He was about to continue in this vein when one of his assistants came up and whispered that he was wanted on the telephone, and he excused himself.

The soft strains of a small dance band came floating in from the supper room, waiters were moving around busily, and the bar was beginning to fill up.

'Well, what do you think of our Mr Luigi?' asked Wyatt.

'I wouldn't trust him as far as I could throw him!' retorted Sally.

'Yes, he's a wily bird and no mistake,' mused Wyatt. 'I'm always meaning to ask at the Yard if they have anything against him in the files.'

Sally had now recovered from the shock of her experience in the taxi, and was beginning to feel hungry, so they went down into the dining-room, where the head-waiter conducted them to a table on the edge of the tiny dance floor. Wyatt would have preferred somewhere less conspicuous, but it was the only table vacant at that moment.

As they sat down a dance ended, and Sally noticed a small group of girls returning to a table near the band. They were obviously dance hostesses, very carefully chosen for their contrasting styles. There was a willowy brunette, a graceful blonde, a petite redhead, and a platinum blonde whose hair appeared to be almost silver when she stepped into the bright lighting.

After Wyatt had ordered their meal, Sally sat watching the girls until the next number started. They were joined by a tall, fair-haired girl, who carried herself with assurance. She sat down and looked around the room, and her eye caught Sally's almost at once. As soon as the music started, the blonde girl came over towards them. She was wearing a striking green and silver dress, and her poise and air of sophistication would have made many women envious. She stopped at their table, and said in a low, husky voice:

'Can I talk to you for a minute, Mr Wyatt?'

'Certainly,' said Wyatt, rising. 'I'll get another chair.' He found one at once, and brought it over.

'I mustn't stay long – it isn't safe,' she said.

Wyatt tried to recall where he had seen her before, but was unable to do so.

'Did you come here to try to find Lauren Beaumont?'

'What do you know about Lauren Beaumont?' demanded Wyatt, somewhat surprised.

She was about to speak when a waiter arrived. When the waiter had gone she said:

'Lauren Beaumont was here last night – she was with a thick-set little man – a Scotsman, I think ...'

'Yes, that's right,' said Wyatt encouragingly. 'What else do you know about her?'

'She's disappeared, hasn't she?'

The girl looked round furtively as she spoke, obviously anxious not to be overheard, though this was extremely unlikely, as conversation was none too easy amidst the music and the chatter of the dancers. Wyatt gave a quick nod in reply to her question, but did not speak.

'I knew she would!' said the girl tensely. 'Listen, Mr Wyatt, we can't talk here – my name is Coral Salter – I'm a dance hostess here, and I happen to have found out—'

She broke off again as the waiter came to the table. Wyatt dismissed him as quickly as possible, and turned to Coral Salter again.

'You were about to say you've found out something, Miss Salter. Why are you telling me this?'

'Because I swore I'd get even with that rotter!' There was a vicious note in her voice. 'Anyhow, we can't talk here. Could you meet me in my flat in about an hour? The cabaret comes on then, and I can slip out ...'

'Of course,' he agreed.

'I'll tell you everything I know ... I reckon I'll level up some old scores ...'

'You didn't tell me the address,' Wyatt reminded her, noticing that Charles Luigi was making his way over to their table. The girl noticed it too.

'I'll give it to the cloakroom attendant – pick it up on your way out, Mrs Wyatt,' she concluded hastily, and a second later Luigi was standing at her elbow.

'What is this – a family party?' he began on a note of *bonhomie*. 'I didn't know you had met Mr and Mrs Wyatt, Coral.'

'They asked me to have a drink,' she explained with a touch of defiance.

'That was very kind of them, my dear. But I am sure you have a number of clients waiting. I like to see those pretty legs of yours on the dance floor.'

Coral Salter rose rather sulkily, nodded to Wyatt and Sally, and went off to the table by the band.

Luigi turned to Wyatt with a helpless gesture.

'Tut! Tut! These young ladies – they're too temperamental for words.'

Sally smiled understandingly and complimented him upon the band. After chatting with them for a minute or two, he excused himself and went off to greet a small party that was just coming in.

Sally watched Coral Salter dancing.

'That girl knows something; I'm pretty sure of that,' she told her husband. 'What are we going to do, darling?'

'Finish dinner first,' he decided. 'Nothing like a solid foundation if there's anything unpleasant to be tackled.'

'We'll still have some time to wait before she's free.'

'H'm,' murmured Wyatt, eyeing the very limited floor space somewhat dubiously. 'I suppose we could dance. It's supposed to be wonderful exercise, even for old crocks like me.'

By the time they had finished dinner the floor was even more crowded, but they made some pretence of dancing a waltz and a couple of fox-trots.

Sally was glad when Wyatt at last decided it was time to be moving, for she did not like the atmosphere of the Madrid. She couldn't help feeling that it was liable to be raided at any moment.

In the cloakroom, she asked the girl rather tentatively if Coral Salter had left her any message, and was given a somewhat grubby envelope. She opened it when they were outside in the taxi. It contained a latchkey and a scrap of paper on which was scrawled in pencil the address: 14 Sutton Mansions, Milton Rd., St John's Wood.

They found the flat was one of a recently erected block, standing well back from the road. The flat they sought was on the second floor, and both the hallway and stairs were deserted when they went up.

'I wonder what her idea was in giving you the key,' mused Wyatt, as they mounted the stairs.

'She may have anticipated having a bit of trouble in getting away, and didn't want us to be left standing on the stairs.'

'H'm ... well, it was a good idea of hers to come back here separately, anyhow.'

He opened the flat door, and they went into a thickly carpeted hallway. Wyatt fumbled for the light switch, and they found their way through a half-open door into a very expensively furnished lounge.

'By Jove! This is certainly home sweet home, and no mistake,' said Wyatt, appraising a mahogany cocktail cabinet that must have cost at least a hundred pounds. Sally went over to the window and drew the heavy velvet curtains.

'I wonder how Coral Salter can afford a flat like this?' she speculated.

'Sally, this is hardly the time and place to start examining the facts of life,' smiled Wyatt.

'All the same, I shouldn't have thought she earned a great deal in that job,' murmured Sally.

'My dear Sally,' said her husband patiently, 'Coral Salter is an extremely beautiful girl. Attractive girls have many peculiar ways of their own of augmenting their incomes. Didn't you discover that when you were at the Yard?'

'Stop acting the fool, dear. Look at this enormous set – it's a radiogram – and there's television, too ... why, it must have cost hundreds ...'

She suddenly realized he was not listening to her. He was standing beside a small table on which was a pale green telephone. He picked up the pad and began flicking over the pages.

'This is interesting, Sally,' he said presently. 'There's a friend of ours down here. Doctor Fraser – Welbeck 55568.' He stood quietly tapping the pad with his finger-nail.

'Lionel, how far do you think this girl Coral Salter is mixed up in this affair?'

'Pretty deeply, I should imagine,' said Wyatt, lighting a cigarette.

'I can't think how she comes to know so much,' said Sally in puzzled tone. 'Have you any idea?'

'I have a feeling she's rather a close friend of Mr Charles Luigi – or has been in the past. Maybe it's a case of a woman scorned. There's a lot goes on at the Madrid that the police never get to hear of.'

Sally settled herself in the most comfortable armchair.

'It's rather odd that she should have made a note of Doctor Fraser's telephone number, isn't it?' she reflected. 'I can't make up my mind about Doctor Fraser – that was a queer story of hers about the girls who impersonated Barbara Willis and Mildred Gillow—'

'And Lauren Beaumont.'

Sally sat bolt upright.

'Lionel, you don't think Coral Salter was one of those girls? She may have got scared when she heard of the disappearances.'

'Now don't get worked up about it, Sally.'

Sally relaxed again.

'It's all very well for you to say that,' she grumbled, 'but remember what Luigi said about getting involved in things which don't concern you.'

Wyatt slowly blew out a stream of smoke, then said quietly: 'You're not suggesting I should throw up the case, are you, Sally?'

'Of course not!' she replied with an impatient gesture.

'You've got to see it through now you've got so far. But, for Pete's sake, don't start telling me not to get worked up over things.'

'Darling! You look quite hot and bothered,' said Wyatt in some amusement. 'I think you'd better go in the bedroom and powder your nose. I should imagine it's the door at the end of the hall.'

'I refuse to powder my nose,' said Sally, 'but I would like to see that bedroom. If it's anything like this lounge, it'll be worth coming a long way to see.'

She picked up her bag and went out, while Wyatt resumed his study of the telephone pad, which contained a mass of closely written names and numbers. He had just managed to decipher the name "Barbara Willis" when he heard a scream from outside. He dropped the pad and ran to the bedroom.

Sally was standing by the dressing-table, her hand to her mouth, staring at something which Wyatt could not see.

'Sally! What is it?'

'Look!' she cried in a strange little voice. 'The other side of the bed!'

Wyatt moved into the room and walked past the foot of the bed.

On the far side lay the inert form of Coral Salter. Her eyes were closed, and there were ominous red marks around her neck. There had obviously been a struggle, for her dress was torn off her right shoulder, and there was a thin stream of blood from her mouth.

'Is she dead?' asked Sally in a breathless whisper. Wyatt lifted one of the girl's eyelids, then felt her pulse.

'She's dead all right – strangled,' he pronounced. 'She must have been dead about twenty minutes.'

'Then she might have been killed at the Madrid and brought here afterwards.'

'That's quite possible,' he agreed, 'though I should imagine it wouldn't be too easy to do that without attracting attention. Alternatively, the killer could have followed her here, done the job, and got away down the fire-escape ... that would be much simpler.'

Sally beat her fist in her palm.

'This is horrible, what are we going to do?'

'Don't panic, Sally,' he said, going over to her. He picked up a bottle of smelling salts from the dressing-table.

'Here, take a sniff of this, then listen to me. I want you to go out and get a taxi if you can – drive straight to the Yard and get Lathom. Then—'

He paused, and they both listened intently. Somebody was fitting a latchkey into the outside door of the flat. A second later, the door opened and was closed again after the newcomer had entered.

A man began humming to himself in a pleasant baritone voice. He went into the lounge, and presently they heard the clink of glasses and the subdued music of a radio programme.

Wyatt and Sally, who had moved towards the bedroom door, looked at each other questioningly. Finally, Wyatt made up his mind. He squeezed Sally's hand reassuringly, and whispered: 'Let me have that revolver from your bag.'

Her hands trembled a little as she unfastened the clasp and handed him the tiny .22.

'Do be careful, Lionel,' she whispered.

'All right, darling. When I go into the lounge, you can pass behind me and get to the outside door. If there's any trouble, hop out and get some help. Ready now?'

She nodded. Wyatt opened the bedroom door cautiously

and moved softly in the direction of the lounge, the door of which was almost closed. Sally had no difficulty in getting to the outside door of the flat, and waited there nervously for him to go into the lounge. He hesitated for some moments, trying to ascertain the movements of the man inside. But he heard nothing beyond the swish of a soda syphon and the sound of a glass being set down on a tray.

He would have liked to wait a few minutes longer, but he could see that Sally could not stand much more of this suspense, so he slowly pushed open the door.

'Why, Mr Wyatt,' cried a familiar voice. 'How on earth did you get here?'

'What's more to the point, Mr Linder,' replied Wyatt in level tones, 'what are you doing here?'

Linder swung round in the armchair in apparent bewilderment.

'Are you crazy?' he snapped. 'This happens to be my flat!'

CHAPTER VI

Mr Linder has an Alibi

Sally had softly turned the knob of the Yale lock in readiness to make a quick getaway. She stood listening to the conversation, and on hearing Linder claim that it was his flat she gave a little exclamation and released the latch with an audible click.

'Who's that outside, Mr Wyatt?' she heard Linder ejaculate.

'It's all right, Mr Linder,' came Wyatt's reassuring voice. 'My wife is in the hall outside.'

Wyatt put his head round the door and beckoned to Sally, who came into the lounge.

'Mr Wyatt, what is the meaning of this?' demanded Linder sternly. 'Are you in the habit of breaking into people's flats? You wouldn't have a search warrant, I suppose?'

'Before we go into all that, Mr Linder,' replied Wyatt, 'you'd better come into the bedroom. There's something I'd like you to see.'

'The bedroom?' stuttered Linder. 'What can there possibly be in the bedroom …?'

'If you don't mind, Mr Linder – there's no time to be lost,' persisted Wyatt.

Linder looked from one to the other in some mystification, then rose and followed Wyatt into the bedroom. The detective watched him as they came round the bed and saw the figure of the dead girl. If Linder knew what he would find there, then he certainly simulated surprise and horror in a manner that would have done credit to any West End actor.

'Who is this girl?' he gasped. 'Who is she?'

'You don't know her, Mr Linder?' asked Sally, who was standing by the bedroom door.

'Of course I don't know her!' he declared vehemently. 'I have never seen her in my life before.'

Wyatt sat on a corner of the bed and looked down at the dead girl.

'Her name is Coral Salter, Mr Linder. She is, or rather she was, a professional dancer at the Madrid.'

'Then she's ... dead?'

'Strangled,' said Wyatt, eyeing him closely.

Linder took an involuntary step forward.

'But look here, what the devil's she doing in my flat?' he protested in a frightened voice. 'How did she get here? Mr Wyatt, for God's sake, tell me what's been going on!'

'It isn't as simple as all that, Mr Linder,' said Wyatt quietly. 'All I can tell you is that we met Miss Salter for the first time at the Madrid about two hours back. She told me that she wanted a confidential chat with me, and suggested that we should go to her flat.'

'But this is not her flat!' insisted Linder. 'You mean she gave you this address?'

'She left a note for my wife with the cloakroom attendant, and this address was on the paper. There was a key in the envelope, too.'

'Then it's quite obvious what has happened,' said Linder

81

tensely. 'Someone must have known that she intended to see you – someone must have known about the note ...'

'You mean they substituted another note, with this address on it,' said Wyatt slowly.

'That's quite possible,' said Sally excitedly. 'Someone must have seen Coral Salter talking to us, and followed her when she went to the ladies' cloakroom ...'

'Then it was a lady who was responsible?'

Sally shook her head impatiently. 'I don't know. She could have been intercepted before she went to the cloakroom, and then somebody else could have given the envelope to the cloakroom attendant.'

'But what about the key, Sally?' said Wyatt. 'It isn't as easy as all that to duplicate a Yale key, is it, Mr Linder?'

Linder frowned with annoyance.

'I don't care if there were fifty keys!' he said wildly. 'This is my flat, and you've only to go down to the head porter if you want to prove it.'

'I don't doubt it's your flat,' replied Wyatt calmly. 'And I dare say the police will be quite satisfied about that. What they will want to know is—'

'What is this girl doing here?'

'Exactly!'

Linder paced thoughtfully over to the window and stood there for a few moments without speaking. Then he turned and said:

'Mr Wyatt, you don't seriously think I had anything to do with this business, do you? You don't think I murdered this girl?'

'It's rather difficult to know what to think,' said Wyatt. 'The fact remains that you'll have to do quite a lot of explaining to the police.'

'But I've no motive for killing her. I've never even seen her before,' repeated Linder with considerable emotion. He made an obvious effort to control himself, then asked in a quieter tone:

'Have you any idea what time she died?'

'She's been dead about twenty minutes – perhaps half-an-hour.'

'And you say you saw her at The Madrid?'

'That is so.'

'After eight o'clock?'

'Yes, of course. We met her over an hour ago.'

Linder breathed a sigh of relief. 'Thank God, that lets me out!'

'Then I take it you have a pretty satisfactory alibi, Mr Linder?'

'Fortunately for me, Mr Wyatt, it's the perfect alibi,' he announced with complete assurance. 'An acquaintance of mine called for me just after eight. We strolled down to the Hanover Restaurant near Baker Street, and stayed there till about a quarter past ten. We left the restaurant together and went to my friend's flat for a drink. Then we strolled back here – he left me just outside. So you can see we've been together all the evening, and he can testify to that. In fact, it's the perfect alibi.'

'I shouldn't be too sure about that, Mr Linder,' said Wyatt mildly. 'Doesn't it rather depend upon the integrity of your companion?'

'Naturally,' smiled Linder.

'Then the person in question is reliable?'

'Undoubtedly, Mr Wyatt. It was Chief Inspector Lathom.'

Wyatt telephoned Lathom's flat immediately and received full corroboration of Linder's story. He also arranged for

Lathom to come over and take charge of everything, and the inspector arrived by taxi ten minutes later. After Wyatt and Sally had told him all they knew, they left him to contact the nearest station, arrange for removal of the body, and gather any further information he could obtain. In fact it seemed that Lathom would get very little sleep that night, but he agreed to meet Wyatt with Sir James at ten the following morning.

When Wyatt arrived he found that Lathom had already given Sir James a summary of the events of the previous night, and they had come to the conclusion that it would have been a physical impossibility for Linder to have killed Coral Salter.

Sir James had a little stack of files in front of him on his desk, and looked more worried than ever.

'What about this fellow Knight?' he asked, almost as soon as Wyatt had propped his stick against the desk and sat down.

'Well, he was certainly at the Madrid; we had a talk to him,' said Wyatt.

'Could he have murdered the girl and then taken her to the flat?'

'Yes,' said Wyatt, 'I suppose he could. But, of course, the same applies to Charles Luigi or anyone else at the club.'

Lathom looked up from his note-pad, on which he was drafting out a report.

'What exactly was Mr Knight doing at the Madrid?' he queried.

'Apparently, he found out that the car which tried to force him over the bridge belonged to Charles Luigi, and he wanted to interview him.'

Lathom sniffed.

'I'm always suspicious of these amateur detectives; maybe it's time we had a word with Mr Knight,' he murmured.

'That's an idea,' agreed Perivale, taking a well-worn pipe from his pocket and slowly filling it. 'By the way, Lathom, did you check up on that car of Luigi's?'

'Yes, sir, there's a report in the blue file. The car was laid up and never left the garage. If Knight got the number right, then the number must have been faked.'

'That would mean somebody is trying to throw suspicion on Luigi,' suggested Perivale.

Wyatt leaned back in his chair. 'Unless, of course, the garage people are pulling a fast one on us, and Luigi really did use the car. That little man has a finger in so many pies, he might quite easily own that garage.'

Perivale slowly digested this as he carefully rammed the tobacco into his pipe.

Wyatt was in rather a contrary mood on this particular morning. For one thing, Lathom had vouchsafed no explanation as to why he had spent an entire evening with Hugo Linder; he had a feeling that the inspector was holding something back so as to accumulate kudos for himself.

'What made you spend the evening with Hugo Linder, Inspector?' he suddenly demanded in as casual a tone as possible.

'What made you spend the evening at the Madrid, Mr Wyatt?' countered the inspector.

'I thought you knew why. I simply wanted to have a talk to Luigi.'

'I wanted to have a talk with Hugo Linder,' countered Lathom again.

'Is he a friend of yours?'

The inspector shrugged. 'A policeman has no friends,' he

said. Sir James looked from one protagonist to the other, but said nothing. Lathom was obviously, in Wyatt's opinion, determined to give as little away as possible. The tension was relieved at length by the arrival of a sergeant to inform them that Victor Taylor, the taxi driver who had tried to kidnap Sally, was downstairs in Superintendent Bradley's room.

'Have you seen this man?' Wyatt asked Sir James.

'No, Lathom's questioned him.'

'Any luck, Inspector?'

Lathom shook his head.

'He's as scared as a jack-rabbit and sullen as they make 'em. I couldn't get much out of him.'

'D'you mind if I have a chat with him?' asked Wyatt politely. Lathom shrugged as if to wash his hands of any such proceedings, and it was Perivale who said:

'Go ahead, Wyatt; that's why I had him brought from the station. You know Bradley's office, don't you?'

Wyatt nodded and went out.

He found Vic Taylor in a truculent mood. He was looking shabbier than ever, perhaps because he had slept in his clothes and had not shaved. When Wyatt offered him a cigarette, he refused it with a violent gesture.

'Keep your ruddy cigarettes!' he snapped. 'What's the game, mister? I've already been 'ere once answerin' a lot o' cock-eyed questions, an' I'm just abart browned off. What are you goin' to do wiv me?'

Wyatt perched on a corner of the desk and thoughtfully rubbed the hook of his stick.

'What would you like us to do with you, Mr Taylor?' he said easily.

'Come orf it!' snapped Vic Taylor. 'You ain't paid for bein' funny.'

'I was only asking you a civil question,' said Wyatt pleasantly. 'What would you like us to do with you?'

'What the hell do I care!' snarled Taylor, with a note of desperation. 'You can shove me in jug and have done wiv' it!'

'Yes, I suppose we could do that,' ruminated Wyatt. 'At least, you'd be safe there.'

'Safe? What d'yer mean?'

'From the gentleman who gave you that job last night – the job you fell down on,' Wyatt reminded him. 'I hope my wife didn't upset you – your nerves seem to be in a bad way this morning.'

'I was a ruddy fool to take that job,' admitted the taxi driver with some show of reluctance. 'I'm sorry if your wife was frightened, guv'nor – though I must say I reckon she can look after 'erself all right.'

'She was brought up in a hard school, Mr Taylor,' said Wyatt with a smile. 'Were you well paid for that job?'

Taylor eyed him suspiciously.

'I've 'ad that long-faced "dick" askin' me all them questions, an' a fat lot I told 'im. If you want to know what I was paid, you'd better go and ask him yerself.'

Wyatt laughed, then lighted a cigarette.

'I'm afraid I don't hit it off very well with Inspector Lathom,' he confided, 'so I don't suppose he'd tell me very much, even if he knew anything. All the same, I do happen to know that Lathom has a theory about you. He thinks that you are mixed up in this "Rossiter" affair.'

The little man's hands clutched frantically at his shabby cap.

'Blimey! You don't think I 'ad anything to do wi' any o' them jobs ...' he stuttered.

'I don't, Mr Taylor,' replied Wyatt indifferently. 'But I'm just telling you that Inspector Lathom does!'

The little driver looked round the room like a cornered animal.

'I swear I got nothing to do with this "Rossiter" business,' he repeated hoarsely.

'I'll take your word for it,' nodded Wyatt. 'Providing you'll take my word that I'll treat your story with confidence. Now, what happened last night?'

Taylor swallowed hard, then said in a low voice:

'I was paid fifty quid and told to pick up Mrs Wyatt an' take 'er to an address in the East End.'

'Who paid you the money?' demanded Wyatt.

'I dunno ... and that's the truth, guv'nor.'

Wyatt was quite sure that he was lying, but he was determined to be patient.

'You know, Mr Taylor, the position is really quite simple,' he said reasonably. 'You've got to make a decision, and it's entirely up to you. I'm certainly not going to influence you one way or the other. But this is the point: if you don't tell me what really happened yesterday, there's a sporting chance that Inspector Lathom might convince me, and a whole lot of other people, that you're one of the leading lights in this "Rossiter" business. Maybe you don't know that it's already involved four murders to date. On the other hand, if you do come clean with me, then I don't doubt that I can convince Inspector Lathom, and others, that you have no connection with "Mr Rossiter".'

Taylor seemed to hesitate for several seconds, obviously weighing up the pros and cons of the situation.

'Could I have a cigarette now, guv'nor?' he said eventually. Wyatt passed over his case, and with his other hand flicked open his lighter. Taylor inhaled deeply several times, then expelled a long stream of smoke.

'It was like this, guv'nor,' he began in a rather more convincing manner. 'I park my car at Layman's Garage, the other side o' Vauxhall Bridge, and I was fillin' up there yesterday mornin' when I saw a bloke watchin' me. 'E was a funny-lookin' customer – swarthy sort of bloke, gettin' on for fifty I should think. Just as I was gettin' ready to move orf, he comes over and makes me a proposition ... fifty quid to pick up Mrs Wyatt and take 'er to an address down East. Made out it was a sort o' practical joke, though I 'ad me suspicions all along.'

'What was the address?' interposed Wyatt.

''E said it was a vet's place – a sort of shop – the address was 28 Coster Row, Shadwell Basin.'

Wyatt hastily scrawled it on the back of an envelope.

'Had you ever been there before?'

Taylor shook his head.

'Don't often go down that way. They ain't got much use for taxis there as a rule.'

'And what about this man who gave you the money – had you ever seen him before?'

'Never set eyes on the bloke. Jolly sort of feller in a way. Foreign, of course.'

'How tall?'

'About five-feet-eight, I should think.'

'You'd be able to recognize him again, of course.'

'Blimey, not arf! I could pick 'im out of a regiment.'

Wyatt stubbed out his cigarette. He felt reasonably certain that Taylor was telling the truth.

'Look here, Taylor,' he said amiably, 'I'm going to take a chance and get Sir James to release you. Mrs Wyatt won't be bringing any charge against you, if you'll just do one little thing for me.'

'OK, Mr Wyatt,' said the little man eagerly. 'What is it you want?'

'I want you to pick me up at my flat this evening at eight o'clock and take me to the Madrid – you know, where my wife directed you last night.'

'I know it, guv'nor. Is that all?'

'Not quite,' said Wyatt deliberately. 'When we get there, I shall want you to come in with me and have a look at the proprietor, a man named Charles Luigi ...'

Wyatt was just knotting his tie when the bedroom door opened and Sally came in.

'Mr Knight's outside,' she said. 'He seems to be het up about something. From what I can gather, Inspector Lathom has been putting him through a mild form of third degree.'

Wyatt peered at himself in the mirror, adjusted the tie to his satisfaction, picked up his stick and went into the lounge.

Maurice Knight was pacing to and fro.

'Hello, Mr Knight, what's the trouble?' he asked pleasantly. 'Afraid I haven't much time – I've a taxi ordered for eight.'

Knight seemed to have some difficulty in controlling his temper. His hair was unruly, his tie a little on one side, and his coat unbuttoned.

'Mr Wyatt, did you know they were going to send for me?' he demanded flatly, facing Wyatt as he came through the door.

'Who were going to send for you?'

'Scotland Yard! I've been there this afternoon. They've been hurling questions at me for two hours. Good heavens, anyone would think that I was a suspicious character—'

90

'But you are a suspicious character, Mr Knight,' replied Wyatt pleasantly. 'Would you like a drink?'

He went over to the cocktail cabinet.

'What did you say?' demanded Knight.

'I said would you like a drink?'

'Wyatt, let's put our cards on the table,' said Knight abruptly. 'Why was I forced to visit Scotland Yard this afternoon? Why do you consider me a suspicious character?'

Wyatt handed him a glass in which there was a generous measure of whisky.

'Drink that first; then I'll tell you.'

Knight took a long drink.

'Now,' said Wyatt. 'In the first place, you were not forced to visit Scotland Yard: you were invited to do so. Secondly, I did not say I considered you a suspicious character: I say that you *are* a suspicious character. Would you like to know why?'

'I should be extremely grateful if you would tell me why,' replied Knight, not without some bitterness.

'All right then ...' Wyatt took a sip at his own glass. 'The first girl to be murdered by "Mr Rossiter" was your own fiancée, Barbara Willis. Now that, in itself, is quite an interesting point, Mr Knight. Then we must add to it the fact that when Tyson committed suicide, or was murdered, you were in the vicinity. You were actually staying at Teignmouth.'

Knight slumped into an armchair and gazed moodily out of the window, but did not speak, so Wyatt went on in a level tone:

'Last night, a professional dancer named Coral Salter was murdered. Although the body was discovered in a flat at Sutton Mansions, the police are fairly certain that she was murdered at the Madrid Club. You see the connection?'

91

'Yes,' said Knight reluctantly, 'I was at the Madrid last night. It was quite a coincidence, of course.'

'I have only your word for that,' said Wyatt smoothly.

'But you know why I went there – to see Luigi about the car.'

Wyatt nodded.

'You may have had a good reason for going to the Madrid, but the fact remains that you went, and were obviously there when the girl was murdered. I happened to catch sight of you myself about that time.'

Knight drained his glass and set it down on a side table. Then he produced a cigarette-case, offered Wyatt a cigarette and took one himself.

'I'm sorry I was rude just now,' he apologized. 'I've been rather upset this afternoon in one way or another. Though it's a matter of complete indifference to me what you or Scotland Yard or anyone else thinks about me.'

There was a note of defiance in his voice now, and he drew upon his cigarette before continuing.

'When Barbara was murdered, I made up my mind to investigate this case. It wasn't that I fancied myself as an amateur detective; I'm well aware I'm not cut out for that sort of thing. But I made up my mind that if Scotland Yard didn't get this "Mr Rossiter" by orthodox methods, then, by jove, I'd try the unorthodox. And I shall keep on trying, Mr Wyatt, whether you or Sir James or the Big Five like it or not!'

Wyatt smiled.

'Well, that seems fair enough, Mr Knight. But do you realize the risks you're running?'

Before Knight could reply, Sally came in to say that Wyatt's taxi had just turned the corner.

Wyatt asked his visitor if he could drop him anywhere on the way to the Madrid, and his visitor said he was due at a party in Bond Street. Knight showed some curiosity as to Wyatt's reasons for revisiting the Madrid, but did not pry too obviously into the matter. Wyatt advised Sally not to wait up for him, picked up his coat and went out with Knight.

'Shall we walk down?' asked the visitor.

'No, we may as well use the lift,' said Wyatt, pressing the button.

There was a soft whirring, and presently the lift slid gently into view. As the light inside was switched off, it was not until Wyatt had his hand on the gate that he realized it was occupied.

In the far corner a figure of a man had slumped on to his knees, and as the lift came to a standstill with a slight jerk, he toppled over and lay full length on the floor.

Wyatt wrenched the gate open, then switched on the light. He immediately caught the gleam of metal, and saw the long knife between the man's shoulder blades. He bent down and turned the man's face towards him, gave a low whistle of recognition.

'Who is it? Do you know him?' Knight queried anxiously.

'Yes – it's a taxi driver named Victor Taylor. He was going to take me to the Madrid.'

'Is he dead?'

Wyatt made a quick examination, then slowly nodded.

'I'm afraid so ...'

Wyatt left the gates open so that the lift could not be summoned from any other floor, then rushed downstairs, leaving Knight on guard. The hall of the flats was quite deserted, and Wyatt had some difficulty in finding the head porter. The porter swore that he had seen no visitors. There was nothing for it but to go back upstairs and telephone Scotland Yard.

He found Inspector Lathom in his office and briefly related the facts to him.

'Well, well, murder on your own doorstep now, eh, Mr Wyatt?' he commented, and Wyatt thought he could detect a note of smugness in his tone. However, Lathom promised to come round immediately and bring a police surgeon and ambulance.

When he arrived he also had Sir James Perivale and a sergeant with the 'murder bag', who immediately busied himself taking photos of the body and any likely fingerprints.

All this time Sally had remained in her bedroom, in a state of considerable agitation. Wyatt forbade her to leave the flat.

However, after Lathom and his assistants had left, Sir James asked Wyatt if he could have a word with Sally, and they went into the lounge.

'Now, Sally, I take it you've a rough idea what's happened,' began Sir James.

'Well, Lionel told me the taxi driver had met with an accident, then I heard him on the phone to Inspector Lathom.'

'That's right,' nodded Perivale. 'Now, there's just one little point I want to check up with you. I understand that Wyatt and Mr Knight were here in the lounge when you came in and said the taxi had arrived.'

'That's right, Sir James,' nodded Sally. 'I happened to be crossing the hall and caught sight of the taxi driving up.'

'Ah, you saw the taxi,' agreed Perivale. 'But did you see Taylor?'

'I'm afraid I couldn't swear to that, I didn't take particular notice of the driver.'

Wyatt leaned his elbows on the radiogram and frowned thoughtfully.

'It's quite obvious that Taylor wasn't driving,' he declared. 'Someone else brought him here and dumped him in the lift.'

Sir James rubbed his chin.

'You say you dashed downstairs as soon as you found the body?'

'And didn't see a soul. Of course, I didn't search everywhere. Somebody might have been hiding. But I brought out Jerrams, the porter, and he hasn't seen anyone go out since, apart from Knight and your people.'

'You looked in the cab, I take it?'

'Just a quick glance,' nodded Wyatt. 'It seemed to me quite empty: your man has examined it pretty thoroughly.'

Perivale sat back in his chair and tried to piece the evidence together. This latest development seemed to point directly to Luigi. Wyatt had intended to take Taylor to the Madrid for the purpose of identifying Luigi as the man who had paid him to kidnap Sally.

Perivale's reflections were cut short by the ringing of the telephone. Wyatt answered it and heard the distinctive voice of Doctor Fraser.

'I'm sorry to disturb you, Mr Wyatt,' she said, 'but they gave me your number at Scotland Yard, and I'm in something of a quandary. Maybe it's just my imagination making a mountain out of a molehill, but I can't get the thing off my mind.'

'Surely a psychiatrist should be able to cope with a little problem like that,' said Wyatt.

'It isn't as easy as all that,' she assured him. 'You remember I told you about those mysterious cases, and how the girls disappeared ...'

'Yes,' said Wyatt at once. 'Are there any more developments?'

'There's just been a new one – about half an hour ago. I had a telephone call from a man who said he was Professor Reed. He told me that his daughter had been taken seriously ill, and that he had been recommended to me by his local practitioner, Doctor Stenman.'

'You know Doctor Stenman?'

'I do not, Mr Wyatt. And I have certainly never heard of Professor Reed. To be quite frank with you, Mr Wyatt, he didn't sound very much like a professor.'

'I see,' said Wyatt. 'So you're highly suspicious about the whole business?'

'I've been trying for some time to trace Doctor Stenman, both in the phone book and the Medical Directory, and I'm getting more and more suspicious.'

'You sound a bit upset, Doctor.'

'Wouldn't you be upset, Mr Wyatt? In view of what I told you had happened before?'

'All right,' said Wyatt. 'We'll try to prevent it from happening again. I take it this Professor Reed gave you an address?'

'Yes, that's another thing. The address was – well – unusual, to say the least. It was 28 Coster Row, Shadwell Basin. Isn't that in the East End?'

'Just a minute,' said Wyatt, fumbling in his pocket for an envelope on which he had scrawled the address Victor Taylor had given him. It was exactly the same.

'Twenty-eight Coster Row ...' he repeated slowly. 'Yes, it's the East End all right.'

'Well, what do you think I should do, Mr Wyatt? I mean, should I make the call? If there really is a girl who's very ill ...'

'Leave it for tonight,' said Wyatt. 'If you'll telephone me first thing in the morning, I'll probably have something more definite for you then.'

'Very well, Mr Wyatt. I'll do that. Thanks a lot.'

Wyatt thoughtfully cradled the receiver. He was about to tell the others what had happened when Lathom came in to inform them that Sir Donald Angus was outside.

'I thought you went back to the Yard, Lathom,' said Sir James.

'Yes, sir, he was waiting there, and I thought I'd better bring him back here. He's had some rather important news.'

'Bring him in,' said Wyatt, and Lathom went out to return with Sir Donald, who looked a little whiter than usual. There was a strained expression in his eyes.

Wyatt noted all these signs, and was the more surprised to find Sir Donald inclined to be somewhat aggressively cheerful. His eye caught the whisky decanter and regarded it so longingly that Wyatt was impelled to ask him to have a drink.

'That's verra nice of you, Mr Wyatt. I don't indulge much, but seeing as this is rather a special occasion, I think, perhaps, just a small one ...'

Perivale swung round in his chair.

'Did you say a special occasion?' he asked.

'That's right, Sir James. I don't mind telling you this business has been a great strain on me, but it's all over now, thank goodness.'

'You mean you've heard from "Mr Rossiter"?'

The little Scotsman tossed down his drink.

'No, and I won't be hearing from him, either. It's all over and done with now. The lassie's turned up again. It was all a practical joke.'

'Practical joke?' stuttered Perivale.

'Rather a queer sense of humour,' said Wyatt quietly.

'Perhaps you'll explain yourself, Sir Donald,' said Lathom.

Angus was making strenuous efforts to be hearty, but Wyatt noticed that the worried look was still in his eyes.

'Has Lauren Beaumont come back?' asked Sally.

'Yes, she's back, and she's all right … quite safe and sound. That's what I want to explain. It was all a practical joke. You see, she never really disappeared at all; she simply decided to pay a surprise visit to some old friends of hers.

'You mean she walked out on you?' demanded Perivale with some annoyance.

'Aye, I suppose you could put it that way,' replied Sir Donald, apparently unperturbed. 'She's a girl who acts a good deal on impulse.'

He switched on a smile that was as patently artificial as the teeth it displayed.

'But what about the note?' asked Sally. 'And then there was the ear-ring.'

'Ah, yes, I must tell you about that,' said Angus with a noticeable effort. 'You see, Lauren's got rather a queer sense of humour – as Mr Wyatt said. She'd been reading in the papers about this mysterious "Mr Rossiter", so she thought it would be rather a lark if she played a joke on me. She's a girl who's very fond of the limelight, ye understand,' he added somewhat apologetically. 'She's always wanted to go on the stage, and she likes to dramatize her private life.'

'I can quite appreciate all that,' said Perivale rather frigidly.

'The point is that this case is no joke at all – it has already involved five deaths ...'

'Yes, Sir James, I can see your point, and I'm very sorry indeed to have put you to all this trouble, but after all, Miss Beaumont is a free woman; if she likes to disappear for a few days I presume she's at liberty to do so.'

'Certainly, Sir Donald, she can do that. It's leaving notes and ear-rings and misleading the police in the execution of their duty that I object to.'

'Is Miss Beaumont with you, Sir Donald?' quietly interposed Wyatt.

'Yes, she's waiting outside in my car.'

Wyatt turned to Lathom.

'Would you mind asking her to come up here, Inspector?' he asked. Perivale nodded his agreement.

'I think we should talk to that young lady very seriously,' he said, and Lathom went out at once.

Angus looked a trifle disgruntled and turned to Sir James.

'Really, I see no need for you to question Lauren. I can give you all the information you require,' he said somewhat stiffly.

'I'd like to talk to her just the same,' said Sir James.

'So would I,' said Wyatt, coming over to Sir Donald's chair to take his empty glass. He paused for a moment, then said:

'Sir Donald, why do you think "Mr Rossiter" murdered Barbara Willis?'

'I haven't the faintest idea,' replied Angus, looking surprised and bewildered.

'Why do you think he murdered Mildred Gillow?'

'How can I tell that any more than—'

'All right,' said Wyatt sharply. 'I'd better enlighten you. He murdered them because he had every intention of getting his name splashed across the front page of all the papers. Because he knew that from that moment the name "Mr Rossiter" would strike fear and desperation into the heart of his potential victims.'

'What are you getting at?' shouted Angus, his veneer of *bonhomie* quite forgotten.

'I'll tell you what I'm getting at, Sir Donald. In my opinion, you received a second note from "Mr Rossiter" demanding a certain sum of money. You kept that note secret because you were scared, and you paid over the money demanded, so your friend Miss Beaumont has been allowed to go free.'

'That's a lie!' cried Angus fiercely. 'It's a dirty lie!'

'Where did you take the money?' persisted Wyatt.

'I tell you I didn't! ... It's a lie!'

'Very well, Sir Donald. You're a pretty powerful man in your own world, and I dare say you're accustomed to getting your own way. But Sir James and I have quite a number of friends in Fleet Street, and we may decide that this little escapade of Miss Beaumont's should be published in its fullest details – as a warning to other young girls ...'

He hesitated. Angus looked from one to the other of the faces of the two men. They were quite inscrutable.

'All right,' he said at last. 'What did you want to know, Mr Wyatt?'

'Simply the address where you handed over the money,' said Wyatt.

Sir Donald licked his lips nervously. He had gone very pale indeed.

'I can't ... I promised ... you see – they threatened that if I told ... if I told they'd ...' His voice trailed away.

'All right, Sir Donald,' said Wyatt forcefully. 'Supposing I tell you, then if I'm wrong you can correct me.' Once again he paused, then said:

'You took the money to a man named Professor Reed – at 28 Coster Row, Shadwell Basin.'

CHAPTER VII

Miss Beaumont Remembers

Inspector Lathom tapped softly on the door, but Perivale went over to it and asked him to wait a few minutes before bringing in Lauren Beaumont. Then he returned and faced Sir Donald Angus.

'Well, Sir Donald?' he challenged. 'Is Wyatt telling the truth?'

Angus looked frightened now. He slipped a finger round his collar to ease it, and tried to face the Assistant Commissioner's accusing stare.

'Yes ... that was the address,' he admitted at last.

'You damn fool!' exploded Perivale. 'Didn't I tell you to get in touch with us the moment you heard?'

'You don't understand,' protested Angus. 'They'd have killed her, as they did the others. I couldn't stand the scandal ... it would have ruined me.'

'Never mind the poor girl's life,' put in Wyatt ironically. 'How much did it cost you to preserve your reputation, Sir Donald?'

The Scotsman did not reply, and Wyatt repeated the

102

question rather more insistently. Sir Donald swallowed hard, and said in a low voice:

'Fifteen thousand pounds.'

Perivale thumped the arm of his chair with an imprecation.

'How the devil do you expect us to clear up this business when you play right into their hands?' he snapped.

'I'd got no choice!' said Angus desperately. 'I've got a big deal on involving over half a million, and the slightest scandal would ruin everything.'

Sir James sighed and made a gesture of helplessness. He turned to Wyatt.

'How did you find that address?' he asked.

'It was the place where Taylor was supposed to take my wife; and I've just had the same address over the telephone from another source,' replied Wyatt. 'It wasn't very difficult to put two and two together.'

Sir James made a note of the address and said:

'Well, I suppose we'd better send a couple of Squad cars down there, but it's a hundred to one the birds have flown.'

'If you don't mind, Sir James,' said Wyatt, 'I'd like to pop down there myself – it would attract less attention. If there should be any trouble, I'll arrange with Lathom to have some of your men within easy call.'

'All right, Wyatt, suit yourself,' grunted Perivale, who suspected that Wyatt had one or two of his own theories that he wanted to follow up in Shadwell Basin.

'Before Miss Beaumont comes in,' continued Wyatt, 'I think it might be a good idea if Sir Donald told us what happened that afternoon when we last saw him, and he went back to his hotel.'

Wyatt suggested this so that Angus and the girl should have no opportunity of hearing each other's story; he was by no means sure of either of them as a witness, and this was the safest way of getting at the truth.

Angus agreed with some reluctance, for he was still plainly terrified at the repercussions that might follow.

'Did you go back to the hotel, Sir Donald?' asked Perivale, in a tone which sounded a trifle sceptical.

'Most certainly I did, Sir James,' Angus assured him. 'I intended to follow your instructions to the letter. When I got back to my room, rather a surprising thing happened. I'd been there about five minutes – lying on the bed and trying to relax – when the telephone rang, and I was amazed to hear the voice of that man Luigi, who owns the Madrid Club.'

'It doesn't surprise us, Sir Donald,' Wyatt informed him. 'What did he want?'

'Well, first of all he asked me if I had enjoyed my visit to Scotland Yard, then he began talking about Lauren.'

Wyatt refilled Angus' glass and brought it back to him.

'What did he have to say about Miss Beaumont?' he inquired.

'He reminded me of what had happened to Barbara Willis – and he talked about another unfortunate accident unless ...'

'Unless?'

'I was to pay over fifteen thousand pounds the next afternoon at four o'clock – I had to lock the money in a suitcase and deliver it personally at the address you mentioned. In return I would get full information about the whereabouts of Miss Beaumont.'

He took a large gulp at his whisky.

'So you went to Shadwell Basin,' prompted Wyatt.

'Yes, it was a small, dirty shop, with a board over the

door which said: "Professor Reed, Veterinary Surgeon". One of the window-panes had been broken and was blocked up with cardboard. In the window there were a couple of boxes with little terriers inside. It didn't look at all the sort of place to be mixed up in ... The moment I opened the door about a dozen dogs started howling. Somebody swore at them, then the shabby curtain in the far corner was pulled aside and a big man in shirt-sleeves – no collar or tie – came lurching in. He was obviously the worse for drink.'

'He didn't look much like a professor, eh, Sir Donald?' murmured Wyatt.

'I was very dubious about that myself, and I asked him twice if he were Professor Reed. He got a bit indignant the second time, and I thought for a moment he was going to make a scene. So I thought I'd better tell him my name.'

'Did he recognize it?'

'He was so stupefied with drink that I'm very doubtful if he did – though he had been given his instructions. At first he didn't see the suitcase – it was rather gloomy in the shop. So I put it on the counter in front of him, and that seemed to refresh his memory. He said he had a message for me, and asked me to have a drink. He poured himself one, and I kept asking him about the message. It was a long time before he could recall it – his brain seemed quite fuddled. However, I held on to the case until I got the message, so he made an effort at last and mumbled something about a seat in St James's Park near the Admiralty Arch – and said that Miss Beaumont would be waiting there for me. I tried to pump him for more information, but that was obviously all he knew, and he kept repeating it like a parrot. So I gave him the suitcase, came out and got into my taxi again and drove straight to Town. Quite honestly I never expected to see

Lauren again, and I was almost out of my mind when we arrived at the park.'

'It must have been a great strain,' said Sally sympathetically. He looked at her gratefully, then went on with his story.

'Suddenly I saw her. She was sitting on a seat just inside the Park, looking straight in front of her with a queer expressionless sort of gaze. She was very pale, and I immediately had the impression that she'd been drugged.'

'But you said just now that she was perfectly all right,' Sally reminded him.

'That was before ... before I decided to tell the truth, Mrs Wyatt. She was in a terrible condition; at first, she didn't even recognize me. She seemed quite lifeless, as if someone had beaten the sense out of her.'

He drummed his fingers on the arm of his chair.

'I didn't know what to do,' he confessed. Naturally, I was very relieved to see her again, to find that she was alive, but I knew that something had to be done. It was obvious that she would have to see a doctor as soon as possible, but it would be none too easy to explain ...'

'Wasn't she well enough to walk?' asked Wyatt.

'She seemed to recover slightly in the fresh air, and after a time I got a taxi and we went back to the hotel. We were walking through the lounge on the way to the lift, when Lauren stumbled and I thought for a moment she was going to fall. There was a girl at a nearby table having tea with a young man, and she jumped up at once and came over to us. As luck would have it, she turned out to be a doctor.'

'She didn't mention her name, by any chance?' murmured Wyatt.

'Later on she told me she was a Doctor Fraser – she has

a place in Wimpole Street. She was a very efficient young woman, and she took Lauren up to my room at once—'

He broke off and said rather nervously:

'Perhaps I ought to tell you that I introduced Lauren as Miss Smith, and told the doctor she was my secretary.'

'Why did you do that?' asked Perivale.

'It was all on the spur of the moment. I'd had so many upsets these last few days I felt suspicious of all strangers – for all I knew she was one of that gang. Of course, I realized later that she was quite above board. The doctor examined Lauren pretty thoroughly, and although I couldn't tell her very much she seemed to know what was wrong. She asked me to wait downstairs in the lounge, and said she'd join me shortly. So I went downstairs, and was hanging about, wondering whether to order some tea, when the young man who was with the doctor invited me to his table. He seemed quite an agreeable sort, though he was obviously a foreigner. He realized I was worried about Lauren, and tried to set my mind at rest by telling me Doctor Fraser was extremely capable.'

'Did the doctor join you eventually?' asked Wyatt.

'Oh, yes, she came down in about twenty minutes' time and began to ask me a number of rather awkward questions, because she said it was a most unusual case, and she obviously suspected that Lauren had been a victim of some sort of foul play.'

'How right she was!' put in Wyatt. 'What sort of questions did Doctor Fraser ask?'

'Oh, she was obviously trying to establish some sort of background to the case. Then she suddenly asked me if I had heard of a drug called Amashyer, which induces light-headedness and a loss of memory.'

'Did she think Miss Beaumont had been injected with it?' interposed Perivale sharply.

'She seemed fairly certain about it. I rather got the idea that she had jumped to the conclusion that *I* had given the girl an overdose of this drug, and I had to tell her that Miss Beaumont had only just returned after two days holiday. So she wrote out a prescription at once, and said that she didn't think the injection would have any serious effect. She left me her telephone number, just in case, but refused to take any fee.'

'That was very generous of her,' said Wyatt. 'Did the tablets she prescribed have any effect?'

'Yes, indeed. An hour after taking a couple of them, Lauren seemed almost normal again. She was still a bit groggy on her feet, but the dizziness had gone. We began to talk over the situation and decided that the best thing we could do was to tell the police that the whole affair had been a sort of practical joke. We didn't want any further trouble with "Mr Rossiter" ...'

Angus relapsed into silence, regarding the faces of his listeners somewhat anxiously.

'Well, Sir Donald,' said Wyatt at last, 'you've taken an extremely selfish attitude throughout this business, but I suppose we can hardly blame you for that.'

'I told you before, Mr Wyatt, that I'm in the middle of a very delicate financial transaction, and any breath of scandal would ruin everything. Wouldn't you have done the same in my place?'

'In your place, Sir Donald,' replied Wyatt gravely, 'I rather doubt if I should have become so – er – deeply involved with Miss Beaumont.'

'Talking of Miss Beaumont,' put in Perivale, 'I think we

might see her now.' He went to the door and called to Lathom, who came in at once with the lady in question.

Lauren Beaumont was what some American fiction writers would probably describe as a sultry blonde. Her corn-coloured hair was rolled high above her forehead; she had a lean, rather sallow face beneath her carefully applied make-up. She still appeared a trifle dazed and slow of speech, but Wyatt was not at all sure whether she was exaggerating in this respect, and had come prepared to "act dumb". As Lathom came through the door behind her, he made an expressive gesture intended to convey that he had made no progress as far as his own questioning was concerned.

She looked round the assembled group somewhat uncertainly, then addressed herself to Angus.

'I thought you said we were going back right away, Donald,' she said in a feeble voice. Angus led her to a chair.

'It's all right, Lauren,' he reassured her. 'There's nothing to worry about; we're just having a little talk, that's all.'

He introduced the various members of the party, and Perivale and Wyatt began to ask questions as informally as possible.

'There's no need to be nervous, Miss Beaumont,' began Perivale. 'We know you've had a pretty trying time, and we don't intend to worry you with a lot of unnecessary questions. You see, we know what really happened.'

The girl looked worried.

'You mean Sir Donald has told you the truth?' she said in a half-whisper.

'I told them everything,' put in Angus.

'He told us a very interesting story, Miss Beaumont,' said Wyatt, 'but without your side of the adventure, it's rather incomplete. Have you any clear recollections of what has been happening to you?'

She passed a hand over her forehead.

'I've been trying hard to think of everything – while I was waiting outside,' she replied somewhat mechanically. 'I've got the first part all right; that's quite clear in my mind. But after that it's just as if there were a curtain in front of me.'

'All right,' said Wyatt soothingly. 'Perhaps it'll help if we go right back to the beginning and take it in easy stages. You remember you had an appointment at a shop in Bond Street for a fitting?'

She looked blank for a moment, then her memory appeared to function.

'That's it,' she said quickly. 'It was a grey costume ... I had a fitting for my new grey costume ... I remember it quite well now. There was a neat little hat in the window that caught my eye just as I was going in, and as I went through for my fitting I asked the price of it. It was rather expensive – eighteen guineas I remember ...'

'Splendid!' applauded Wyatt. 'You're coming along nicely. Did you buy the hat?'

Again she hesitated for a second, then said:

'No ... I decided to leave it until after I'd had my fitting. They took me to the little room at the far end of the shop, and I tried the costume on. It wasn't quite right, and the woman started making some alterations.'

'You don't remember this woman's name?'

'I never knew it. They just called her "Madame" – she seemed to be the one in charge. She moved behind me, pinning up the costume here and there, and suddenly I felt a sharp jab in the top of my left arm. She apologized and said she couldn't think how it happened; then she went on to talk about the hat in the window and I'd almost forgotten about the pin when I suddenly noticed my left arm had gone completely numb.'

'You didn't see this pin?' queried Wyatt.

'No, she was behind me at the time.'

'Obviously it was a hypodermic,' said Lathom.

'I remember sinking on to a chair,' continued Lauren Beaumont, 'and after that I've only a hazy idea of what happened. I seem to remember the woman giving orders about a car, and somebody wrapping a coat round me.'

'You can't recall actually being in a car – or getting into one?' suggested Wyatt persuasively. She was obviously making a considerable effort, judging by the strained expression on her face, but she finally shook her head.

'No ... I couldn't be sure about the car ... but there must have been one ... the next clear recollection I have is Donald coming up to me in the Park ... it's all like one of those dreams when you're half-awake and trying to wake up properly ...'

'All right, Miss Beaumont,' nodded Perivale after a moment. 'You've been very helpful.' He turned to Lathom.

'We'll need a warrant for the arrest of Charles Luigi,' he decided. 'And one for this man who calls himself Professor Reed. And I want a couple of plain-clothes men down at the shop in Bond Street as soon as it opens. By the way, Miss Beaumont, do you remember the name of that shop?'

'I've a receipt for a deposit,' she told him, taking a slip of paper out of her bag.

Perivale took the paper and scrutinized it. The name was unfamiliar to him, but doubtless they'd know something about the people at Savile Row.

'Sir James,' interposed Wyatt quietly, 'you haven't forgotten what I asked about this man Reed?'

Perivale jerked himself out of his reflections.

'Oh, yes, you wanted to have a go at him yourself first, didn't you, Wyatt?'

'Do you know the man, Mr Wyatt?' asked Lathom curiously.

'I only know what Sir Donald has told us,' replied Wyatt.

'Then you've never met him,' persisted Lathom suspiciously.

'Not yet. But that is roughly the idea, Inspector. Sally and I thought we might do the sights in the East End again quite soon. It's some time since we were down that way.'

Half an hour later Wyatt and Sally were steering through the deserted streets of the City on their way to Shadwell Basin. It was quite dark now and Wyatt was driving with the speedometer needle flickering around the thirty mark. They met a little traffic from the docks, but nothing to delay them. Both of them were busy with their thoughts, and their conversation was spasmodic for some time. As they were passing Liverpool Street Station, Sally suddenly asked:

'Why do you think this man Reed telephoned Doctor Fraser?'

Wyatt steered the car deftly round a bus parked near the station.

'It could be that Reed has a sick daughter and the local practitioner advised Doctor Fraser as a consultant,' he murmured absently.

'Yes, it could be,' said Sally sceptically. 'Is that what you really think?'

'Haven't you got any theories of your own, Mrs Wyatt?' he smiled. 'Remember, you used to be on the force as well as the old man!'

'Lots,' said Sally. 'For one thing, I had a pet theory about "Mr Rossiter's" identity. Unfortunately, it's been knocked on the head.'

'That's interesting,' said Wyatt. 'What was the theory?'

Sally hesitated a moment then said, with a trace of reluctance: 'Well, if you must know, I suspected Sir Donald Angus.'

'Phew! That's a bit steep!' said Wyatt. 'What on earth made you suspect Angus?'

'Oh, it doesn't matter now,' replied Sally impatiently. 'He can't possibly be "Mr Rossiter".'

'Can't he, indeed?' queried Wyatt, his eyebrows lifting a fraction. 'Just because he told a very interesting and extremely convincing story about delivering fifteen thousand pounds doesn't necessarily mean that he was telling the whole truth.'

'But, darling,' protested Sally, plainly taken aback, 'after all he's told us you can't think that Sir Donald could possibly be "Mr Rossiter".'

'It was your pet theory in the first place,' laughed Wyatt, gazing intently ahead as he picked his way along a series of narrow slum streets. At last he slowed down the car and drove on to a piece of waste land at the side of a public house.

'I'll leave it here,' he said. 'It won't be so noticeable.'

He took the ignition key and locked all the doors.

'Have you any idea where this shop is?' asked Sally.

'I've a rough idea. But we're meeting a bloke in this pub first,' said Wyatt, leading the way into the saloon bar.

He caught sight of the man he sought almost at once. He was a dapper little cockney in rather a loud suit with noticeably padded shoulders.

'I got yer message,' he said, coming over to them. 'Ain't

113

'eard of yer for quite a while now, since you tipped me off about steerin' clear of that Hoxton gang.'

'I've been busy in one way and another,' smiled Wyatt. 'I didn't recognize you for a minute.'

'Ah, that'll be the dirty piece ... the moustache.'

'Oh, yes. Well, have a drink, Lanny. And what about you, Sally? By the way, Sally, this is Lanny Kitson – my wife. I've brought her down here to see the sights.'

'Is that so?' said Lanny with a disbelieving wink. 'You'll be bringing your grandma next week, I shouldn't wonder. Mine's a pint of wallop, if it's all the same to you, Inspector.'

Wyatt gave his order to the barmaid who was regarding them with some interest. He manœuvred Lanny out of earshot of the other customers.

'Lanny,' he said quietly, 'you wouldn't happen to know a man who calls himself Professor Reed?'

Lanny wiped his mouth with the back of his hand, and said:

'Prof Reed? Of course I know the old so-and-so!'

'Tell me more about him,' urged Wyatt.

Lanny thoughtfully considered his beer.

'The old prof's a clever cove in his way. Gone to seed, o' course. Bin mixed up in one or two shady bits of business of late years.'

'Such as what?'

'Well, he's been pinched once or twice for receivin' ... and not long ago a valuable greyhound that got stolen was traced to 'im. Turns 'is hand to almost anything in a manner of speakin'.'

He took a drink, then went on: 'Of course, it's the booze that's the trouble with the old prof. Too late to reform now, I reckon. Funny thing, you're the second bloke tonight who's been askin' me about him.'

'Really?' said Wyatt. 'That's quite a coincidence.'

Lanny spoke in an even lower tone.

'You ain't tryin' to tell me the prof's gone and done another job, 'as 'e?'

'Well, I've no actual evidence at the moment,' replied Wyatt with a smile. 'But I'm curious to know about this other person who's been making inquiries. Where did you meet this man?'

'In the pub down the road – the Queen's Arms – we just got talking, and the conversation got round to dogs, and, of course, the prof is a bit of a vet, so that's how it 'appened. All the time, I kept tryin' to think where I'd seen this bloke's face before. It might 'ave been in the papers ...'

Wyatt took a wallet from his pocket and selected a newspaper cutting.

'Would that be the man?' he asked.

'Yes, that's 'im! Spittin' image!' pronounced Lanny.

Wyatt slowly returned the cutting to his wallet. It was a picture of Maurice Knight and Barbara Willis.

'Thanks, Lanny – you've been very helpful,' said Wyatt. 'Now, can you give me some idea where Coster Row is? And the professor's place?'

'That's easy,' nodded Lanny. 'You just turn left when you go out of 'ere, keep on for about fifty yards – it's the second turnin' on your right.'

They finished their drinks, wished Lanny good night, and went out into the chilly autumn air. There was a slight mist swirling up from the river and Sally shivered and pulled her coat more tightly around her. They followed Lanny's instructions and soon came to Coster Row, which was a cul-de-sac ending in the canal embankment. It was a short street, with one lamp half-way down and another at the far end, and they had some difficulty in seeing the numbers on the shops and houses. It was Sally who finally spotted the place they were looking for. She caught sight of a large model of a terrier in the window, which seemed to contain little else except a carton of dog powders and a couple of empty boxes.

'What a dreadful-looking place!' exclaimed Sally. 'You'd think the authorities would step in and do something.'

'It certainly isn't my idea of a vet's establishment,' nodded Wyatt, trying the door gently. It was locked. He peered through the window to see if he could detect some form of activity at the back of the shop.

He stepped back and looked up at the first-floor windows: there was no sign of life there either.

He rattled the latch of the door more noisily this time, so that the sound echoed through the deserted shop.

'I'm surprised we haven't heard the dog bark that Sir Donald mentioned,' said Sally. 'He'd surely have barked at all this noise.'

'If the old boy's out he may have taken the dog with him,' said Wyatt, looking up and down the street, which appeared to be quite deserted.

'Yes, this is about the time one would take a dog for a stroll,' said Sally. 'What are you going to do?'

'I think I'll just nose around a bit,' Wyatt decided. 'It might be a good idea if you went back to the car and waited for me.'

'What are you going to do?' repeated Sally, suspiciously.

'Oh, I just thought I'd try and see if there's a way into the place,' he answered lightly.

'I'd much sooner stay here,' she told him. 'Besides, you might need help of some sort.'

Wyatt considered this for a few moments. He hardly relished the idea of involving Sally in an unauthorized entry of enclosed premises, and he had no official search warrant, but he was equally chary of leaving her on her own.

'All right, come along then,' he decided at last. 'But don't make a sound.'

She followed him down an entry which divided the shop from the house next door. It was very dark in this narrow passage, and Wyatt was tempted to use the tiny pocket torch he carried for such emergencies, but after a few seconds his eyes became more accustomed to the gloom, and he was able to discern the shape of a doorway in the wall of Professor Reed's house about twenty feet along the passage. They moved towards it as silently as possible, and after a little fumbling, Wyatt found the door handle.

To his surprise the door was unlocked. It creaked noisily as he slowly pushed it inwards.

The darkness was more intense than ever as Wyatt moved in a step or two and tried to get his bearings. After a pause he whispered: 'Stand just inside the door, Sally, and keep clear of the passageway if you can.'

'All right,' she said quietly. 'Don't worry about me.'

Wyatt now decided to take a chance and shine his torch for a second, so that he could establish the layout of the house. When he did so, he saw a door on his left, apparently leading to a kitchen or sitting-room, and a curtain on his right which concealed the entrance to the shop. Then he felt a tug on his sleeve, and Sally whispered:

'Lionel ... I think this door has been broken open ... there are splinters near the keyhole ...'

She referred to the outer door from the passage, and a quick glance at it proved her surmise to be correct.

'Do be careful,' she whispered. 'Whoever did it may be somewhere in the house now. They may be armed and ...'

He patted her hand reassuringly.

'All right, darling, don't worry. Take that toy pistol of yours out of your bag and hold on to it just in case – but I've a feeling the bird has flown.' He moved towards the left-hand door. The kitchen-sitting-room proved to be deserted at a first glance: then Wyatt caught sight of something protruding from beneath the table.

He directed the torch at the object and saw that it was the hindquarters of a large mongrel dog. The dog, which was obviously dead, was stretched on a mat under the table.

Looking up, he saw Sally was standing in the doorway.

'Is it dead?' she whispered.

'I'm afraid so. Seems to have been poisoned – or maybe gassed ... someone must have taken the dog by surprise ...'

'Unless Reed did it himself,' suggested Sally. 'It may have been brought here to be destroyed.'

'That's possible, of course. Though it's hardly usual to leave a dead dog lying under the table.'

'Yes, it is queer,' Sally agreed.

'All right, stay outside the door, just in case,' ordered Wyatt, slowly continuing his investigation of the room. Apart from an overturned chair in one corner there appeared to be nothing else unusual, though the room had obviously not been cleaned for weeks. The fire was still smouldering in the grate, and there was a smell of cheap pipe tobacco hanging in the air. Wyatt could not discover any letters or papers of any description which would afford a clue to the owner, and he was about to explore the drawers of a shabby bureau when he heard a stifled exclamation from Sally, who had moved out into the passage and was standing by the curtain leading into the shop.

'Lionel!' she gasped. 'There's somebody there!'

He crossed over to where she was standing, and thrust her behind him.

'Where?' he snapped.

'The – the curtain—' she gulped. 'There's someone standing the other side. I touched him. I tell you I ...'

'Stand clear, Sally,' he ordered. Then he called out sharply: 'Come out of there ... whoever you are!'

There was no sound from the other side of the curtain.

They looked at each other in complete mystification.

After five or ten seconds, Wyatt called out again.

'Come out! D'you hear me? Come out!'

Again there was silence.

With a sudden, quick movement, Wyatt snatched at the curtain. The material was quite rotten and tore away in his hands.

On the other side, the shirt-sleeved body of a man was hanging lifelessly from a rope fastened to the curtain rod.

CHAPTER VIII

A Warrant for Mr Luigi

Wyatt switched out his torch immediately the ghastly features of the man in shirt-sleeves had become visible.

'Get out of here, Sally!' he said forcefully. 'Wait in the passage outside.'

Sally backed away, still tense from the shock of their discovery. It had taken all her self-control to suppress a piercing scream.

A man's footstep echoed past the end of the entry.

Wyatt took a small penknife from his pocket, and reaching above the dead man's head sawed vigorously at the rope. He had cut about halfway through it when the dead weight of the body snapped the remaining strands, and it toppled forward into Wyatt's arms. It almost caught him unawares, and he had some difficulty in lowering it to the floor. As he did so, he noticed a faint smell of perfume, which appeared to emanate from the man's clothing.

The scent was vaguely familiar to him, but he could not connect it immediately with any other person or situation, and he forgot it almost at once as he stooped to examine the body.

He shone his torch on the bloated features, and decided that, according to Angus' description, this must have been Professor Reed. The cord had bitten deeply into the neck, and it took Wyatt a little time to remove it, working by the dim light of his pocket torch. He called to Sally from time to time to see if she was all right. The fresh air outside had revived her, and presently she called to her husband in a low voice:

'How long has he been dead?'

'It's difficult to say,' replied Wyatt.

'I suppose it's Reed?'

'Yes, it must be,' replied Wyatt. 'Are you sure you're OK, darling?'

'Yes, yes, I'm all right now. What are you going to do?'

'Well, the first thing I shall do is search him,' he replied briskly, 'although I don't have much hope of finding anything.' He dragged the body into the back room and lighted the gas which shed a greenish glare on the untidy kitchen.

He began carefully examining the numerous pockets in the dead man's clothing, including a jacket he found flung across a chair behind the counter.

The main contents of the dead man's pockets appeared to be grubby betting slips, and there was a small notebook in his hip pocket which was full of cryptic jottings on what appeared to be the form of various greyhounds.

Wyatt was still frowning over this when there was a sudden quick step in the passage outside, and almost immediately Wyatt looked up to see Maurice Knight standing in the doorway. There was an unpleasant glitter in his deep brown eyes.

'Well, we meet in some unexpected places, Mr Wyatt,' he began, with a noticeable edge to his voice.

Wyatt slowly rose to his feet.

'You're certainly with us in times of trouble, Mr Knight,' he replied in a similar ironical vein.

The newcomer rolled his cigarette to the side of his mouth and blew out a stream of smoke.

'That fellow looks in a pretty bad way,' he observed. 'I take it you were applying artificial respiration.'

'I'm afraid it's too late for that, Knight. This man is dead.'

'Oh ... how unpleasant for you, Mrs Wyatt,' said Knight with a glance in Sally's direction.

'Did you come here for any special reason?' asked Wyatt.

'Oh, yes, I called to see a man named Professor Reed.'

Wyatt indicated the body on the floor.

'I'm afraid you're too late.'

Knight followed Wyatt's glance at the dead man.

'Is that Reed?' he inquired, somewhat taken aback.

'You don't recognize him, then?'

'Never set eyes on him before in my life. Poor devil ...' He suddenly changed his tone and asked:

'How long have you two been here?'

'About ten minutes,' replied Wyatt.

'I see ...'

Knight bent down and picked up the dead man's hand, held it for a moment, then let it fall to the floor with a soft thud.

'What are you suggesting?' said Sally quietly.

Maurice Knight shrugged.

'It's obvious that this man has been murdered,' he said, indicating the red marks on the neck of the corpse with his stick.

'And you think we murdered him?' queried Wyatt. 'Is that it, Knight?'

122

'I'm entitled to my opinion.'

Sally suppressed an exclamation, but Wyatt only smiled.

'Don't you think we owe each other an explanation, Knight?' he demanded pleasantly.

'I shall be very pleased to listen to yours, Mr Wyatt,' said Knight in a non-committal tone.

'All right, I came here tonight for two reasons. The first was to follow up a visit made by a man named Sir Donald Angus – perhaps you haven't heard of him ...'

'Of course I've heard of him,' said Knight, taking a folded evening paper from his coat pocket and opening it out. 'Perhaps you haven't seen the last editions of the evening paper, Mr Wyatt?'

He indicated a banner headline across the front page.

'They've got the whole story!' whispered Sally, taking a quick glance at the left-hand column.

Wyatt's eye roved rapidly over the heavy type ... 'We learn from a reliable source that Miss Lauren Beaumont, a personal friend of Sir Donald Angus, the Scottish millionaire shipowner, was abducted by the notorious "Mr Rossiter", and was today returned to the hotel where she had been staying with him, after Sir Donald had paid over the sum of £15,000 for her release ...'

'How did they get it, Lionel?' breathed Sally. 'Sir Donald will be frantic – it's just what he wanted to avoid.'

'Did Angus really pay all that money?' inquired Knight curiously.

Wyatt hesitated a moment, then said:

'Yes, he came here this afternoon at four o'clock, and brought the money with him in a suitcase.'

'You don't mean he gave it to this man Reed?' demanded Knight incredulously.

'That's the plain truth, Mr Knight.'

Knight perched on the corner of the grimy kitchen table. 'So that's why you came here, is it?'

'That's one very good reason,' said Wyatt. 'Now perhaps you'll give me one good reason why you came.'

Knight smiled a trifle ruefully.

'I'm sorry to have doubted you, Mr Wyatt. Of course, I'm just a blundering amateur – I make a hell of a lot of silly mistakes. But I do hit upon something occasionally.'

'You certainly do!' agreed Wyatt a trifle grimly.

'Did you know anything about this man Reed?' asked Sally. Knight shook his head.

'Not till this morning. I was going through some papers that belonged to Barbara, and I came across his name and address. I asked her father about him, and he couldn't throw any light on the matter, though he said he thought Barbara came down to this part of the world several times.'

'Didn't you know about that?'

'No, it came as a complete surprise to me. I can't think why on earth she should visit such a dump like this.'

'If we could find that out, it might be quite a help,' mused Wyatt. 'She never mentioned the name "Reed" to you?'

'Never,' replied Knight positively. Then, after a pause, he went on: 'Have you any idea who killed him?'

'Not the slightest,' replied Wyatt, 'though there must be some connection with "Mr Rossiter" ...'

'Lionel, you don't think Reed could have been "Mr Rossiter", and that Angus didn't hand over the money after all?' said Sally urgently. 'There doesn't seem to be any sign of that suitcase ...'

'You mean that Angus simply killed Reed and rescued his

girl friend?' put in Knight, smiling encouragingly at Sally. 'Then he came back and pitched a yarn—'

'Just a minute,' interrupted Wyatt. 'I'm not absolutely certain, of course, that Sir Donald didn't murder Reed, but I am quite certain that he didn't, strictly speaking, rescue the girl. So I don't think there's much point in pursuing that theory any further.' He turned to Knight and asked: 'What did you expect to find here, Knight?'

Knight shook his head.

'I don't quite know ... some sort of clue to Barbara's murderer. You see, I'm so much in the dark, I'm glad to clutch at any straw ... I've nothing much else to do, and it helps to keep me sane. By the way, have you sent for the police?'

'Not yet,' replied Wyatt, picking up the dead man's coat. He handed it to Sally.

'What do you make of that?' he asked. 'It's some sort of perfume, I'm pretty sure – though it's mixed with one or two other things.'

'Yes, it's perfume all right,' agreed Sally. 'Quite an expensive brand, too.'

'I thought I could smell something, too,' said Knight. 'I thought perhaps it was yours, Mrs Wyatt.'

'No, it isn't mine,' declared Sally positively, handing back the coat. He sniffed it again with a puzzled frown.

'It seems familiar,' he murmured. 'I feel I've come across it before, but I can't think where.'

Wyatt finished going through the dead man's pockets without discovering anything of interest. Then he turned to Knight and said:

'Have you got your car down here, Knight, or can we give you a lift?'

'It's all right, thanks – my car's not far away.'

'Righto, then, come along, Sally. This is a job for the Yard now. I arranged for a couple of plain-clothes men to be on duty at the junction of the main road, so we'll give them the tip on our way back.'

Sally went out with Knight, and Wyatt carefully turned out the gas and closed all the doors behind him.

It appeared that Knight's car was some distance down Coster Row, and he went off in the opposite direction towards the canal, while Sally and Wyatt walked briskly to the piece of waste ground where their own car was parked. They did not talk very much, for they were each sifting a number of theories about the murder which were churning through their minds.

After they had left the East End behind, Sally suddenly snapped her fingers with a triumphant gesture.

'I've got it!' she exclaimed.

'Phew! You gave me quite a start,' he grinned. 'Now, what is it?'

'I've remembered about that perfume.'

'Well?'

'It was Château Number Eight,' she informed him.

'Oh, hell,' said her husband, 'isn't that just like a woman? Worrying herself stiff about a brand of perfume when there's an unsolved murder on our hands.'

'Wait a minute,' said Sally. 'I've remembered something else. I knew I'd come across the stuff before, and now I know where it was.'

'Ah, that's more like it,' nodded Wyatt, slowing the car down to a leisurely fifteen miles an hour. 'I suppose you're going to tell me it's a brand specially recommended by some famous West End actress?'

126

'Oh, dear, no,' replied Sally pointedly. 'I'm quite certain a friend of yours at Shorecombe used it.'

Wyatt sat up rather more attentively, and she went on.

'You remember that we drove back to the inn with Doctor Fraser after the accident?'

Wyatt turned and looked at her.

'You mean Doctor Fraser had the same perfume?'

'I'd bet my last new hat on it,' announced Sally with some emphasis.

'All right,' said Wyatt, 'we'll stop at the next telephone and I'll make a few inquiries.'

They came to an empty telephone box in an alleyway between two city banks, and Wyatt stopped the car.

He got through to Doctor Fraser's number without any delay, and she answered the telephone herself in that cool, attractive Canadian accent.

'I'm so glad you telephoned, Mr Wyatt,' she said at once, and he thought he recognized a note of relief in her tone.

'Why, is anything the matter?' he inquired.

'No, no, there's nothing wrong, but I've been rather worried about that telephone call, and wondering if I'm not acting unprofessionally in not going to Shadwell Basin, as the case was apparently urgent.'

'Then you haven't been down there?' queried Wyatt.

'What do you mean?' she demanded in a puzzled voice. 'You told me not to go until I heard from you.'

'And you're quite certain you followed my instructions?'

'Absolutely. I told you I've been worrying whether I was doing the right thing.' He detected a faint trace of annoyance in her tone.

After a slight pause, she asked:

'Is anything wrong down there? Has – has the girl died or—'

'I've been down to the house,' he told her deliberately. 'And I saw no girl.'

She caught her breath.

'Then it was another trick!' she exclaimed. 'I should have gone down there in the morning and found—'

'You might have found a dead man on the premises – your caller, Professor Reed,' said Wyatt.

'But – but what happened?' she demanded eagerly.

Wyatt ignored the question.

'Have you been out at all this evening?'

'Not since tea. I've been here in my flat ... with a friend of mine. He's here now.' Wyatt hesitated a moment, then said:

'His name wouldn't be Hugo Linder, by any chance?'

There was no reply, and after waiting a few moments Wyatt went on:

'I think you'd better tell me the truth, Doctor.'

'What if it is Mr Linder?' she retorted with a touch of defiance. 'He happens to be a friend of mine.'

'This is most intriguing, Doctor Fraser,' said Wyatt suavely. 'You may remember that when we were at Shorecombe I asked you if you knew a man called Hugo Linder, and you denied all knowledge of such a person.'

'Yes, I know,' she replied. 'I'm very sorry – it was extremely stupid of me.'

'But why did you do it?'

She hesitated a moment, then said: 'I'll explain all that next time I see you, Mr Wyatt. There's nothing terribly sinister about it.'

'I'll be looking forward to hearing the details,' he assured her. 'Oh, there's just one other thing ...'

'Yes?'

'Would you mind telling me what sort of perfume you use?'

'That's a strange question, Mr Wyatt.'

'Believe me, I have a reason for asking, Doctor. You have no objection to telling me?'

'Of course not. I use Château Number Eight. Why do you want to know?'

Wyatt smiled grimly.

'Remind me to explain that next time we meet – when you tell me about Hugo Linder. Good night, Doctor.'

The door of the telephone box slammed after him, and he was crossing the road to rejoin Sally in the car when a high-powered cream saloon swung round the corner. As it passed under the light from one of the new street lamps, Wyatt recognized the driver as Hugo Linder.

Whether Linder had observed this glance of recognition, Wyatt could not be certain, but the car backed to a standstill.

Linder climbed out and came towards them with a polite 'good evening'.

'You're the last person I expected to see, Mr Linder,' ejaculated Wyatt. 'What have you been doing in the East End?'

'Oh, just taking a little run round,' replied Linder evasively.

'Not exactly a salubrious quarter for a joy ride,' was Wyatt's dry comment. 'By the way, I've just been talking to a friend of yours. Doctor Fraser told me you were spending the evening at her flat.' Linder looked a trifle surprised, then recovered.

'I was there earlier on. I had to leave because I'd promised to drive a friend of yours down here.'

'A friend of mine?' It was Wyatt's turn to be surprised.

'Inspector Lathom,' Linder cheerfully informed him. 'He told me he had two plain-clothes men down here he wanted to see.'

'Where is the Inspector?' asked Sally.

'I left him a few minutes ago. It seems the men had received a report from you about a Professor Reed being murdered, and he went along to investigate.'

'That's right,' nodded Wyatt. 'We found the body.'

'How horrible for you, Mrs Wyatt!' sympathized Linder. 'It's a dreadful shock – specially for a woman. I shall never forget the day poor Tyson and I discovered Barbara Willis. It was absolutely ghastly!'

Wyatt noticed Sally's strained expression and abruptly changed the conversation.

'We'd better be getting back, Sally – if Mr Linder will excuse us.'

'Of course,' agreed Linder, with a slight bow. 'I promised to return to Doctor Fraser in time for a supper.'

He went off to his car, which roared on ahead of them.

'I can't make out how he and Lathom come to be on such friendly terms,' said Sally, wrinkling her brow. 'They seem to be practically living in each other's pockets.'

'Maybe Lathom's up to something,' speculated Wyatt, as he drew up with a jerk at the Ludgate Hill traffic lights.

'I never did like—' began Sally.

'I know, darling – you never liked that man's face!' he interrupted with a grin. 'I'm afraid it's too late for him to do anything about it now.'

He lost no time in getting back to the flat, for he had an idea that there might be further developments before the night was out. Sally went into the kitchen to make some coffee and Wyatt was re-reading the evening paper when the telephone rang and he heard the familiar voice of Inspector Lathom.

'I'd no idea you were on your way to Coster Row, or I'd have hung on,' said Wyatt at once. 'I gave your men a pretty full account of everything. Was there anything else you wanted to know?'

'Just one or two small points,' said the inspector. 'In the first place, I find that Reed isn't a registered vet, and never has been.'

'That doesn't surprise me,' said Wyatt. 'I don't suppose he's a registered professor either!'

'You're about right there, Wyatt. He's got a pretty unsavoury reputation from what I hear. By the way, how long d'you think he'd been dead before you found him?'

'I wouldn't like to venture an opinion,' said Wyatt. 'I expect the police will give you a better idea.'

'H'm,' grunted Lathom a trifle sceptically. 'I suppose you're quite sure that he was murdered. It couldn't possibly have been suicide?'

'What do you think yourself?' stalled Wyatt, wondering vaguely if Lathom had hit upon some new clue. But the inspector appeared to be worried about the motive for killing Reed.

'Surely that's fairly obvious,' said Wyatt.

'Not to me it isn't,' replied Lathom doubtfully. 'Perhaps you'd give me your idea.'

'It seems to me to be a plain case of the professor trying to double-cross the gentleman who gave him his instructions, and hoping to get away with the booty himself,' said Wyatt.

'Yes,' said Lathom dubiously, 'I suppose that's the most

likely construction to put upon it. But it doesn't necessarily follow that it's the right one.'

'All right,' said Wyatt urbanely, 'what's your idea of the affair, Inspector?'

Lathom hesitated for a moment, then said:

'I agree that Reed was out to double-cross Mr R., but it's my opinion that he was murdered by another member of the organization.'

'That's all right if you believe in the existence of an organization. Have you found any evidence that points to it?' asked Wyatt quickly.

'Well, no, I can't say I have,' admitted Lathom with some reluctance. 'But, hang it, man, there must be an organization! One man could never cover all that ground on his own. Anyhow, we can't argue that out now, Wyatt. I must be off.'

'You'll want me to give evidence at the inquest, I suppose?'

'Oh, yes, I'll let you know time and place when I see you tomorrow. Good night, Wyatt.'

Wyatt replaced the receiver, and turned to Sally who had been trying to follow the conversation.

'Lathom thinks there's an organization,' he said, with a tiny smile.

'And what about you?' asked Sally.

'I'd like a little more proof of the fact. Of course, it all depends by what one means by "organization".'

'What's your idea?' she asked.

'Well, there's such a thing as one man blackmailing people to do his dirty work for him. But I wouldn't exactly describe that as an organization.'

Sally appeared to be weighing this up for a minute or two, then suddenly she said:

'I wish we could find out how Fleet Street got hold of the Beaumont story. It's in all the evening papers – I've just glanced through them.'

'Sounds as if it came through one of the news agencies.'

'That's about it,' she nodded. 'Do you think "Mr Rossiter" himself gave them the story?'

'It seems highly probable.'

'But why should he do it?'

Wyatt lighted a cigarette and perched on an arm of the settee.

'You might put it down to vanity at a quick guess,' he said, 'but I think it goes rather deeper than that. Three girls disappear mysteriously. Two of them are murdered. In the case of the third, her gentleman friend comes across with fifteen thousand pounds – and she is reprieved. These are the facts as they appear in the papers. Now, what do you think is going to happen when another girl mysteriously disappears and her husband, or friend, or father receives a demand from "Mr Rossiter"?'

'I see,' said Sally slowly. 'You mean they're going to remember what happened to the first two girls – and then how Lauren Beaumont was released ... so they'll think twice before they go to Scotland Yard.'

'Exactly,' nodded Wyatt, flicking the ash from his cigarette. 'If a father or husband has the money that "Mr Rossiter" is asking, he'll simply pay up and keep his mouth shut.'

'It looks as if "Mr Rossiter" will be in clover,' said Sally.

'He'll be in a pretty strong position if we don't get a line on him fairly soon,' agreed Wyatt, moving restlessly around the room. Sally went off to the kitchen to get the coffee, and her husband continued to roam around impatiently. He picked up the evening papers once or twice, then threw them down again. Then she heard him on the telephone, but he finished his conversation when she returned with the coffee.

'Was that Sir James you were talking to?' she asked.

'It was. I was anxious to know what he's done about Luigi.'

'Didn't he say he was issuing a warrant?' asked Sally, pouring the coffee.

'That's right. He's just got it made out – says he'll serve it in about an hour's time. So drink your coffee as quickly as possible, Sally, and we'll get down there.'

'You're going to the Madrid tonight?' she asked in some surprise.

'Yes, I want to see Luigi before they serve that warrant. It's rather important.'

'You don't think he's "Mr Rossiter", do you?' asked Sally, rather anxiously. 'Because if he is, I'm afraid there might be some trouble.'

Wyatt patted her arm.

'Don't worry, darling; there won't be any rough house at the Madrid. Luigi knows better than that.'

He gulped down his strong, black coffee and waited somewhat impatiently for Sally to finish hers. He could not repress a feeling of excitement; Perivale had sounded somewhat tense in their brief conversation, and Wyatt had the impression that matters might well come to a head in the Rossiter affair before the night was out.

'Get your hat on, and I'll ring for the lift,' he said as soon as Sally had finished her coffee. When she came out of the hall five minutes later he was chafing impatiently, for he had already summoned the lift twice, and other occupants of the flats had summoned it from his floor. However, when it returned they went down to the street, where Wyatt had left the car.

Sally still seemed a trifle dubious about the expedition, but she made no comment. However, she felt carefully in her handbag to make sure that her tiny .22 was still there.

As they moved along Hill Street, she suddenly turned to her husband and asked:

'Lionel, why were you so surprised to see Hugo Linder when he came up in his car this evening?'

'Did I look surprised?'

'You certainly did! His headlamps caught you full face, and you were obviously pretty startled.'

'Well,' said Wyatt slowly, 'I suppose it was understandable considering that Doctor Fraser had just told me on the telephone that Linder had been with her all the evening.'

It was Sally's turn to look surprised.

'But I thought Doctor Fraser didn't know Linder,' she said. 'That's what she told us at Shorecombe.'

'She's apparently decided he's worth knowing after all,' he murmured, switching on the dashboard light to ascertain the time. Then he added quite casually: 'By the way, you were right about the perfume. She does use Château Number Eight.'

Sally caught her breath as she ranged over the possible implications of this development.

'Do you think she went to see Reed tonight?'

Wyatt shrugged.

'She says she didn't ... but she's already told us one lie, so we can only reserve our opinion.'

Sally brooded over this for a little while.

'I can't think she's as sinister as all that,' she said at

last. 'In fact, she impressed me as being quite a nice sort of person.'

'Maybe that was just her bedside manner,' smiled Wyatt, manœuvring the car into a car park just round the corner from the Madrid Club.

Business was apparently proceeding as usual at the club, for they could hear the throb of the dance orchestra as they entered the vestibule.

'We may as well have supper while we're here,' Wyatt decided.

He caught the head waiter's attention, and they were shown to a table in a corner. As the waiter held the chairs for them Wyatt said:

'Is Luigi here this evening?'

'I think he is in his office, sir. He usually is about this time. It's at the top of the balcony staircase.'

Wyatt nodded and sat down while he gave the order.

The waiter had just made a note of it when Sally, who had been looking round the dancers, caught sight of the bulky figure of Sir James Perivale in the outer lounge. She drew Wyatt's attention to him as soon as the waiter had gone, and he rose at once.

'I won't be a minute, Sally,' he promised, and went over to the door. Perivale was surprised to see him, as Wyatt had made no mention on the telephone that he intended to visit the Madrid. He had hoped to see Luigi before Perivale arrived on the scene, but the latter was ahead of schedule.

After some discussion Sir James agreed to let Wyatt have a short talk with Luigi, and they arranged to meet at the table in the supper-room ten minutes later. Perivale passed the word to the superintendent who was with him and went off to join Sally.

Just before he left him at the foot of the balcony stairs, Wyatt said:

'By the way, have you got the whole place covered?'

Perivale nodded.

'I thought I saw one or two of your stalwarts on the dance floor,' said Wyatt, somewhat amused. 'You really should arrange for them to take dancing lessons, Sir James.'

'I have a feeling Luigi might make a dash for it,' said Perivale, ignoring Wyatt's levity.

'No, he's much too shrewd for that,' Wyatt assured him. 'See you later.'

He moved lightly up the stairs and knocked discreetly at a door marked "Private".

'Come in!' called a voice that was unmistakably Luigi's.

It was an expensively furnished office, with an elaborate glass-topped desk, concealed lighting, and heavy green velvet curtains. One wall was covered with signed photos of cabaret stars who had appeared at the Madrid. Wyatt noticed a door in the opposite wall which looked as if it might lead to a fire-escape.

Luigi was as affable as usual; he could not have appeared more charming if Wyatt had been his most regular client.

'I did not expect to see you here, my friend – it is quite a pleasant surprise,' he began, clasping his slim, well-manicured hands in a gesture of welcome. 'How are you, Inspector?'

'I'm fine,' replied Wyatt blandly. 'How are you?'

'Never better, my friend. Business is good just lately.' He stooped and opened a drawer to bring out a large cigar box.

'Try one of them, Mr Wyatt.'

'No, thanks,' said Wyatt. 'I'm going down to supper shortly. I just wanted a word with you first.'

Luigi indicated a chair with a lavish gesture.

'Sit down, Mr Wyatt. What can I do for you?'

Wyatt accepted the invitation, and sat looking round the office for a few seconds before he spoke.

'You must have been here nine or ten years now, Luigi,' he began in a conversational tone.

'Nearly ten years.'

'H'm ... it's a long life for a night club. You've done pretty well.'

Luigi nodded and rubbed his hands together. Wyatt noticed that he was wearing two rings, one with a diamond and the other a ruby.

'I hope you have not been sent here by the Ministry of Food, Mr Wyatt,' Luigi was saying with the merest suggestion of an acid tone.

'Oh, dear, no. I'm just a comparatively harmless copper, Luigi.'

Luigi showed his even teeth as he switched on his expansive smile. 'You will have your little joke, Mr Wyatt.'

'I'm afraid there's nothing particularly funny about the question I want to ask you,' said Wyatt quietly.

Luigi became more serious.

'Ah, you mean about poor Coral Salter, of course. That was all most unfortunate.'

'Unfortunate?' queried Wyatt with a slight lift of the eyebrows.

'Yes, indeed. She was a very good dancer – extremely popular with the gentlemen.'

'She was very unpopular with at least one gentleman – the fellow who killed her.'

Luigi looked at Wyatt quizzically with a helpless little gesture.

'It was all most unfortunate,' he repeated, 'but I am afraid Miss Salter was perhaps a little too generous with her favours, and not particular enough in the choice of her gentlemen friends. I am sorry I cannot throw any more light on the matter.'

'The police seem to think you might be able to throw quite a bit of light on several matters, including a certain telephone call.'

For the first time, Luigi appeared to be visibly taken aback.

'Which telephone call was that?' he demanded quickly.

'The one you made to Sir Donald Angus.'

'I don't know what you are talking about,' said Luigi in what appeared to be genuine bewilderment. 'I have nothing to do with Sir Donald Angus ...'

'Well, I hope you can prove it,' said Wyatt calmly, 'because the police are so convinced you're mixed up in that affair that they've issued a warrant for your arrest.'

Luigi leapt to his feet.

'But what am I supposed to have done?' he demanded, thumping his fist on the desk.

'Do you deny that you telephoned Sir Donald Angus and instructed him to deliver fifteen thousand pounds to Professor Reed?'

'Of course I deny it! I have never heard of this man Reed.'

Wyatt leaned back a little in his comfortable chair and endeavoured to decide whether or not Luigi was acting.

'Angus recognized your voice,' he went on presently. 'He'd spoken to you the previous night when he came here with Miss Beaumont, and he's positive that it was you.'

'Then quite obviously the man is lying!' exclaimed Luigi

angrily. 'This is a trap of some sort ... somebody is trying to get the club closed down ... they are always trying ...' He broke off as a thought seemed to strike him, and he began to talk more reasonably.

'You say Sir Donald Angus is absolutely convinced that it was my voice?' he asked.

'That's what he says. And the police believe him.'

'Do you believe him, Mr Wyatt?'

'I'm prepared to keep an open mind,' said Wyatt cautiously, wondering what was coming next.

With a sudden movement, Luigi snatched up his house telephone.

'Is that you, Jules? Will you send Carver into me ... yes, right away.'

He slammed down the receiver. 'Now we shall see what's been going on behind my back, Mr Wyatt,' he said triumphantly.

'May I ask who is Carver?' inquired Wyatt.

'He is a young man who has been working here as a waiter for the last few weeks, although he is obviously a person with some education and no doubt better suited for something more responsible. Yes, he is a young man of considerable talents.'

The object of their conversation suddenly knocked and opened the door. Wyatt turned to look at him with considerable interest.

Carver was in his twenties, pale, expressionless face and lemon-coloured hair.

He seemed in no way overawed by Luigi and his opulent surroundings, but stood quietly at the door and said:

'You wanted to see me, sir?' His voice was almost as characterless as his face.

140

'Come in, Carver, and close the door,' said Luigi, coming from behind his desk. 'This is Mr Wyatt of New Scotland Yard. We've been having a little argument about you, Carver.'

'Indeed, sir?' The young waiter hardly seemed to be interested.

'Mr Wyatt refuses to believe that you have this particular flair for imitating people. I want you to prove to him that he's wrong.'

'I'm afraid I'm not professional, sir,' replied the young man deprecatingly.

'Go on,' urged Luigi. 'I have been boosting you for nearly ten minutes ... telling Mr Wyatt that I shall put you in my next floor show. He's one of my customers, and I am anxious to get his reaction.'

The waiter looked vaguely uncomfortable, as if he did not know where to begin.

'Say something, Wyatt! Recite a little poem, so that he can hear your voice,' urged Luigi.

Wyatt laughed. 'Poems aren't very much in my line, but here's a little limerick if that's any use ...

> 'There was a young lady named Bright,
> Who could travel much faster than light;
> She started one day in the relative way,
> And came back the previous night.'

'That's fine!' applauded Luigi. 'Now, Carver ...'

The young waiter cleared his throat rather nervously then slowly began to repeat the poem with an air of intense concentration. Towards the middle, he was speaking at a normal pace, and although it is extremely difficult to recognize an imitation of one's own voice, Luigi recognized the resemblance at once. When Carver repeated the poem again as Luigi would have spoken it, Wyatt could hardly believe his ears, so uncanny was the mimicry.

'There! You see?' cried Luigi.

The young man seemed much more animated and confident now. 'Is there anyone else you'd like me to do, Mr Luigi?' he asked.

Luigi ignored him completely and addressed himself to Wyatt.

'Now perhaps you see what I was trying to get at, Mr Wyatt,' he said deliberately. Wyatt looked from Luigi to Carver, but did not reply. Luigi suddenly swung round upon the waiter.

'You do a very good impersonation of me, Carver. How long have you been practising?' he barked.

Carver was completely taken aback by his employer's change of demeanour.

'Not very long, sir,' he stammered.

'It wouldn't be you who impersonated me on the telephone this week, would it, Carver?' persisted Luigi with growing intensity.

'No, sir, of course not,' replied Carver nervously.

'You are quite sure?'

'Why, yes, sir ... quite sure ...' The waiter shifted uneasily from one foot to the other.

'You are lying!' shouted Luigi, advancing upon him. 'You are lying!'

He raised his arm as if to strike Carver.

'Who paid you to impersonate me?' screamed Luigi. 'Who paid you? Answer me!'

The young man licked his lips nervously, then said in a low tone:

'It was a woman ...'

'A woman, eh? You mean Coral Salter?'

'No, Mr Luigi ... a woman called Doctor Fraser.'

CHAPTER IX

A Woman's Intuition

'Just a minute,' said Wyatt.

He went over and restrained Luigi, gently pushing him into a chair, where he sat mopping his forehead with a silk handkerchief. Wyatt turned to Carver.

'So you know Doctor Fraser?' he asked quietly.

The young man nodded without speaking.

'Who is this Doctor Fraser?' cried Luigi. 'Why does she want people to impersonate me? I have never set eyes on the woman!'

'You've set eyes on a lot of people you can't put names to, Luigi,' Wyatt reminded him grimly.

'Do you know this woman, Mr Wyatt?' queried Luigi in a slightly injured tone.

'Yes,' said Wyatt slowly. 'I know her.'

'Then who is she?'

'She is a very attractive woman,' replied Wyatt evasively. He turned to Carver again. 'When did you see Doctor Fraser?' Carver seemed to hesitate, then said:

'About a week ago.'

144

'Where did you meet her?'

'At her flat in Wimpole Street,' replied Carver rather reluctantly. 'I don't remember the number.'

'You went there by appointment?'

Carver nodded. 'Perhaps I'd better explain it all from the beginning,' he offered, and Wyatt motioned him to a chair. He sat down, clasping the arms of the chair.

'It was like this, Mr Wyatt,' he began hoarsely. 'I've always been keen on impersonating people and that sort of thing, and I thought that if I got a job here as a waiter, then I might get a chance in cabaret. And that's what happened about a week back, when Walter Haylor – he does songs at the piano – got a touch of food poisoning and was off for a couple of nights.'

'And you took his place,' put in Wyatt.

'That's right, sir. My little act went rather well—'

'Never mind that,' snapped Luigi. 'Get on with your story!'

'Yes, Mr Luigi. Well, it seems that this Doctor Fraser happened to catch the act one night, and the next day she phoned and asked me to go round to her flat. She didn't say what she wanted – just that it was a little business matter. I suppose I must have sounded a bit doubtful, because she immediately went on to ask if I'd be interested in two hundred pounds.'

'H'm, that's quite a lot of money,' commented Wyatt.

'It's a hell of a lot of money,' retorted the waiter with sudden emphasis. 'And God knows I can do with it. You see, I'm thinking of getting married,' he added, half-apologetically.

'Congratulations,' said Wyatt dryly. 'So you made an appointment to see Doctor Fraser?'

'Of course! Catch me turning down a chance like that!'

Wyatt went and stood over the young waiter.

'Now this is rather important, Carver,' he said. 'We've had Doctor Fraser under observation for some time, and I want to check up as many details as possible. Could you remember, for instance, the dress she was wearing when you saw her?'

Carver looked somewhat puzzled.

'It wouldn't be a sort of honey colour – to match her blonde hair,' prompted Wyatt.

'Yes ... yes, I believe it was,' nodded the waiter.

'Go on!' said Luigi. 'What happened?'

'Well, she asked me inside ... there was no one else there. We went into a sort of consulting-room – I remember there was a big couch under the window. As soon as I got inside she said she'd put her cards on the table without wasting any time.'

'And what was the little job she wanted you to do?'

Carver spoke with an effort.

'She wanted me to telephone Sir Donald Angus and give him a message, using Mr Luigi's voice. She had the message all written out on a slip of paper ...'

'You didn't bring that away with you, by any chance?'

Carver shook his head.

'No, I had to do the telephoning there, so that she had a check on what I said. She burnt the paper immediately afterwards.'

'So you accepted her offer, of course.'

'I couldn't afford to refuse, Mr Wyatt. I needed the money pretty badly, and she told me it was only a sort of practical joke.'

'Practical joke!' shrieked Luigi, shaking his fist. 'You ruin my name and think it is a practical joke!' A casual observer would have received the impression that the little *restaurateur* was on the verge of an apoplectic seizure.

'Get out!' he shouted. 'You are fired! I will have you black-listed in every club in London!'

The waiter half turned to go, but Wyatt detained him.

'Wait a minute, Carver,' he said quietly. 'I'm afraid you can't leave yet.'

'What do you mean?' said Luigi sharply. 'I've told him to get out; I never want to see him again.'

'I don't think you understand, Luigi, that I wasn't joking about that warrant. Sir James is downstairs now with Superintendent Bradley.'

'Well, what of it?'

'Don't you think Carver is rather an important witness on your behalf?'

'But you are a witness, Mr Wyatt. You have seen and heard all this. Sir James will take your word.'

'Yes, that may be so,' agreed Wyatt. 'But I don't think he'd agree with my letting Carver get out of here.'

Luigi rubbed his forehead with his hand, then said thoughtfully: 'Perhaps you are right, Wyatt. They had better come in here and he shall tell them the truth about that telephone call – it will serve him right—'

Wyatt went over to the door and opened it.

'All right, I'll fetch them up now. I shan't be two minutes.'

The moment the door had closed, Carver seemed to be about to speak, but Luigi quickly put his finger to his lips. They waited for some seconds. Then Carver said quietly:

'Do you think he believed it?'

Luigi shrugged.

'I don't know whether he did or not, but you've got to tell the police exactly the same story – word for word. And you've got to stick to it.'

Carver nodded.

'All right, Mr Luigi ...'

As Wyatt came up to their table, he noticed Perivale was reflectively sipping a liqueur brandy and listening to Sally who was chatting away with considerable animation. He looked up as Wyatt approached and asked:

'Did you see Luigi?'

'I've just left him in his office. He's waiting for you.'

'Right,' nodded Perivale, getting to his feet. 'I'll just warn Bradley, then I'll go up.' As he was moving away, Wyatt laid a hand on his arm.

'I spoke to him about that telephone call – he said it was faked.'

'Faked!' stuttered Perivale. 'How could it be?'

'He says he was impersonated by a man called Carver, one of the waiters here.'

Perivale gave a short laugh.

'Good lord, Wyatt, you don't mean to tell me you fell for an old story like that!'

'Then you think he was lying?' said Wyatt with a faint smile.

Perivale patted him on the shoulder.

'No question about it. We know that the night before Lauren Beaumont disappeared she came here and spoke to Luigi. We know that Luigi phoned Angus with that message about paying ransom to Reed. We know that the car which tried to force Maurice Knight over the bridge was Luigi's car. Why man, it's an open and shut case!'

'Just a minute,' said Wyatt, trying to detain him.

'There's no time to be lost. This man Luigi is obviously "Mr Rossiter", and the sooner we pull him in the better. See you later, Wyatt.'

Wyatt stood staring after him as he collected Bradley and

briskly climbed the staircase to the balcony. He hesitated for a moment outside the door, then opened it and went in with Bradley. The door closed, and Wyatt went back to their table.

Sally smiled across at him as he sat down.

'I can guess what Sir James has been saying,' she murmured. 'I've been trying to argue him out of it.'

'Then you don't think Luigi's such a desperate character?' queried Wyatt.

'He's obviously mixed up in this case – but I'm convinced he isn't "Mr Rossiter",' announced Sally positively.

'Any particular reason?' smiled Wyatt.

'Well, if you must know, I think "Mr Rossiter" is Maurice Knight. I suspected Sir Donald at first, but now I've got a strange sort of feeling about Knight,' said Sally. 'Of course, you always pull my theories to pieces, and I admit I haven't any cast-iron evidence.'

'Nobody has much evidence against anyone, apart from Luigi, and even he has a get-out. He claims that he was impersonated over the telephone by one of his waiters – a young fellow called Carver.'

Sally was interested at once.

'Have you met this waiter?' she asked.

'Yes,' said Wyatt. 'He's got rather a good story ... says Doctor Fraser paid him a couple of hundred to impersonate Luigi.'

'Do you believe him?'

'I do not,' said Wyatt. He waited for the waiter to place an omelette in front of him, and when they were alone again, he said: 'In the first place, I happened to find out that Carver has never set eyes on Doctor Fraser.'

'That was very clever of you, darling,' said Sally. 'How did you work it out?'

'I simply asked him if she was wearing a dress to match her blonde hair, and he agreed that she was.'

'And she's a brunette ... that was pretty smart of you, darling.'

'Ah, but that isn't the end of the story by any means,' said Wyatt, busy with his omelette. He leaned a little to his left to see the door of Luigi's office at the top of the balcony.

'All the same, I think Carver did impersonate Luigi.'

'Really, Lionel, you are exasperating,' said Sally, accepting a light for her cigarette. 'You always start at the wrong end of a story.'

Wyatt laughed.

'Very well, darling, I'll begin at the beginning. Once upon a time there was a night club proprietor who had several little sidelines that enabled him to keep his club open even when it ran at a loss. Then one day he met ...'

At that moment the door of Luigi's office opened and Perivale came running down the balcony steps. He came over to their table at once.

'We've got Luigi,' he announced somewhat breathlessly, 'but that waiter fellow lost his nerve and made a dash for it ...'

'Where is he?' demanded Wyatt quickly.

'He rushed out through the far door – it leads on to some sort of fire-escape that runs along the building. There are other doors that open on to it, so he may have doubled back. Bradley's gone after him ... the young fool's got a revolver. He threatened us; that's how he got out.'

'Well, he can't get very far if you've got the outside of the building covered,' said Wyatt.

Perivale nodded. 'All the same, I'm worried about that gun. The young fool's pretty desperate.'

There were sudden sounds of a scuffle, and a police whistle sounded from one of the outer rooms. The dancers eyed each other uncertainly. Perivale took command of the situation, and ordered everyone back to their seats.

Everyone was talking in rather frightened voices, and for a moment they did not see Carver suddenly reappear through a door in the far corner of the balcony, followed a second later by the stalwart figure of Superintendent Bradley. The white-faced waiter made for a corner of the balcony, and swung himself on to an iron girder which supported the roof. When Bradley made as if to follow him, he fired wildly. Bradley clutched his arm. Perivale shouted to him to abandon the pursuit, for he imagined that it was only a question of waiting until Carver had tired of perching up in the girders.

Then Wyatt drew his attention to a small skylight in the centre of the roof, which was obviously the man's objective. He clambered along the framework of girders with frantic haste.

'If he gets on that roof, we'll lose him,' said Perivale, hurrying away to warn his outside men.

Carver continued his hazardous climb, and rapidly neared his objective. He paused for a moment and looked down below. Then he stretched out an arm and pushed open the skylight.

Six plain-clothes detectives looked on helplessly from the dance floor.

Carver poised a little uncertainly, for his foothold on the narrow cross-span was none too sure, and he had no support to hold on to while he levered himself up to the skylight.

Finally he clutched at the frame with one hand, held on for a moment, then got a hold with his other hand and slowly began to lift himself into the aperture. The plain-clothes men were already moving towards the doors to try and intercept him outside or join in the chase across the roof-tops, when there was a sound of splintering wood.

The frame of the skylight had proved to be rotten through long exposure to the weather, and although Carver tried to get a grip on the roof itself, he was unsuccessful.

A little group of men and women in evening dress rushed wildly to the side of the dance floor as the black figure came hurtling down.

Carver clutched frantically at a cross-girder, held on to it for several breathless moments, then let go. He struck another of the girders and fell on the side of the dance floor farthest from Wyatt and Sally.

The plain-clothes men at once surrounded the waiter, and Wyatt went over to the little group. One of the detectives, who recognized Wyatt, shook his head.

'The poor devil's done for, I'm afraid, Wyatt,' he said quietly. Wyatt nodded and returned to Sally, whom he immediately conducted back to their waiting car. She was very silent on the journey back to the flat, still overcome with the horror of the incident, and Wyatt's mind was busy with the strange problems presented by Mr Luigi.

They were both a little surprised to find that two visitors were waiting for them in the entrance hall to the mansions. As they came in they saw Doctor Fraser and Hugo Linder sitting near the lift.

Wyatt invited them inside, and they all managed to squeeze into the tiny lift.

In the flat Sally went off to her bedroom to take off her hat, and Wyatt took his visitors in the lounge.

'This is an unexpected pleasure,' he began politely. 'I'm sorry to have kept you waiting.'

Linder accepted a chair, leaned back and said quietly:

'It's rather presumptuous of us calling at this time of night, Mr Wyatt. But I felt we both owed you an apology and an explanation.'

'That's very generous of you, Mr Linder,' said Wyatt pleasantly. 'Would you like a drink?'

They both refused.

'In that case, do try these cigarettes,' begged Wyatt. 'I'm very glad you came, because I feel there are quite a few things we might clear up together.'

Doctor Fraser played with the clasp of her bag a trifle nervously.

'I'm sorry I didn't tell you the truth when you asked me if I knew Hugo, Mr Wyatt, but believe me there was a very good reason,' she began earnestly.

'It was entirely my fault,' Linder interrupted her. 'You see, Doctor Fraser and I are sort of unofficially engaged ...'

'Please accept my congratulations,' said Wyatt politely.

'It's quite unofficial as yet,' put in Doctor Fraser hastily. 'In fact, we're not telling anyone—'

'I quite understand,' nodded Wyatt.

'You see, Mr Wyatt,' went on Linder, 'we didn't want Scotland Yard to associate our names ... when I found the body of Barbara Willis ... and she was suspected of being mixed up with the "Mr Rossiter" affair, well it all looked ...'

He made a helpless gesture.

'You mean it looked as if you two might be running a little organization, eh, Mr Linder?'

Linder rubbed the back of his head with a worried air.

'Yes. I advised Doctor Fraser not to say anything to anyone, and then I gave the show away myself. It was darned stupid of me.'

153

Wyatt frowned thoughtfully. These two seemed genuine enough, and there was something quite likeable about them. It was quite obvious that Linder was very much in love with Doctor Fraser, and that part of their story might well be true. But there was still that business with Sir Donald Angus to be considered.

Wyatt perched on the arm of the settee and addressed himself to Doctor Fraser.

'I believe that you had tea with Mr Linder at the Royal Astoria Hotel this afternoon. And while you were there you met Sir Donald Angus.'

'Why, yes, that's true,' replied Doctor Fraser, looking slightly puzzled. 'How did you know that?'

He evaded her question by asking:

'Haven't you read about Sir Donald in the papers this evening?'

'I rarely see the evening papers,' she replied.

'And I missed 'em this evening,' said Linder. 'What has Sir Donald been doing?'

'He has paid over rather a large sum of money for the return of a lady friend of his who was abducted.' He watched the doctor closely as he added: 'Her name was Lauren Beaumont.'

'Lauren Beaumont!' she echoed in an astonished voice.

'Not a name one would forget easily, eh, Doctor?' said Wyatt casually. 'And I don't suppose Sir Donald will forget that £15,000 or this unpleasant publicity for quite a long time.'

'Then she was returned?' asked Doctor Fraser.

'But of course; you saw her for yourself; in fact, Sir Donald told us you looked after her very capably.'

Doctor Fraser's expression changed again.

'You mean *that* girl!' she exclaimed. 'But that wasn't the girl I saw previously who gave me the same name.'

'Did you expect it to be?'

'Well, no ... no, I guess not,' she replied in a bewildered tone. 'I thought there was something odd about that set-up ... she didn't look like his secretary or anybody else's. Of course, she was pretty badly doped.'

'That's another thing,' said Wyatt. 'You diagnosed the drug that had been injected as "Amashyer". Now, I know quite a lot about "Amashyer", and one of the things about it is that it's none too easy to diagnose compared with most of the other narcotics.'

'Well, I happen to specialize in that sort of thing,' replied Doctor Fraser somewhat stiffly. 'We psychiatrists use drugs quite a bit you know, Mr Wyatt – and I read an article on "Amashyer" in the *Medical Times* only a month ago. It gave the after-effects in considerable detail.'

'I'm quite prepared to believe all that,' nodded Wyatt, 'but you have to admit, Doctor, that it was rather a remarkable coincidence that you should be having tea at Sir Donald's hotel when he brought this girl back. Do you usually go there for tea?'

'Why, no,' she replied candidly, 'and we wouldn't have been there today if Hugo hadn't telephoned and asked me to meet him there instead of the Ritz.'

It was Linder's turn to look surprised.

'I telephoned?' he queried sharply.

'Why, yes, darling ... this morning, just after I was through with my last patient ...'

'But, Gail, I did nothing of the sort!' he protested.

'Then why do you think I turned up at the Royal Astoria? And how did you come to be there?' she demanded.

'Because of the note you sent, saying would I make it the Royal Astoria, instead of the Ritz.'

'I sent you a note?' she repeated, plainly staggered.

'But of course you did. It came by messenger at midday.'

'Have you got the note?' asked Wyatt.

'No, I'm afraid I burnt it. But what does all this mean, Mr Wyatt?'

Wyatt went over to the fireplace to get an ashtray from the shelf. He returned and leaned against the mantelpiece.

'It could mean,' he began slowly, 'that "Mr Rossiter" somehow discovered that you two were meeting at the Ritz, and decided that it would suit his purpose better if you met at the Royal Astoria. So he forged a note to Linder – that wouldn't be too difficult, as he probably has at least one of the doctor's prescriptions in his possession – and he got a young man named Carver to telephone Doctor Fraser.'

'Who is Carver?' asked Doctor Fraser.

'You've never met him?'

'That's why I'm asking, Mr Wyatt.'

'Then I'm afraid you won't now. He met with an accident this evening that's almost certain to be fatal. Pity, because the young fellow was quite a remarkable mimic ... yes, quite remarkable.'

'Then you think that "Mr Rossiter" got him to imitate my voice over the telephone?' asked Linder.

'I said that's what might have happened,' replied Wyatt deliberately.

Over breakfast the next morning, Wyatt read the accounts of the affair at the Madrid Club in three different papers. They tallied in the essential details, but he was relieved to see that none of them connected the death of Carver with the Rossiter affair; possibly because Inspector Lathom had not been present on this occasion.

'Have you had any news about Bradley?' asked Sally, whose appetite seemed in no way impaired by the unpleasant experience of the previous evening.

'No,' replied Wyatt. 'I'll telephone the hospital presently. It was only a flesh wound, and Bradley's pretty tough, so I imagine he'll be out and about by the end of the week.'

He picked up Sally's picture paper and saw a large photo of Sir Donald Angus and Lauren Beaumont staring up from the back page.

'Phew!' he whistled softly, 'this isn't exactly going to oil the machinery of high finance. He'll soon be wishing he'd left his lady friend to fight her own battles. H'm ... I see she's described as his secretary, so that's something ...'

'I wonder how they got that picture ...' said Sally. 'One of "Mr Rossiter's" men must have followed them round with a camera.'

'Poor old Angus certainly ran into Trouble with a capital T on this trip,' nodded Wyatt, passing his cup over to Sally. 'However, it's a waste of time to sympathize with big business men – they always seem to find a way out of their scrapes.'

The telephone cut short any further discussion on this subject, and Wyatt went to answer it. He was not altogether surprised to hear the surly tones of Lathom at the other end. The inspector had paid a visit to the dress shop in Bond Street, and had cross-questioned the assistants. He had satisfied himself that the only one who had any connection with the abduction of Lauren Beaumont was a girl who was known as Miss Marcia, and he had taken her into custody.

'Sir James thought you might like to have a chat with her,

Mr Wyatt,' said Lathom, in a manner which seemed to disassociate himself from the idea.

'I would, very much,' replied Wyatt politely. 'Would it be all right if I came along in about half an hour?'

'I'll tell Sir James,' said Lathom and rang off.

Wyatt passed on the news to Sally, who was excitedly discussing its possibilities when Maurice Knight called. The moment Sally brought him in it was obvious that he was under some stress. His mouth twitched nervously and he looked as if he had not slept the previous night. He refused the coffee Sally offered him, then changed his mind and said he would like a cup if she could make it black and strong.

When she passed it to him his hand jerked and knocked the spoon to the floor.

'What's the matter, Mr Knight?' asked Wyatt curiously. 'You're like a man expecting a bomb to go off at any second.'

Knight said: 'I'm scared, Wyatt – just plain scared. And I don't mind admitting it.'

'Tell us all about it,' invited Wyatt. 'What are you frightened of exactly?'

Knight made an obvious effort, then began with some difficulty:

'When I first began to investigate Barbara's murder, I never thought of the danger it would involve – at least, I didn't think of my own danger.'

'You can't come up against a man of "Mr Rossiter's" calibre without running into danger sometime,' said Wyatt seriously. 'Well, what's happened this time?'

'Someone – I've no idea who it could be – someone tried to kill me last night,' said Knight moodily.

'Well, you're still alive to tell the tale,' said Wyatt encouragingly. 'Let's hear it.'

Knight took a drink of coffee and accepted a cigarette. Then, with some hesitation, he continued:

'After I left you last night I went back to my flat. I was standing outside, feeling for my latchkey, when suddenly a car went past. I heard what I took to be a backfire from the exhaust, but it must have been a revolver shot. The glass panel of the door splintered just above my head.'

'Didn't you even get a glimpse of the car?' asked Sally, a note of indignation in her voice.

'I'm afraid not. I was so dazed, I didn't know what to do. It completely took my breath away.'

'You were more scared than you were by the car accident at Shorecombe?' asked Wyatt.

'I certainly was. You see, I had something to occupy my mind immediately at Shorecombe. I had to keep driving the car. Besides, although I knew it couldn't have been an accident, at the back of my mind there was still the thought that it might have been. But there's nothing accidental about a bullet a few inches above one's head.'

'Did you inform the police?' inquired Wyatt.

Knight shook his head.

'In the first place, I was so upset ... I thought I'd sleep on it. Then this morning, I got a note ...'

He fumbled in his inside coat pocket and produced a folded slip of paper, which he passed to Wyatt, who smoothed it out and read:

'Do not interfere in matters which do not concern you. This is the last warning. Mr Rossiter.'

Wyatt passed the note to Sally, who read it and returned it to Knight.

'You say this arrived by the first post?' asked Wyatt.

'Yes, apparently it was posted last night in St John's Wood, though I suppose that isn't much help.'

'Not the slightest,' said Wyatt cheerfully.

Sally looked across at her husband, a tiny frown puckering her smooth forehead.

'Darling, I can't understand why "Mr Rossiter" bothers to plan an attempt on Mr Knight's life, when he has so many other fish to fry,' she murmured. 'After all, Mr Knight admits himself that he's only an amateur, and without the help of Scotland Yard he can't possibly—'

'Don't you believe that someone tried to kill me last night, Mrs Wyatt?' interrupted Knight in an unnatural voice. 'Perhaps you'd care to come and examine my front door ...'

'That's all right, Mr Knight,' said Wyatt soothingly. 'We believe you all right. Someone did try to murder you last night, and someone sent you that note. Now, why did they do that? Obviously because they are beginning to feel that your interference – or investigations if you like – are something of a nuisance. You're beginning to get under their feet; you're starting to spell danger. It may be only a fluke, but there's just a chance that you've stumbled across something that "Mr Rossiter" doesn't like.'

'Do you really think so, Mr Wyatt?' queried Knight anxiously.

'That's just a sort of hunch,' Wyatt assured him. 'I don't suppose for a minute you know yourself what it is you've found out ... but there's probably something.'

Knight looked perplexed.

'I can't think of anything,' he had to admit.

'Think back over the last day or two,' urged Wyatt, as

160

Sally refilled Knight's cup. 'Go over all the little details you can call to mind. For instance, those papers you went through – the ones that belonged to your fiancée. Did you find anything else of importance besides that address?'

Knight shook his head.

'As far as I could see, it was just a lot of odds and ends. I didn't look at it very carefully. Of course, I could go through it again, if you think it would be any use.'

'That's up to you,' said Wyatt. 'In the meantime, I don't quite know what we can do about your own personal safety.'

'You could drop a word to Sir James,' said Sally almost indifferently.

'Yes, I could do that. Then, first of all, they'd have Mr Knight on the carpet for poking his nose into matters which don't concern him – and after they'd detail a couple of men to act as unofficial bodyguard. Would you be in favour of that, Mr Knight?'

'Good lord, no!' exclaimed Knight in alarm. 'That would only make me more scared than ever.'

'That's just what I thought,' smiled Wyatt, glancing at his wrist-watch. 'Look here, I'm on my way to the Yard now, and I'll put it to Sir James strictly off the record. I'll let you know what he thinks about it.'

'All right,' agreed Knight. 'I'm very grateful to you, Wyatt. I'm terribly sorry to have bored you with all this – I must sound an awful coward ...'

'All brave men are cowards,' said Wyatt gravely. 'And I've yet to meet anyone who likes being shot at.'

He put on his coat and scarf and picked up his walking-stick.

'I've got my car here if you'd let me drop you at the Yard,' offered Knight.

'Could you? That'd be a great help … I'm a bit late, I'm afraid, and it's rather urgent.'

Knight rose and moved to the door.

'I'll go on first, just in case she won't start. See you down there.'

He went out, nodding good morning to Sally, and looking rather more confident than when he had come in twenty minutes earlier.

Sally walked with her husband out to the lift and they waited for it while Knight dashed down the stairs.

'Do you believe that story?' she inquired, after making sure that Knight was out of earshot.

'You mean about the revolver shot?' Wyatt asked, adjusting his scarf. 'Don't you?'

'You know what I think about Knight,' she replied quietly.

'Oh, yes, I was forgetting,' said Wyatt, pressing the lift button. 'Do you still think he's "Mr Rossiter"?'

'Don't you?' said Sally.

Wyatt carefully fastened the belt of his coat.

'Well, if he is, then all this business is going to take a lot of explaining away, isn't it?'

'He could be lying,' suggested Sally.

Wyatt shook his head reprovingly.

'You ex-policewomen have no faith in human nature,' he said sadly. 'There's no time to argue now. Work up your case against Knight and maybe we'll talk about it at lunch-time.'

The lift arrived and he got in and slammed the gates. Sally waved to him as he disappeared from view, then returned thoughtfully to the flat.

Wyatt found Knight sitting in a pre-war sports model, with an aluminium bonnet which was vibrating jerkily to the beat of the engine.

'This is rather a swell-looking tub,' he commented, settling himself into the bucket seat. 'Where did you get it?'

'Oh, I've had it for some time now. It's pretty ancient, I'm afraid,' replied Knight, revving the engine and slipping into bottom gear. 'Still, it holds together and keeps going.'

'It's certainly roomy,' said Wyatt, placing his stick by his side and luxuriously stretching out his legs.

'Yes, it's a bit too roomy, if anything. You've got to sit up pretty straight or you can't see the road.'

The car roared towards Piccadilly. Wyatt noticed that Knight still seemed a trifle upset. Once he missed his gears badly and cursed under his breath.

'You're sure I'm not taking you out of your way?' said Wyatt politely.

'No, no, that's all right – I've plenty of time.'

Knight suddenly began looking intently at his driving mirror, and his conversation became vague and disjointed. Wyatt peered at the mirror, too, then looked behind, but could see nothing unusual in the traffic at their rear. Suddenly Knight clutched his arm.

'That van – the one right behind us,' he said hoarsely. 'It's been on our tail almost since we started.'

Wyatt looked round again.

The van referred to was painted in a drab grey, and bore no indication of its owners.

'It looks like a laundry van,' said Wyatt, trying to get a good view of the driver, who wore a cap pulled down rather low.

'Do you think so?' said Knight, with a worried frown. 'Sorry I'm so jumpy – I keep imagining myself in the most ghastly situations.'

Wyatt smiled reassuringly.

'Well, if the van worries you, why not let it pass? If you slow down, we shall soon see if they're tailing us.'

'That's an idea,' nodded Knight, taking his foot off the accelerator and drawing in slightly. Sure enough, the van sounded its horn and slid quietly ahead.

'There you are,' said Wyatt.

'Yes, it was stupid of me,' murmured Knight somewhat ruefully. 'I don't know what gave me the idea that he was following us.'

'What you need is a good stiff drink,' suggested Wyatt. Knight nodded.

'There's a little pub on the Embankment – I'll call in there when I've dropped you at the Yard.'

They were moving slowly along Piccadilly when Wyatt noticed the rear doors of the van open about a foot. Without warning, the van turned abruptly into Sackville Street, and at that precise moment a man's hand appeared in the aperture at the back.

When he saw that the hand was grasping a small, round object about the size of a tennis ball, Wyatt quickly grabbed at the hand-brake, at the same time shouting:

'Pull up!'

Knight, his face deathly white, trod hard on the foot-brake, so that the round object which came hurtling towards them fell about three yards in front of the car.

Wyatt pulled Knight on to the floor, which seemed to rise up like a small boat on a heavy wave: they were flung in different directions to the accompaniment of a deafening explosion. Glass flew everywhere; the car turning over on its side, the wheels spinning.

The van roared up Sackville Street and disappeared.

Wyatt was vaguely conscious of people running from all

directions, police whistles blowing. Knight was flung clear, but Wyatt was still underneath the car, pinned down by the steering wheel, for the steering column had buckled with the force of the explosion.

He had just begun to feel a stabbing pain in his left shoulder when he heard a voice that was somehow familiar call out:

'Give me a hand, officer. Take the other side and we'll turn the car over ...'

Almost at once, the floor of the car began to move over from its upright position.

'Good lord!' said the voice of the constable. 'There's a man down here in the bottom of the car. Are you all right, sir?'

Wyatt painfully levered himself into an upright position.

'I – I think I'm all right,' he replied a trifle breathlessly, feeling round his shoulders with a certain caution. He moved his head gingerly to the right and saw Knight supported by a stalwart constable and looking more scared than ever.

Then he moved his head in the opposite direction and met a familiar pair of steely grey eyes.

'Sir Donald Angus!' he exclaimed in surprise. 'What are you doing here?'

CHAPTER X

Guest Night at the Palais

Sir Donald seemed equally surprised at the question.

'I was just strolling down towards the Haymarket to see a man I know ... lucky I was on the other side of the road or I might have caught a packet.'

'Very lucky,' agreed Wyatt, rubbing his bruised arm.

He looked round once again. Two pedestrians had been hurt by the bomb explosion, and an ambulance was rushing along Piccadilly. Wyatt walked rather painfully over to Knight.

'Are you all right?' he asked.

Knight's left arm hung limply.

'I got a nasty jar,' he replied, 'but I'm pretty sure there's nothing broken. The car seemed to take the worst of the shock.' He turned to look at the battered bonnet of the racing car.

'Well, she was on her last legs, and I dare say I'll get something from the insurance people,' he reflected grimly. 'How are you, Wyatt?'

'All in one piece,' said Wyatt. 'We were lucky to escape the flying glass. What happened to that van?'

'The last I saw of it they were going hell for leather up yonder.' He nodded in the direction of Sackville Street. Wyatt went up to the police sergeant who had taken charge of the situation, and gave him all the details, together with his name and address and a description of the van. Neither he nor Knight had noticed the number. Knight came up and gave his own address, but could add nothing to Wyatt's information, for neither of them had recognized the driver. The sergeant seemed rather puzzled, and not at all sure that it was indeed a bomb which some criminal had had the effrontery to throw into the heart of Piccadilly. It was something quite new in his experience, and he was inclined to regard his witnesses with a certain amount of suspicion, as if they were the members of a criminal gang which had been receiving drastic treatment from a rival organization. He asked a number of what appeared to be trivial questions with no direct bearing on the incident, but he seemed satisfied at last, and promised Wyatt that he would put out an 'all stations' call to try and trace the van.

When this was completed and most of the crowd had drifted on after the wreck of the car had been hauled away, Wyatt was a trifle surprised to see that Sir Donald was still hovering around the outskirts of their little group.

'I'd like to know what happened exactly, Mr Wyatt,' he said curiously. 'I was on the other side of the road, and the first I knew about it was the explosion ...'

Wyatt smiled a little wryly.

'Why are you so anxious to know, Sir Donald?'

'I – I was just wondering if it would be anything to do with – well, with a certain gentleman ...'

Wyatt gathered that he referred to "Mr Rossiter". Knight seemed to guess what Sir Donald was referring to.

'It was him all right – or one of his damned underlings,' he said bitterly. 'They must have been waiting for me at your flat. Didn't I tell you the swine was after me?' His voice rose to a hysterical note.

'Take it easy, old man,' said Wyatt soothingly.

'Aye, get a grip on yourself, laddie,' urged Angus. 'Ye're not the only one that rascal's put through it. If ye ask me, Mr Wyatt, it's high time the police did something about it.'

'I don't have to ask you to appreciate that, Sir Donald,' retorted Wyatt.

Knight moved about uneasily. 'I'm sorry to have landed you in this mess, Wyatt,' he apologized. 'I'm afraid you'll be late for your appointment after all.'

'That's all right, Knight. It wasn't your fault – and the appointment will wait I dare say. All the same, I'd better be getting along. Are you sure you'll be all right?'

'If ye'll allow me,' put in Angus, 'I know a little pub called the Three Stars just off Piccadilly here ... Mr Knight looks as if a good, strong Scotch wouldn't do him any harm.'

'That's an idea, Sir Donald,' nodded Wyatt approvingly. He watched them cross the road talking together, reflecting that he hadn't introduced them. Then he began wondering about Angus. Supposing he were mixed up with "Mr Rossiter", he had certainly appeared on the scene of the accident with remarkable celerity, as if he had been standing there waiting for it to happen ... should he have allowed Angus to take Maurice Knight off like that?

An empty taxi approached and cut short his reflections. He ordered the driver to take him to Scotland Yard as quickly as possible.

He found Sir James in rather an irritable mood. It appeared that a member of the Cabinet had buttonholed the Home

Secretary on the question of the Rossiter affair. The Home Secretary had asked the Chief Commissioner for a detailed report, and Perivale had no wish to make one at this stage in the case.

On top of all this, two crime reporters of the big daily papers had been on the telephone with some rather pertinent questions about the affair at the Madrid Club, anxious to confirm a report that Luigi was under arrest and curious to know exactly what the charge was. He had been rather curt with them, and was a little worried as to what they were going to print.

When Wyatt came in, he was chewing an unlighted cigar and turning the pages of a report on the affair at the Madrid. It had been written by one of the detective-sergeants, and was none too clearly worded. He had already pencilled in two or three extra sentences and was trying to decide whether he should send it down again to be completely rewritten.

'I expected you a quarter of an hour ago,' he said somewhat abruptly as Wyatt closed the door.

Wyatt quickly recounted the details of the accident in Piccadilly.

Perivale laid the cigar on his ashtray and passed a hand over his forehead.

'More trouble!' he muttered. 'There's no ending to this damned case. I must say it looks pretty fishy Angus being there. Did he give any good reason?'

'Well, his hotel isn't very far away, and he was walking down to the Haymarket, so he says.'

'H'm ... I've had him on the phone this morning. Wanted to know if it'd be all right if he went back to Scotland tomorrow. Seems he's had enough of London.'

'You can hardly blame him,' smiled Wyatt. 'This must be his most expensive trip to date. What did you tell him?'

'I said I'll let him know,' replied Perivale moodily. 'It might simplify things a bit if he's three hundred miles away. He wouldn't get into trouble so easily perhaps.'

He picked up his cigar again and eyed it distastefully.

'Pity you didn't get the number of that van,' he grumbled. 'I'll bet a hundred to one it's tucked away at the back of some garage, or abandoned on a piece of waste ground by this time.'

He picked up his telephone and asked to be connected with Lathom's office.

'Wyatt's here,' he told his colleague. 'Bring that woman in as soon as you like.' He put down the receiver and said:

'We'll have to handle this girl pretty carefully, Wyatt. She may be a valuable witness.'

'She certainly seems to be a very likely contact with "Mr Rossiter",' nodded Wyatt. 'I wouldn't be surprised if he has some sort of hold over her. He seems to manage to poke his finger into a lot of pies.'

'Yes, apparently her name is Christie, but she is usually known as Miss Marcia. Lathom has already had a talk to her, but he hasn't got very much information.'

'Has Miss Beaumont identified the girl?'

'Oh, yes, we had a special parade for her benefit.'

'And what did Miss Marcia say to that?'

'Swore she'd never set eyes on Beaumont ... she would, of course,' grunted Perivale. 'Ah, here she is ...'

Lathom opened the door and Miss Christie came in. She was a willowy brunette with a faintly supercilious stare.

'Miss Christie, sir,' said Lathom

'I should prefer it if you called me Miss Marcia.'

'Certainly, Miss Marcia,' agreed Perivale a trifle wearily. 'Perhaps you'll be good enough to sit down and answer a few questions.'

'This man,' replied Miss Marcia with a languid wave of her perfectly manicured hand, 'has already asked me a great number of quite futile questions, and I fail to see why I should be humiliated in this manner ... prying into my private affairs.'

'I'm very sorry, Miss Marcia,' replied Perivale gravely, 'but I must ask you to appreciate that we have had very definite proof that you are concerned in this case.'

'In what case, may I ask?' she demanded, with a lift of her delicately pencilled eyebrows.

Perivale waved aside the question and said:

'This is ex-Inspector Wyatt – Miss Marcia. He may have a few questions to ask you.'

'Indeed,' she replied coldly.

There was a vestige of a smile around Wyatt's mouth as he exchanged a glance with Perivale.

Perivale said: 'Miss Marcia, I don't think you realize the seriousness of the situation. You're aware that young lady identified you as the person who drugged and abducted her?'

'I've told you a dozen times I have never seen her in my life before,' retorted Miss Marcia with visible signs of irritation.

'Do you seriously expect us to believe that?' said Perivale.

'It's a matter of complete indifference to me what you believe,' she said, with a shrug of her elegant shoulders. Wyatt watched her closely, trying to decide to what extent her attitude was insolent bravado. At last, he walked over to her and said:

'You know, Miss Marcia, I've had a feeling for some weeks

that this "Mr Rossiter" we're after might quite easily turn out to be a woman.'

She sniffed.

'I've a suspicion that you get your ideas from reading novels, Mr Wyatt.'

Wyatt smiled, then became serious once more.

'I take it then you'd feel insulted if I suggested that *you* were "Mr Rossiter",' he suggested.

She gave a little artificial laugh. 'Good heavens, you can't be serious!'

'Perfectly. There's a pretty strong chain of evidence against you, Miss Marcia. Miss Beaumont visited your shop one afternoon to purchase a costume and made arrangements for a fitting the following morning. Now, it's my guess that she talked too much. You got her on to the subject of men, and she probably told you about her friendship with Sir Donald Angus. So you decided that she was a pretty safe victim for one of your little coups, "Mr Rossiter".'

'Don't call me "Rossiter"!' she snapped, recoiling at the accusation. 'You know it's all utter nonsense. If that's what you really believe, then you must be a complete idiot.'

Wyatt regarded her with a faint smile.

'Shall I tell you what I really believe, Miss Marcia?' he asked. 'It doesn't take much imagination to suggest that when Lauren Beaumont boasted to you of her gentleman admirer, you probably hinted that she might like to get him to take her to the Madrid Club, which had lately become the fashion again, and that if she mentioned your name to the proprietor, Charles Luigi, he might be able to supply her with several pairs of silk stockings.'

'And why should I want her to go to the Madrid?'

'Simply for Luigi to get a good look at the girl before you went ahead with your plans.'

Miss Marcia favoured him with a cynical stare.

'I don't know who you are, Mr Wyatt, but it's obvious to me that you ought to write novels, with your imagination.'

'Thank you, Miss Marcia; I'll keep it in mind,' replied Wyatt politely. 'Though there isn't as much fiction in that story as you might think. You see, we picked up Luigi last night.'

'What has this man to do with me?'

'Quite a bit, Miss Marcia,' replied Wyatt suavely. 'Because he decided to tell us all he knew.'

'I don't believe it!' she cried in a tense voice. 'Luigi would never talk! What did he tell you?'

'Everything,' replied Wyatt curtly.

She slumped into her chair, and her face suddenly looked old beneath the elaborate make-up.

'In that case, there's nothing else for me to say,' she murmured.

'I should be interested to hear your side of the story, Miss Marcia,' said Wyatt.

'You're bluffing!' she cried suddenly in a suspicious tone. 'I don't believe Luigi said a word.'

'All right,' said Wyatt vaguely, 'if you'd prefer not to go into the matter. It won't take us long to check up his statements for ourselves.'

She became apprehensive again.

'What did Luigi say?' she demanded hoarsely.

Perivale flashed a warning glance at Wyatt.

'What did Luigi tell you?' queried the girl again.

Wyatt sat back and studied her thoughtfully.

'You were right just now when you said I was bluffing

about your being "Mr Rossiter",' he said. 'Luigi told us enough to satisfy us that you couldn't possibly be.'

'Luigi knows the identity of "Mr Rossiter" as well as I do!' she exclaimed angrily. 'Didn't he tell you that – didn't he tell you how it all started?'

'I'd prefer to hear your version of the affair,' replied Wyatt quietly.

There was a long pause. She looked round the little group of men and found each face inscrutable.

'Could I have a drink of water?' she said at last.

Lathom went over and filled a glass from a jug which stood on a side-table in the far corner. He brought it over to her and she began to sip it.

'Why are you so anxious to hear my side of the story, Mr Wyatt?' she demanded slowly.

'Just for the records, Miss Marcia. And I might add that it will be greatly to your own advantage when your case comes to be considered.'

She shook her head. There was a new look of decision in her eyes as she snapped:

'I'm afraid that'll never happen.'

As she finished speaking she seemed to bite upon something solid, then she took a drink of water. Almost immediately she began gasping for breath and the men rushed over to her. They lowered her gently to the floor as she relapsed into unconsciousness.

'Get the first aid people!' Perivale ordered.

'She must have had a pellet of some kind in her mouth, ready for an emergency of this sort,' said Wyatt grimly.

Perivale said: 'I thought you were overdoing that bluff about Luigi.'

'But you told me last night you picked him up,' said Wyatt quickly.

'That's true enough,' grunted Perivale. 'But we had to let him go again.'

'You let him go!' echoed Wyatt.

'Yes, he was brought up at a special court first thing this morning,' put in Lathom. 'He asked for bail, and I put it at £10,000, thinking no one would find it for him. To our amazement, two men came forward.'

'So Mr Luigi is back in circulation,' said Wyatt thoughtfully. 'That certainly complicates matters.'

Sally was sitting at the piano playing a series of Jerome Kern numbers, while her husband sat moodily gazing into the fire. Since his return from the Yard, after the interview with Miss Marcia, Sally had been worried about him, for he had been strangely uncommunicative. Time and again, he made monosyllabic replies to her questions, and apart from a brief account of the girl's death and the fact that Luigi was still at large, he had enlightened her on no further developments of the case.

'Lionel!' she called from the piano. 'Will you open a window?'

He did not hear her, and she repeated the request. As if reluctant to be dragged out of his reverie, he limped across to the window and flung it open with a bang.

Sally indulged in another furious burst of rhythm, then swung round on the piano stool.

'What's the matter, Lionel?' she asked.

He shifted impatiently in his armchair.

'Nothing's the matter, darling; I'm perfectly all right,' he assured her somewhat ill-humouredly.

She came over to him and perched on the arm of his chair.

'You've had a long face ever since you got up this morning, and you came back tonight like a politician who's just lost a safe seat. What is it? Are you worried about something?'

'Well, perhaps, in a way,' he confessed.

'Are you still upset about that girl at Scotland Yard yesterday morning?'

'I'm very puzzled about the whole business,' he admitted. 'Not to mention feeling uncomfortable that Luigi is still at large.'

'I should imagine he'll lie low for a bit if he has any sense,' said Sally.

'He'll probably have to obey orders, the same as the rest of the outfit,' brooded Wyatt.

'Then you don't think he's "Mr Rossiter"?'

'I can't imagine Luigi as a master mind somehow. He strikes me more as a petty trafficker in drugs or smuggled merchandise. Sir James has put a couple of men on his tail, but I don't suppose they'll find out very much.'

Sally picked up two evening papers he had flung on the floor and folded them tidily.

'Well, what have you been up to all day, darling? Or is it a top secret?' she said lightly.

'Oh, no, it isn't as vital as all that.'

He took a notebook from his pocket and turned the pages.

'You remember I found this on Reed's body,' he reminded her, flattening out the little book at a page towards the end, and indicating a scribbled entry.

'Royston – 10.30,' she read slowly. 'What's it mean, Lionel? Is Royston a man or a racehorse? Or maybe a greyhound?'

He shook his head. 'I'm pretty sure it's neither. For one

thing, there's no race run at that time. Royston is obviously a man whom Reed was to meet at 10.30.'

'Well, have you tried to find him?' asked Sally.

Wyatt sighed.

'I have spent the whole of the morning and the better part of the afternoon in some of the shadiest quarters of the East End, asking all my disreputable acquaintances if they know a man named Royston.'

'Phew!' said Sally. 'No wonder you're depressed! Did you run the gentleman to earth?'

He shook his head sadly.

'Not a trace! No one had ever heard of a man named Royston.' He snapped the notebook shut and thrust it back in his pocket.

'So you're feeling pretty frustrated, eh?' smiled Sally. 'Is it really as vital as all that, darling?'

'My dear girl,' said Wyatt patiently. 'I don't trudge round East End pubs all day unless I'm after something fairly important. It seems more than probable to me that Royston was the man who gave Reed his orders for the Angus job.'

'Then it's probably an assumed name,' suggested Sally. 'Which makes the whole thing fairly hopeless.'

They were still discussing ways and means of following up the inquiry when the front-door bell rang. Wyatt went out to find Doctor Fraser and Hugo Linder.

The doctor looked ill at ease, and Linder was certainly none too happy.

'We were on our way to the St James' Theatre,' began Doctor Fraser, 'and as we walked through the park we were discussing the affair at Shadwell Basin.'

'The doctor told me about your telephone call to her that evening when I was away,' said Linder.

'Yes – he takes rather a serious view of it,' she nodded. 'In fact, nothing would do but that we should come straight here.'

Wyatt looked from one to the other, then inquired:

'What are you referring to exactly?'

'You asked Doctor Fraser what sort of perfume she used,' Linder reminded him.

'Ah, yes, the perfume,' said Wyatt lightly. 'I'd almost forgotten.'

'Why did you ask her that question?' persisted Linder in a somewhat ominous tone.

'Simply because I wanted to know what sort of perfume she used,' replied Wyatt airily.

'I'm serious about this, Mr Wyatt,' said Linder coldly. 'It happens to be quite important.'

'I'm glad you think so, Mr Linder.'

Linder paced across to the window and back again, then thrusting his hands deep in his trouser pockets, said:

'About a week ago I bought Gail a bottle of perfume for her birthday. It was the brand she always used – Château Number Eight. Two days later, she had a visit from Inspector Lathom about a prescription she had given to a Miss Gillow.'

'Mr Wyatt knows all about that,' put in the doctor.

'Mr Wyatt doesn't know that the bottle of scent was missing from your dressing-table after the inspector's visit.'

Wyatt offered them a cigarette and snapped open his lighter.

'I take it the inspector wasn't shown into your bedroom,' he said to Doctor Fraser.

'Of course not ... and I think perhaps Hugo is exaggerating about all this. But I have to admit that the inspector was alone in my flat for about ten minutes. My maid let him in, and as I was out at the time, he said he would wait. She told him I was due back quite soon.'

'But your maid would surely have heard him move from one room to the other – wouldn't he have had to cross the hall?'

She shook her head.

'As it happens, my bedroom leads out of the sitting-room the inspector was shown into.'

Wyatt blew a ring of smoke into the air.

'Have you asked your maid about this stolen bottle?' he inquired.

'She says she knows nothing about it. If you're suggesting she stole it, well, I'm afraid I can't believe that. She's been with me eight years now ...'

'Then you think Inspector Lathom took it?' demanded Wyatt mildly.

'Of course not,' she replied emphatically. 'The whole idea is quite absurd. But why did you ask me about the perfume in the first place? That seems to be Hugo's chief worry.'

'I asked you,' said Wyatt deliberately, 'because someone who used Château Number Eight visited Professor Reed on the night he was murdered.'

There was a look of fear in her eyes as she sank into the nearest chair.

'But I told you! I never went near Shadwell Basin that night,' she said in what was almost a whisper.

'I never said you did, Doctor,' was Wyatt's reasonable reply. 'I was only relating the facts of the case.'

Linder laid a hand on Wyatt's arm.

'Supposing the person who killed that man wanted to throw suspicion on Doctor Fraser,' he began urgently. 'If he

179

knew what perfume the doctor used, then the obvious thing would be to spray some of it on the dead man …'

'As you say, Mr Linder, it's quite an obvious trick,' nodded Wyatt. 'That was why I didn't follow it up too closely. But there is a rather more subtle aspect of it, if you'll think for a minute.'

'Well?' said Linder, in a challenging tone.

'Let us suppose, just for sake of argument, that Doctor Fraser *did* go to Shadwell Basin that evening, and then later – because of what I said on the telephone – began to get rather worried about the perfume. Wouldn't it be rather a neat bit of camouflage if you came along with the doctor and spun me a story about the perfume being stolen?'

'Mr Wyatt!' exclaimed the doctor, half rising to her feet. Wyatt put up a restraining hand.

'Don't be alarmed; this is only a supposition, Doctor Fraser.'

Linder swung round.

'It's not the sort of supposition I care for!' he snapped.

'No?' said Wyatt, with the merest lift of his eyebrows. 'In that case, let's just forget all about it. Unless you'd like me to mention the matter to Lathom.'

'That's up to you, Mr Wyatt,' said Linder indifferently. 'The fact remains that the perfume was stolen. If you care to pursue the matter further, I'm sure the doctor will be only too glad to help in any way.'

He looked across at Doctor Fraser, who nodded her agreement.

'That's all right, then,' smiled Wyatt, going over to the fireplace and flicking the ash from his cigarette.

Then he turned and leaned against the mantelpiece as he asked:

'By the way, Mr Linder, you don't happen to know anyone named Royston, I suppose?'

Linder repeated the name thoughtfully, then shook his head.

'What about you, Doctor?'

The doctor seemed to be equally positive.

The front-door bell rang again, and Sally answered it, returning a few moments later. She went across to Wyatt and said in a low tone:

'It's Inspector Lathom. I put him in the dining-room.'

'OK,' replied Wyatt with a sigh of resignation. 'Tell him I won't be a minute.'

Wyatt turned to find his callers already proposing to leave.

He saw them to the door, and then went into the study, where Sally had turned on the electric fire, and was chatting with some effort to Inspector Lathom.

Never very cheerful at the best of times, the Inspector's features were more gloomy than ever. He had been none too keen on the idea of calling on Wyatt, but Perivale had insisted that the latest complication in the Rossiter affair needed the co-operative concentration of every available man.

It did not take him long to enlighten Wyatt as to the reason for his visit. Another girl had disappeared. Her name was Marjorie Faber, and her father was head of a large firm of manufacturing chemists.

Wyatt sat at his desk and jotted down one or two notes. He got the impression that Lathom was beginning to feel the strain of this case and had been under fire from his superiors, who were anxious to see results.

'How did you know about this girl disappearing?' Wyatt inquired.

'Her father telephoned us about an hour ago, and Sir James and I saw him and he told us all he knew. The poor devil's very upset – he practically worships his daughter.'

'When did he last see her?'

'Just before she went off to the Palais de Danse at Rammersford last night. Since then she's completely vanished. She never went home, and this morning, by midday post, her father had a note from "Mr Rossiter" – exactly the same as Angus'. It just said: "Wait – Mr Rossiter".'

'H'm ... looks pretty grim,' mused Wyatt, scribbling a design on his blotter. 'You say her father is well off?'

'He'll pay; no doubt about that, even if it takes his last penny. But we've got to find her, Mr Wyatt, if we have to put every man in the Force on the job and comb out every house in the country. If this goes on much longer, we shall be the laughing-stock of Europe.'

The inspector's face was drawn and there was a note of anxiety in his voice. Even Sally was inclined to feel a little sorry for him.

'How much do you know about this girl?' asked Wyatt.

'Only what her father told us. She's been expensively educated, but I got the impression that she's inclined to be a bit flighty. Seems she went to the dance with a young man named Phil Dark. I managed to get him on the telephone, but he stuck to it that he had a bit of a tiff with the girl about half-way through the evening, and he went home by himself. He said he could prove all that, so I'm going to check up as soon as possible.'

'And you've no idea what happened to Marjorie Faber after this fellow left her?'

'That's where we're up against it. Of course, I haven't had much time to look into it yet; I've got two men making inquiries at the Palais, but it isn't easy to trace one girl in such a large crowd.'

Wyatt sat back in his chair.

'So now what?' he asked.

'Sir James wondered if you could come down to the Yard at once, Wyatt. He's holding an urgent conference, and he wants to make a big push on the case right away ... before Mr Faber gets a demand from "Mr Rossiter" if possible.'

Wyatt looked across at Sally.

'Can you amuse yourself for an hour?' he asked.

'Considering I've been amusing myself all day ...' she smiled. 'Off you go, darling, and don't be too late.'

As they were going down in the lift, Wyatt said to Lathom in a casual tone:

'By the way, Lathom, when you went to see Doctor Fraser a few days back, I suppose you didn't get a chance to take a good look round her flat.'

Lathom shook his head.

'No, as a matter of fact, all I had time for was a quick peep into her bedroom. It was next door to the sitting-room the maid showed me into.'

'What made you look in the bedroom?'

'Well, in the first place, I didn't know what it was; I simply opened the door to see, more out of curiosity than anything.'

'You didn't happen to notice a bottle of perfume on the dressing-table, I suppose?'

'As a matter of fact, I did,' nodded Lathom. 'I remember it had a vivid green label on it. I also noticed a comb, a hand mirror, a diamante clip, a pair of ear-rings and a powder bowl on the dressing-table, Mr Wyatt. I've got rather a knack of remembering these things. Why, is there anything wrong in that quarter?'

'Nothing at all …' murmured Wyatt blandly. 'And I must say I envy you your powers of observation.'

Sally went back to the lounge after switching off the electric fire in the dining-room, wondering how she could fill in the rest of the evening. There was a film at the Plaza she rather wanted to see, but she somehow didn't feel like going by herself.

She sat down at the piano and idly picked out a tune with one finger, reflecting that the flat suddenly seemed more empty than it had done for some time. On a sudden impulse she decided to go into the kitchen and try out a recipe she had just come across that afternoon in a new cookery book.

She was just putting on an apron when the telephone rang, and on answering it she was delighted to hear the friendly voice of Janet Cape, an old colleague who had been on the office staff at the Yard before resigning to get married.

'Why, Janet!' exclaimed Sally. 'How did you know I was here?'

'I rang up the farm, and Fred gave me your number. Why ever didn't you let me know before?'

'It's been such a rush, and Lionel is mixed up with a big case; we hardly get time to breathe. This is the first evening I've had free since we got here. Lionel's gone off to the Yard again.'

'Then why don't you come over?' replied Janet at once. 'You can be here in half an hour.'

Janet and her husband, a tea merchant, had a flat in Holland Park.

Sally hesitated for a moment, then decided to accept. She might not get another opportunity of seeing Janet while she was in Town.

When she had agreed, Janet added hurriedly:

'Oh, I forgot … we're going along to the Rammersford Palais after dinner. You'll join us, of course. It's only a small party.'

'I haven't an evening frock,' began Sally doubtfully, but Janet waved this objection aside.

'That doesn't matter in the least. Nobody stands on ceremony at the Palais. They're a lovely crowd there – and you'll see Roy Antonio in person.'

'You mean the man who croons on the wireless?'

'Yes, he plays the trumpet, too.'

'Sounds quite a character.'

'He is. My cousin knew him when he was Georgie Royston from Clapham, only too glad to make ten bob a night at a village dance.'

'Did you say Royston?' queried Sally, the name sounding vaguely familiar.

'That's right – Georgie Royston. Of course, that's kept very dark nowadays.'

Janet chattered on merrily until Sally interrupted:

'I must rush and change, darling – you can tell me all the news over dinner.'

She replaced the receiver with a tiny sigh. Janet's exuberance was sometimes a trifle overwhelming, particularly if you had not seen her for some time. Sally went to the bedroom and examined her somewhat limited wardrobe.

Two hours later the party drove up to the Rammersford Palais. As they parked the cars Sally could hear the brassy blare of Frankie Wayne's Wildcats, whose glossy pictures were displayed so effectively in the showcases in front of the dance hall.

'That's Roy Antonio,' said Janet, as the first trumpet player came to the microphone to sing a vocal refrain. Sally looked at him closely as they danced past. He seemed to her to be a typical dance band boy: sunburnt complexion, neat little moustache, beady eyes and a flashing artificial grin. She thought it might be an idea to study him a little more closely, so at the end of the dance they found a table near the band and the men in the party went off to get some ices.

After a little desultory conversation amongst themselves the band began the next number. Georgie Royston, alias Antonio, seemed to earn his money, for he either sang a vocal refrain or extracted strange and wonderful noises from his trumpet. He was obviously the band's star performer. Sally was just deciding that it was almost impossible to judge a man's character from the way he behaved when playing in a band when she suddenly caught sight of her husband talking to Sir James in a far corner of the room.

With a brief apology to her companions, she skirted the crowded dance floor and made her way over to them. She was upon them before either had noticed her. When she touched her husband lightly on the arm, the look of amazement on his face when he swung round and saw her was, she felt, worth travelling much further than Rammersford to see.

'Sally! What the devil are you doing here?'

She laughed.

'So this is where you great minds retire to hold your conferences, is it, Mr Wyatt?'

'By Jove, you gave us quite a start, Sally,' said Sir James. 'Didn't expect to see you here.'

'And I certainly never dreamed I'd see you,' said Sally. 'What goes on?'

'We're down here with Lathom, trying to get an idea of

the lie of the land. He's busy checking up with one or two people who saw Marjorie Faber here last night.'

'Isn't he signalling to us – over yonder?' asked Wyatt, indicating the gaunt figure of the inspector standing by a distant exit.

'I'll go,' decided Perivale. 'You stay here and just keep an eye on things in general.'

As soon as he had gone, Wyatt turned to Sally.

'You shouldn't have come here on your own, darling,' he began, with a worried look. 'There's something fishy going on here and ...'

'I didn't exactly come on my own,' said Sally with some diffidence.

'Good lord!' exclaimed Wyatt, slightly taken aback. 'Then who—'

She drew him into a corner where they could not be overheard and spoke in a low and urgent tone.

'Just after you left, Janet Cape 'phoned and told me she was coming here, with a party. She started talking about the band and suddenly came out with something terribly important. I simply had to come here so that I could try and check up on it.'

'What is all this mystery?' he demanded, somewhat puzzled.

'Have you noticed that trumpet player in the band – the one who sings and all the girls gather round ...?'

'Yes, of course,' said Wyatt impatiently. 'He's Roy Antonio, supposed to be one of the highest paid musicians in the country ... a very heavy gambler too, I believe ...'

'His name isn't Antonio at all,' interrupted Sally deliberately. 'It's Royston.'

Wyatt caught his breath.

187

'Are you sure of this?'

'Absolutely. Janet's cousin used to know him when he went by his real name. She can tell you all about him.'

Wyatt stared thoughtfully across the crowded dance floor. The band finished a number and there was some applause.

'Look,' said Sally. 'They're just coming off the stand.'

Wyatt followed her gaze as the band boys put down their instruments and came down the steps on to the floor. For once in a way the trumpet player seemed to have no time for his feminine admirers. A stocky little man in a neat grey lounge suit was waiting to speak to him. His back was to them and it was not until he swung half round in the course of an animated conversation that they recognized the familiar features of Sir Donald Angus.

CHAPTER XI

Exit Mr Luigi

Wyatt took Sally by the elbow and piloted her to the nearest
vacant table.

'Stay here; I'll be back,' he promised, keeping his quarry
in sight.

He began moving around the floor, which was still very
crowded, though it was only a small relief band playing at
that moment. He suddenly felt a tug at his sleeve, and turned
to find Sir James standing there.

Perivale began telling him that he had just seen the manager
of the Palais, who had promised his co-operation, then he
broke off and gripped Wyatt's arm.

'Good lord! That's Sir Donald Angus!'

'That's right, Sir James. I was just going over to him.'

Perivale rubbed his chin, somewhat perplexed.

'What on earth is he doing here?'

'Maybe it's a case of the wealthy man sampling the people's
pleasures ... maybe!' replied Wyatt humorously. At that
moment Lathom came up to them, and addressed himself to
his chief.

'I don't think there's very much more we can do here, sir,' he began briskly, then noticed that the other two were paying little attention. He followed their gaze and gave a low whistle.

'Angus! What the devil's he doing here?'

'I was just on my way to ask him,' replied Wyatt.

'He's talking to one of the band ... now what could he possibly want with him?'

'It's a man named Roy Antonio,' said Lathom shrewdly. 'I've heard one or two things about him ... I've a vague idea he's got a police record ... you don't think he's something to do with Marjorie Faber, do you, Wyatt?'

'I'm pretty sure he is,' said Wyatt abruptly, rather to their surprise.

'What makes you so sure?' asked Perivale curiously.

'Because his name isn't Roy Antonio at all – it's Royston. And Royston is the man who had an appointment with Reed just before he was murdered.'

Wyatt took the little black notebook from his pocket and showed them the entry.

'Ten to one this fellow knows something about Marjorie Faber,' decided Perivale briskly. 'Get him up to the manager's office, Lathom, as soon as he leaves Angus.'

'Very good, sir,' nodded Lathom.

They watched the two men still in close conversation for several minutes, always moving a little nearer and contriving to remain unobserved. Suddenly, they saw Angus swing on his heel and stride over to a small table under the balcony almost level with the platform. Royston gave a little shrug and moved across the floor to join a group of girls. Lathom went in that direction to await an opportune moment for conducting his man to the manager's office.

Wyatt and the Assistant Commissioner concentrated their

attention on Angus, and as they drew nearer the table where he was just sitting down they could hear him quite plainly talking in an angry voice to a girl who sat with her back to them.

'Nothing short of sheer, damnable impertinence!' he was saying. 'Why you should imagine that a man in my position is going to tolerate ...'

He suddenly looked up and caught sight of Perivale, and his jaw dropped. The girl noticed his change of expression and turned round to see what caused it.

'Good evening, Miss Beaumont,' said Wyatt pleasantly.

She replied to his greeting, but there was a sullen expression on her face.

'I didn't expect to see you here, Sir Donald,' continued Wyatt. Angus scowled at him.

'I hope you gentlemen will excuse us. I have just asked Miss Beaumont to dance.' He rose and offered her his arm.

'In that case,' replied Wyatt evenly, 'Sir James and I will sit down and wait till you've finished. We rather wanted to have a little chat with you.'

'Now, look here, Wyatt,' said Angus, the colour suffusing his thick neck, 'if you'll take my advice, you won't interfere in matters that don't concern you.'

The girl laid a restraining hand upon her escort's arm, but he shook it off impatiently.

Wyatt was still smiling.

'I haven't the slightest wish to interfere in what doesn't concern me, but I'm very interested in that young man you were just talking to. A Mr Antonio, isn't he?'

'Who the devil's Antonio?'

'You know quite well, Sir Donald,' interposed Perivale. 'He's the fellow from the orchestra ...'

'Oh … I was just asking him if he had seen Miss Beaumont.'

'Then he's a friend of yours, Miss Beaumont?'

'Certainly not!' she replied, a shade too readily. 'I just happen to know him by sight. He's very popular here.'

'Look here, Wyatt,' broke in Angus again. 'We don't intend to stand here and be cross-questioned. Is there any reason why we shouldn't come and dance at this place? For that matter, what law is there against my having a chat with one of the fellows in the band? It seems to me that you and Sir James should be able to employ your time more profitably than …'

His voice trailed away as he was suddenly aware of Wyatt gazing intently at the lapels of his coat.

'What the devil are you staring at?' he demanded irritably.

'I was just admiring your suit, Sir Donald,' said Wyatt in a casual tone.

Without any further ado, Angus took Lauren Beaumont in his arms and began to dance. When they had moved out of earshot, Perivale said curiously:

'What was it you were staring at, Wyatt?'

'Just a bulge in Sir Donald's inside coat pocket.'

'It was probably only his wallet.'

Wyatt shook his head.

'It would have to be a pretty large wallet stuffed to capacity to make a bulge like that. My guess is that he had a nice fat pile of banknotes tucked away there. Let's hope he's kept a note of the numbers.'

They saw Lathom tap the band boy on the shoulder and take him off to the manager's office. After some discussion, they decided that no useful purpose could be served by waiting to talk to Angus in his present mood, so they made their way down a long corridor that led to the office. It was a very simply furnished room compared with that of Charles Luigi. Most of the chairs looked well-worn, and there was a large but serviceable light oak roll-top desk under the window.

Lathom was obviously having some trouble with Roy Antonio, alias George Royston, for they could hear the musician's angry voice some distance from the door.

'It's no good you saying you've never met Sir Donald Angus,' Lathom was shouting, 'because we know perfectly well you're as thick as thieves!'

'I tell you I've never seen the guy!' came the pseudo-American voice of Royston.

'We saw you talking to him on the dance floor, only a few minutes ago,' said Lathom harshly.

'You must be nuts!' snapped Royston.

'This lying won't get you anywhere,' barked Lathom. 'Three of us saw you.'

'Just a minute now. You don't mean that grey-haired guy with a voice like "Annie Laurie"? He came and asked me if I knew where he could find a girl named Beaumont.'

'Ah, now we're beginning to get somewhere,' said Lathom. 'You do know Miss Beaumont?'

'Sort of.'

At this point the door opened to admit Perivale and Wyatt. Royston swung round and looked them up and down.

'What's this – a police raid?' he rasped.

'You could put it that way, Mr Royston,' said Wyatt smoothly.

Royston turned to Lathom.

'Who are these men?'

'My name is Wyatt, and this is Sir James Perivale – we're delighted to make your acquaintance, Mr Royston.'

There was an angry light in the trumpet player's eye.

'Where d'you get this Royston stuff? The name is Antonio – Roy Antonio.'

'And a very nice romantic sort of name; it must be a great help with the ladies. You seem to be on pretty good terms with them, if I may say so.'

'I get by,' said Royston indifferently.

Wyatt leaned against the desk and said quietly:

'How friendly were you with Miss Marjorie Faber?'

Royston shook his head.

'That's a new one on me, brother. I once knew a dame called Webber who used to sing with a six-piece outfit at Epsom; she won a crooning competition over there and—'

'Listen to me, Royston,' snapped Wyatt abruptly, going over to the musician. 'If you take my advice, you'll drop that phoney American twang and come down to brass tacks. A girl name Marjorie Faber came here last night; she was picked up by someone and she disappeared. That person who picked her up was either the notorious "Mr Rossiter" or a member of his organization.'

'What's all this got to do with me?' demanded Royston insolently, eyeing Wyatt with a shifty glance.

'That's exactly what we're here to find out, Royston. Are you a member of that organization?'

'I've never heard of any organization,' snarled Royston. 'And I'm due back on the stand. There'll be a hell of a row if I'm not there to—'

'Just before you go,' continued Wyatt blandly, 'I want to ask you one or two questions about your old friend, Professor Reed.'

'Who the hell's Professor Reed?'

If Royston was familiar with the name, he did not betray

the fact, though they were watching him closely. Wyatt went on talking in the same level tones.

'The late Professor Reed was particularly well known in the East End, both as an unlicensed vet and also as—'

'What d'you mean – the *late* Professor Reed?' interrupted Royston.

'Didn't you know he was dead?'

'I ... I tell you I never heard of him,' replied Royston sullenly.

'That's a pity in a way. He was quite a character. His death was really most regrettable. Pity he was murdered in cold blood like that.'

'Murdered!' repeated Royston. 'Who murdered him?'

'Why, "Mr Rossiter", of course.'

Royston drew his coat sleeve across his forehead, upon which had appeared tiny beads of perspiration.

'I see you're beginning to call Professor Reed to mind now,' went on Wyatt inexorably. 'You see, Royston, the professor had served his purpose. So far as "Mr Rossiter" was concerned, he was a back number, just as all "Mr Rossiter"'s accomplices become back numbers in time.'

'What are you getting at?'

'I'm merely trying to bring home to you the fact that there's sure to come a day, Mr Royston, when you are in some danger yourself from "Mr Rossiter". You pulled off a big job for him last night, and—'

'Nothing happened here last night as far as I'm concerned,' asserted Royston angrily.

There was a pause.

'All right, Mr Royston, if that's the attitude you propose to take,' said Perivale at last; 'we've no definite evidence against you. But there is something you might like to bear in mind.'

'What's that?' demanded Royston, a hint of curiosity in his voice.

'Just at the moment, we're interested in two things. The identity of "Mr Rossiter", and what happened to that girl last night. But there's quite a possibility that tomorrow we might be interested in – you!' Perivale spoke slowly, weighing every word.

'I've told you! I know nothing about what happened here last night,' repeated Royston.

Wyatt began pacing up and down the room. There was a a steely quality in his voice now as he confronted Royston once more.

'I put it to you, Royston, that for weeks now you've been watching Marjorie Faber. We've discovered that you were on friendly terms with her. It's my bet that you contacted Reed and he promised to get in touch with "Rossiter" and let you know. But Reed couldn't keep that appointment for a very good reason. He was dead. However, someone else kept it … someone else brought you the money, the instructions – and the hypodermic syringe!'

Royston appeared to recoil. He took half a step backwards, then recovered. He licked his lips nervously.

'How did you know about the syringe?' he said in a gruff whisper.

'You injected a dose of "Amashyer",' went on Wyatt quickly, 'and then you smuggled the girl into your car. Now … where did you take her?'

Royston seemed to be thoroughly frightened.

'I – I didn't take her anywhere.'

Lathom went up to him and thrust him down on to a chair, he stood over him menacingly.

'Where did you take her?'

Royston clenched his hands until the knuckles showed white.

'You'd better talk fast!' growled Lathom. 'If that girl's dead, you'll be put on a charge right away. Now – where is she?'

'I – I took her to Shadwell Basin,' said Royston with an effort. 'She was all right when I left her – I swear—'

'Who met you when you got there?' It was Wyatt taking over the questioning again.

'The man who brought the money – he came instead of Reed.'

'Well,' said Wyatt, 'surely you know his name.'

Once again Royston hesitated. He looked round the room as if he was seeking some means of escape. But finally he said quietly: 'Never saw him before, but I think his name is Luigi.'

'H'm, now we're beginning to get somewhere,' nodded Wyatt. 'I don't think you're quite aware of what you've been mixed up with, Royston. It's a much more dangerous game than you imagine. Now, what happened at Shadwell Basin?'

'We got the girl out of the car,' said Royston with some reluctance, 'and there was a launch waiting near Millgate Steps. We put the girl in the boat and Luigi handed over the money.'

'How much?'

Royston paused. 'Two hundred pounds,' he said at last.

'Where did he take the girl?'

'I don't know. I swear I don't know,' said Royston, trying to loosen his collar.

Lathom was on him like a terrier.

'Did you get the impression that he was taking her a long way, or just a short trip?' he persisted.

'I tell you he didn't say anything.'

Lathom stood looking down at him, with his hands on his hips.

'You'd better think hard, Royston. The sooner we find that girl, the better it'll be for you.'

Royston tugged at his collar as if it were choking him.

'I can't say for sure,' he said with an effort. 'I did somehow get the idea they weren't going far. He said something to a man who was steering about a warehouse – I think he said the linseed warehouse … it sounded like that. I swear that's all I can tell you.'

Perivale looked questioningly at Lathom, who had been attached to the river patrol for some years.

'There is an old linseed warehouse about a mile down-river from Millgate Steps,' nodded Lathom. 'It hasn't been used for some time, as far as I know.'

'All right, we'll have to get busy,' decided Perivale. He turned to Royston and said:

'You'd better go back to your band, Royston, and keep your mouth shut. It's lucky for you that you've told us this – it may save that girl's life and yourself from being mixed up in a murder charge. All right, you can go now. We've got your address from the manager and I expect we'll be in touch with you again.'

Royston wiped his forehead once more, muttered something under his breath, then went out. A minute or two later they followed him back into the dance hall, where a riotous samba was in progress. They had to wait until it was finished before they could cross the floor to Sally.

Wyatt told Sally that he was going with Perivale and Lathom to the East End, and did not expect to be back until fairly late.

'That's all right, I'll go back to Janet and the party,' nodded

Sally, looking a trifle anxious. 'Do be careful, Lionel – don't go rushing into things,' she added.

'I'll just limp along behind the others,' said Wyatt with a grin, and he went back to Perivale and Lathom, who had been telephoning the river police.

There was a tang of frost in the air and the moon was lurking behind a bank of clouds as they cast off and made their way downstream. It was chilly on the water, and Wyatt buttoned the collar of his light overcoat closely round his neck.

They did not see much traffic on the river, apart from an occasional tug. Wyatt chatted to the sergeant in charge of the launch, who knew all about the old warehouse, which, he said, had been badly damaged by blast in the air raids.

'I've thought once or twice I saw lights in the little office place at the far end,' he told them, 'but I couldn't be certain. It might have been somebody with a torch inside; on the other hand, it might have been the headlights of a car reflected on the windows. One thing's certain, there's nothing in there worth pinchin', or I might have tipped off the shore men. Anyhow, we'll be seeing for ourselves tonight, maybe.'

They slid past Millgate Steps and reached their objective five minutes later. There was a slight trace of mist curling over the river. The moon was still behind the clouds, so they could only see the dim outlines of a long, narrow structure, when the launch eventually bumped against some wooden steps immediately beneath the warehouse.

Wyatt stood up rather cautiously to get some idea of the lie of the land. The launch's headlight picked up a small rowing boat moored a few yards further on, and he drew Perivale's attention to it at once.

The Assistant Commissioner frowned thoughtfully.

'I think perhaps you'd better stay here with the sergeant, Lathom, just in case somebody tries to make a getaway. Wyatt and I will go and take a quick look round.'

He put one foot on the slimy steps and tested it carefully.

'Don't come up till I'm at the top,' he said to Wyatt, 'just in case they won't stand the weight of both of us.'

He climbed the steps slowly and cautiously, and presently called to Wyatt to follow. They both carried torches, but it was a little lighter now, and they did not use them, to avoid attracting attention. The sergeant had also switched off all the launch's lights and the engine had now stopped its throbbing.

Perivale and Wyatt stood silently on the wooden landing stage for two or three minutes, getting their bearings. They could see that the warehouse was built out over the river, supported by large wooden piles around which the water swished.

'Come on Wyatt – and watch your step!'

They started to walk slowly round the building.

'It looks pretty derelict,' observed Wyatt.

'The perfect hide-out.'

They moved on, picking their way amongst piles of rubbish at the side of the warehouse. Suddenly, they both stopped and listened.

A small object had dropped into the water with a distinct 'plop' a few yards away from them.

'What the devil could that be?' whispered Perivale.

'Sounds like something fallen through the floor of the warehouse ... or maybe one of us kicked a pebble or something.'

'I thought it sounded further underneath ...'

As he spoke, there was another 'plop' which sounded in exactly the same place.

Sir James gripped Wyatt's arm, and they listened tensely. About ten seconds later there was another tiny splash.

They moved in its direction, and the next 'plop' sounded appreciably nearer.

'It might be water rats or something like that,' whispered Perivale, but Wyatt shook his head.

'It wouldn't happen in exactly the same spot,' he murmured.

Wyatt looked round carefully as if he were trying to come to some decision. There were no lights visible within a hundred yards. The dockside appeared to be completely deserted, and the only sounds were the occasional dismal hoot of a ship's siren and the clatter of a train over a bridge nearly a mile away.

When the tiny splash sounded below them yet again, Wyatt seemed to make up his mind. He clenched his fist and hammered the wooden wall of the warehouse.

'Is anyone there?' he called.

There were two tiny 'plops' in quick succession.

'Someone's in there,' said Wyatt at once. 'They're dropping things through the floorboards to attract attention.'

'But surely they could call out,' said Sir James dubiously.

'We'll soon see about that,' replied Wyatt quickly, leading the way along the side of the building until they came to a door. At first it seemed to be locked or bolted, but a little pressure revealed that it was only jammed.

In a few seconds they were inside the building. Sir James laid a restraining hand on Wyatt's arm.

'Take it easy,' he said. 'It might be a trap of some sort.'

They separated from each other until there was about six or seven yards between them. Then each shone his torch alternately for a few moments. The light revealed they were in an enormous shed, which seemed to be practically empty, apart from a few old boxes and a pile of refuse. There were several holes in the roof.

Not far from the door through which they had entered Wyatt spotted a small cabin-like structure which had probably been used as an office in past years, and he directed the beam of his torch upon it at once. They walked round it cautiously, noting that its one small window was heavily boarded up. They returned to the door, and Wyatt called out in a low voice:

'Is anyone there?'

There followed a queer thumping sound which vibrated the floorboards. Without further ado Wyatt turned the knob, but the door was locked. The thumping continued ...

'Put your shoulder to it, Wyatt,' said Sir James. 'Now!'

The door gave at the second attempt, and they burst into the little room. It was practically bare of furniture, except for a cheap table and a broken-back chair. The beam of their torches swung round, until in the far corner they saw a girl, propped against the wall. She was half-lying on the floor, her arms and ankles were bound and she was effectively gagged. Wyatt noted at once that she was wearing an evening gown, which had become very bedraggled. Her hair had tumbled over her forehead, and her make-up had smeared under her eyes.

Near her feet was a small pile of odds and ends, including nuts and bolts and various bits of scrap iron, and she had been pushing these through a fair-sized hole in the floor hoping they would attract attention when they fell into the river below.

Wyatt looked inquiringly at Perivale as they started to untie her and remove the gag.

'It's Marjorie Faber all right,' said Sir James.

The knots were so thoroughly tied that Wyatt had to produce his pocket knife and cut the cords, noticing as he did so that the girl appeared completely dazed.

When they released her, she gave a long-drawn sigh of relief and her head fell forward as she relapsed into semi-consciousness. Sir James produced a small silver brandy flask, and they managed to get her to drink a little, after which she began to show some signs of reviving.

'I – I heard your boat,' she said presently. 'I tried to attract your attention, though I thought it might be – it might be *them* again.'

'It's all right,' said Wyatt reassuringly. 'Just take it easy and don't try to talk.' She drank a little more brandy, and after a while they lifted her to her feet, but they had to support her all the way out of the warehouse. The strain on her nerves had been a heavy one, and she was sobbing half-hysterically as they moved slowly towards the launch.

The cool night air seemed to revive her a little, and after they had walked up and down several times along the front of the warehouse, she began to show some signs of recovering. But it was not going to be easy getting her down the slippery wooden steps and into the launch, and Wyatt began to wonder if it would not be advisable to try and get a taxi. However, as Lathom, who had joined them, pointed out, this would be none too easy at that late hour.

Lathom was very anxious to question the girl, but Wyatt restrained him, pointing out that she might still be under the influence of the drug, and would not be able to recollect details effectively.

Eventually they half-carried her down the steps. The sergeant had produced a padded seat cushion and she sat on this in the well of the launch, looking around her very uncertainly.

'You can turn the light on, Sergeant,' said Lathom, but Wyatt called out:

'Wait a moment! There's something coming this way ...'

They all listened intently, and the distant throb of a motor-boat engine grew gradually louder.

'It wouldn't be the river patrol, would it, Sergeant?' asked Wyatt. The sergeant shook his head.

'He isn't showing a light. Somebody up to no good, if you ask me.'

Whoever it was, the boat was obviously heading in their direction, and Lathom ordered the sergeant to swing round his powerful lamp in line with the oncoming vessel.

When the motor-boat was about fifty yards away, the engine cut out and they could hear the swish of the water around its bows. But the inspector did not order the light to be switched on, for he had an idea that in another two minutes the newcomer would be too close to them to make a getaway when suddenly dazzled by its full glare.

Then without warning a dim figure rose to a kneeling position in the motor-boat and called out:

'Hello! Are you there!'

'Great Scott!' breathed Perivale. 'It's Linder!'

'There seems to be no mistake about that,' nodded Wyatt.

The man in the boat repeated his cry, and at a signal from Perivale the sergeant switched on the lamp.

'Yes, it is Linder!' exclaimed Lathom, who had been rather doubtful before.

The man in the boat suddenly disappeared and there came a sharp crack of a revolver. Almost immediately there was a splintering of glass and the launch's lamp went out.

The sergeant cursed and began to connect up his emergency lamp. It was a little difficult to see what was happening after the powerful light had been extinguished, and it was not until they heard a splash that Wyatt realized that Linder had dived into the water.

Perivale and Wyatt tried to trace his course, but apart from an occasional splash, as he swam with a powerful stroke, they could not be certain. A minute later, the emergency lamp was on, and its beam swept the sullen waters. But there was no trace of Hugo Linder.

'He could have been under the warehouse by this time,' grunted Lathom.

'On the other hand, he might be well downstream,' said Wyatt.

'We could put out a call to H Division,' suggested the sergeant.

'Yes, that would be best,' decided the Chief. 'No point in hanging around here, and Miss Faber should be taken home as soon as possible. Put out the radio call, Sergeant.'

'I'm afraid Linder has got away with it this time,' said Lathom, taking over the lamp himself and swivelling the beam over the river.

'We'll just hang on till the sergeant gets through,' decided Perivale, 'then we'll get back to Westminster as quickly as possible.'

The sergeant busied himself with the small portable transmitter, and meanwhile Lathom continued to rake the waters with the beam from the baby searchlight.

'What do you make of this Linder business, Wyatt?' he said presently. 'Do you think his turning up tonight proves that he's "Mr Rossiter"?'

'Of course he isn't "Rossiter",' interposed Perivale in an irritable tone. 'We know from what Royston said that Luigi must be "Mr Rossiter". It's just a question of getting sufficient evidence to convict him. Don't you agree, Wyatt?'

But Wyatt refused to be drawn.

'I don't think Sally would agree with you, Sir James,' he replied with a faint smile. 'She suspects Mr Knight and nothing will shake her.'

'Good lord!' ejaculated Perivale. 'What on earth's given her the idea that nincompoop could possibly be a master criminal?'

'It's the ladies' prerogative – feminine intuition!'

'I'm afraid we'll need something a bit more concrete than that,' grunted Perivale, straining his eyes to follow the beam of light. 'Dash it all, why Knight was very nearly murdered himself ...'

He realized that no one was listening. Wyatt and Lathom were staring at a dark object floating on the surface which the beam had just picked up.

'It's a body – a man's body!' snapped Lathom. 'It's floating towards us.'

He grabbed the boathook that lay along the port side of the launch.

Wyatt looked across at Marjorie Faber rather anxiously, but she appeared to be quite oblivious to what was going on.

A few minutes later, Lathom had pulled the body towards them and the sergeant, having completed his radio message, stood by to give him a hand.

The man's face was turned from them and the light was none too certain, so that it was not until the body was right alongside that Lathom exclaimed in surprise:

'Good lord! It isn't Linder after all!'

'No,' said Wyatt quietly. It was the body of Charles Luigi.

* * *

Wyatt had spent an hour in his study after breakfast, writing letters and jotting down some notes in a book which he kept locked in a drawer of the writing-desk. He had been very silent over breakfast, and Sally's efforts at conversation had obviously not been welcome.

Sally made no further attempt to start a conversation, and when her husband disappeared into the lounge, she picked up the morning papers with a little sigh of relief and began to read an account of the recovery of Marjorie Faber and the death of Charles Luigi.

At eleven o'clock she went into the kitchen and made some coffee.

Wyatt was obviously in a more pleasant mood, and seemed to welcome the intrusion, or at least the refreshment. As she poured the coffee, she said:

'That wasn't a very good picture of Mr Linder in the paper, was it, Lionel?'

'Maybe he's one of those peculiar people who never photograph very well,' Wyatt replied. Sally passed his coffee, noticed his change of mood, then said with a little hesitation:

'Darling, you didn't really mind my going to the Palais last night?'

Her anxious expression was so comic that he burst out laughing.

'Why, I'd quite forgotten all about it,' he admitted. 'Did you get back at a respectable hour, or are we going to have the neighbours talking?'

'We were back ages before you.'

She sat on the corner of his desk and sipped her coffee.

'Lionel, do you think the police will find Linder?' she asked.

'If he's alive.'

'The paper says that there was an announcement made on the radio.'

'I'm not surprised.'

'Have you any idea what made him turn up at that awful warehouse?' asked Sally.

'Quite obviously he had an appointment.'

'With "Mr Rossiter"?'

He shrugged.

'Lathom seems to think that Linder is "Mr Rossiter",' he told her.

'That's ridiculous!' she scoffed.

Wyatt smiled.

'You're still backing Maurice Knight. I told Sir James about it ... I'm afraid he came down rather heavily.'

'Did he?' said Sally indifferently. 'I don't want to argue ... I tell you I just *know*!'

'All right, darling,' said Wyatt equably, lighting a cigarette and picking up *The Times*.

Sally fidgeted uncomfortably, rearranging the flowers in a vase and replacing a couple of books on the shelves. At last she was unable to contain herself any longer.

'Lionel, how exactly was Luigi murdered?'

Wyatt looked up from his paper.

'He was strangled,' he replied casually.

'Had he been in the water very long?'

'About an hour, the doctor seemed to think.'

Sally went on tidying the room.

'What did Sir James make of it all?' she asked.

'I'm afraid it shook him rather badly. After what Royston told us, he seemed pretty convinced that Luigi was "Mr Rossiter", and that it was simply a question of collecting sufficient evidence. In fact, he seemed to regard the case as practically settled.'

Sally gathered up a small pile of periodicals and neatly stacked them on a corner of the settee, moving over to a side table near the door.

'Darling, you haven't opened your letters,' she said presently, when she noticed them lying under a paper-weight. 'Fred has sent on quite a pile of them from the farm.'

'Good lord! I quite forgot ...' he murmured. 'I've had so many things on my mind this morning ...'

'There's a registered letter, too,' she pointed out, handing him a neat little envelope which appeared to contain a small solid object. He slit open the packet with his paper-cutter and extracted a neat little penknife, with an imitation mother-of-pearl handle. Around it was wrapped a sheet of thick parchment notepaper, which Wyatt unfolded. On it was written:

'DEAR MR WYATT,

I tried to get you at your flat last night, but unfortunately there was no reply. I am sending you this penknife because I think it will be much safer in your hands than mine. I am convinced that it is a valuable clue to the identity of "Mr Rossiter". I will explain exactly what I mean when I see you.

Sincerely,

MAURICE KNIGHT.'

Wyatt passed over the note.

'From your Number One Suspect,' he smiled. 'How does that fit in with your intuition?'

Sally frowned thoughtfully, opening each of the two small blades and closing them. It seemed to be a very ordinary sort of penknife, costing a few shillings at any hardware store.

Then a thought struck her.

'It couldn't be anything to do with fingerprints, could it?'

'I'm afraid it's a bit late in the day to think of that,' he grinned.

'But it can't possibly—'

She was interrupted by the telephone ringing outside; she ran to answer it. Presently, Sally put her head round the door.

'It's Maurice Knight,' she announced.

Wyatt picked up the receiver of his extension and heard the anxious voice of his caller.

'Did you get the penknife all right?'

'I've just this minute opened your letter. It's quite safe. Sorry we were out last night. Now, what's all this about the knife being valuable evidence? Where did you get it?'

There was a slight pause, then Knight said very deliberately:

'I got it from "Mr Rossiter".'

'Then you've actually met him?'

'The swine tried to murder me again last night! It was horrible!'

Wyatt whistled softly.

'How did it happen?'

'I went out about half-past five to post a letter, and when I got back he was waiting for me on the landing outside my flat. Luckily, there's a light there and I spotted his shadow as I came up the stairs. So I hesitated a fraction of a second before I turned the corner at the top of the stairs. Then I felt his hands on my neck.'

'But surely you saw his face,' said Wyatt.

'No, he forced my head right back, and it's only a dim

210

light on the landing. I fought like the devil. I tried to call for help, but he choked every sound out of me. It was terrible! Then, just as everything was going black, he must have heard someone down below, and he was off like a flash. I felt too upset to try to follow him immediately; in fact I stood there, clutching the banisters, trying to get my breath back. But, as he rushed round the bend of the landing below, I thought I heard something fall from his pocket, and afterwards I went down and found the knife lying there.'

'You're quite sure that this person who attacked you was a man?'

'No doubt about that. I'm sorry I can't tell you anything else ... it all happened so suddenly; I was completely taken by surprise ...'

'I quite understand,' said Wyatt sympathetically. 'Well, I'll pass the knife on to the Yard and get their expert on it. Of course, it's a very common type of penknife, but you never know ...'

'Thanks, Wyatt ... I have a feeling that it might lead to something. I hope it does, because I can't stand much more of this – this nerve-racking business.'

'Don't worry,' said Wyatt. 'We're beginning to get results now.'

'So I see from the morning papers. Well, it can't be too soon for my liking. Goodbye.'

As he replaced the receiver, Wyatt realized that Sally had left the room. She came in a moment later.

'I was listening on the other phone,' she informed him shamelessly.

Wyatt picked up the penknife by its edges and dropped it back into the envelope.

'That conversation must have made you change your mind.'

'Not at all,' she persisted defiantly. 'I still think Maurice Knight is the man you're after.'

She was about to enlarge on this, but the front-door bell rang.

'My turn,' said Wyatt, and went to answer it. In the hallway stood Doctor Fraser and Hugo Linder.

'Well, well, this is quite a morning,' said Wyatt, rubbing his hands. 'Come inside.'

He led them into the lounge, where Sally's eyes widened when she saw who the visitors were.

Wyatt was a little surprised to see that Linder showed no outward signs of the previous evening's adventure. It was Doctor Fraser who looked pale and a trifle haggard.

Almost at once she began to apologize for troubling Wyatt, taking the blame on herself.

'It was my idea entirely,' she said. 'I read all the papers this morning, and heard the report on the wireless, and I insisted that Hugo owes you some explanation. So do I, if it comes to that.'

Linder interposed somewhat hastily:

'Gail, please! I won't have you dragged into this ...'

The doctor waved him aside.

'Darling, please don't interrupt,' she begged in a distressed voice. 'I've got to tell the truth now, and it isn't going to be easy.'

He looked at her anxiously for a few moments, then said quietly: 'Very well, Gail.' He went and stood over by the window, with his hands in his trouser pockets. Doctor Fraser turned to Wyatt once more.

'Hugo went to that warehouse last night because I had a telephone call soon after ten-thirty ...'

Wyatt held up his hand and said:

'Before you tell us your story, Doctor, there's just one question I'd like to ask Mr Linder.'

Linder came over from the window.

'What is it?' he asked curiously.

Wyatt took up the registered packet from his desk and emptied the penknife into the palm of his left hand, which he thrust under Linder's eyes.

'Have you seen this before?' he asked quietly.

'But of course,' said Linder in astonishment, 'it's mine!'

'You lost it?' queried Wyatt.

'Well, not exactly. As a matter of fact, I lent it to someone quite a while back, and he rather conveniently forgot to return it.'

'Whom did you lend it to, Hugo?' asked the doctor curiously.

'I think I can answer that now,' said Wyatt, watching both of them closely. 'Correct me if I'm mistaken, Mr Linder, but I have an idea you lent it to Bill Tyson, the fisherman. Am I right?'

Hugo Linder slowly nodded.

CHAPTER XII

Presenting: 'Mr Rossiter'

Wyatt slid the penknife back into the packet.

'How did you know it was Tyson?' asked Linder at last.

'We can come to that presently. What I'm anxious to hear now is Doctor Fraser's side of the story. Try that other chair, Doctor; you'll find you can relax in it. And let me give you a cigarette.'

A few seconds later, Doctor Fraser began her story in a low, earnest tone.

'Hugo went to that warehouse because I got a telephone call at half-past ten from "Mr Rossiter". He told me that he wanted me to go to a deserted warehouse not far from Millgate Steps. He said that if I went there at the time he stipulated he would hand over certain highly confidential letters of mine.'

'You mean letters that you had written?' queried Sally.

'Mrs Wyatt, if only you knew what I've been through trying to get those letters back,' said Doctor Fraser in an anguished tone. 'I've been through absolute hell – I've cursed myself a thousand times for writing them.'

'Before you go any further,' interrupted Wyatt, 'I hope you realize the significance of what you have just told us.'

She nodded.

'You mean that I've admitted that I know the identity of "Mr Rossiter"?'

'Do you?'

'Yes,' she replied bitterly. 'I've known it right from the beginning. You see, it was like this, Mr Wyatt. Several years ago, I was involved in a most unfortunate scandal. It was a euthanasia case, and I won't go into details, except to tell you that if certain aspects were made public I should be ruined. That was when I wrote the letters, which would have incriminated several well-known people and caused a first-class scandal in the profession. I was only going to use them as a last desperate resource if I had to defend myself against certain charges; they were addressed to my solicitors, setting out all the details of the case. It was one of those cases that were hushed up and never came into court, but there was a chance for quite a long time that it might. So I kept the letters locked in a drawer of my desk. One day, that lock was forced and the letters stolen.'

She fingered the clasp of her handbag.

'About a week later,' she went on, 'a certain gentleman telephoned me and read out the first paragraph of two of the letters over the phone. That was when it started ...'

'You mean "Mr Rossiter" began to blackmail you?' said Sally.

'It was a form of blackmail ... but he never wanted money. That was the cunning part of the whole business. You see, "Mr Rossiter" had made up his mind that a qualified doctor could be of far more use to him – shall I say professionally? – than financially. He knew only too well that as long as he had those letters, his word was law as far as I was concerned. At first I couldn't quite see what he was getting at. He asked me to do the most extraordinary things. One morning he rang up and ordered me to make out two prescriptions – one for a girl named Barbara Willis and another for Mildred Gillow. At that time I'd never seen or heard of either of them. Then, a little while later, I had a telephone call from a girl who called herself Barbara Willis.'

She inhaled deeply and slowly expelled a stream of smoke.

'Why, of course!' exclaimed Sally. 'You mean that "Mr Rossiter" was out to make Scotland Yard believe that Doctor Fraser and "Mr Rossiter" were the same person.'

'That's about it, Mrs Wyatt. I was the one who was going to take the rap.'

'Then "Mr Rossiter" planted those prescriptions on the two girls?' queried Wyatt. The doctor shook her head.

'Not exactly "planted" them, Mr Wyatt. He simply handed them over. He was on friendly terms with both of them.'

'In that case, what was the point in making those two other girls impersonate Barbara Willis and Mildred Gillow, as you told us up at Shorecombe?'

'Don't you see, Mr Wyatt? That's the fiendishly clever part of the whole plan! When the police came to me to trace those prescriptions, I should have to admit that I had been in contact with *a* Barbara Willis and a Mildred Gillow. My receptionist could testify to that effect.'

'But they were impostors!' interposed Linder. 'And you can just imagine the police believing that story, Mr Wyatt; especially when they knew the doctor had supplied the real Barbara Willis and Mildred Gillow with prescriptions. If she had told them the truth, it would have made them more suspicious of her than ever.'

'I think we went into that at the time,' nodded Wyatt. 'Go on with your story, Doctor.'

'I just didn't know what to do,' she confessed. 'Then, one day, "Mr Rossiter" sent a girl to see me who called herself Lauren Beaumont. I felt instinctively that she wasn't the real girl, and that he was playing precisely the same game again. I became very frightened, and in the end I decided to tell Hugo everything. He had always been a great friend of mine, and I knew he could be trusted.'

'And I advised her to get in touch with you, Mr Wyatt,' said Linder. 'I knew that if her supposition was right about Lauren Beaumont, and that the girl who visited her was an impostor, then she might be able to forestall "Mr Rossiter's" next move by telling you her story. I wanted her to tell you about the stolen letters as well, but she held back.'

'Pity,' said Wyatt. 'That meant that "Mr Rossiter" still had an ace up his sleeve. Anyhow, what about last night?'

Doctor Fraser resumed her story.

'I thought "Mr Rossiter" sounded rather overwrought when he spoke to me on the telephone and said that he would hand over my letters if I would go to the warehouse near Millgate Steps. Hugo was with me when the call came through, and he was very emphatic that the message was a trap. He persuaded me to ignore it.'

'Yet you went there yourself, Linder?'

'Yes,' said Linder, with great deliberation. 'I went there myself. I had made up my mind that this persecution had got to stop, no matter what happened. It has reduced Gail to a nervous wreck, and I couldn't bear to see her tortured like that. How would you like to see Mrs Wyatt in a similar position?'

'There's something in that,'conceded Wyatt, 'but there are one or two other things that need explaining. For instance, there was the Château Number Eight.'

'Oh, yes, the perfume,' nodded Linder. 'That was another of "Mr Rossiter's" little tricks to throw suspicion on Gail. He tried to get her down there by a ruse – the telephone call purporting to come from Professor Reed. The perfume was intended as one of the finishing touches.'

Doctor Fraser nodded eagerly.

'That's right, Mr Wyatt. And then again there was that afternoon when Lauren Beaumont returned. You know how we were both tricked into going to the Royal Astoria. If someone had followed the girl back to the hotel, the first person he would have seen there would have been me. It's not a very pleasant thought.'

'I sympathize with you there, Doctor,' said Wyatt evenly. 'But there is one major question you've left unanswered.'

'What's that?'

'Simply – who is "Mr Rossiter"?'

Doctor Fraser looked nervously at her companion, who shook his head.

'I'm afraid we can't answer that, Mr Wyatt,' he said definitely. 'You see, as far as we know, he still has those letters, and if we give away his identity, then the letters will be made public. You do appreciate that, don't you?'

Wyatt hesitated.

'Don't you believe us, Mr Wyatt?' demanded the doctor anxiously.

'I shall have to think it over,' said Wyatt quietly.

'But it's true – every word of it!' insisted Linder in considerable agitation. 'Whether you believe it or not, I tell you it's the absolute truth.'

Wyatt picked up his paper-cutter and traced a design on his blotting pad.

'Well, if it isn't the truth, Mr Linder,' he replied in a thoughtful tone, 'then there is only one other explanation of everything you've told us.'

'What do you mean, Mr Wyatt?' asked the doctor suspiciously.

'I mean that, in that case, you're both lying, and "Mr Rossiter" is not one person, but two – Doctor Fraser and Mr Hugo Linder.'

It was Inspector Lathom's afternoon off. He had worked right through the previous weekend on the Rossiter affair, and as he had been sleeping none too well of late he felt he deserved a few hours relaxation after the hectic events of the night at Millgate Steps. Maybe he wouldn't be able to sleep, but at least he could lie on the bed and read *Wisden*. For Inspector Lathom was a keen devotee of the art of the willow.

Lathom kept his passion for cricket to himself like some secret vice, and many of his colleagues would have been surprised to learn that when he sometimes snatched a few hours off on a summer's afternoon he spent them at Lord's or the Oval. And he whiled away many an hour on winter evenings slowly and methodically ploughing his way through *Wisden* or old copies of *The Cricketer*. He could tell you Denis Compton's batting average for the last Tests against Australia or Laker's bowling average in the West Indies without hardly stopping to think. This strange predilection was even more unaccountable because Lathom had never played cricket himself since the days when he wielded a home-made bat in an alley in Camberwell, with an ever-present dread of being chased off by the police. But there was something about those white figures on the greensward that entranced the matter-of-fact inspector as surely as the silver screen fascinates the movie-fan.

He had been reading for the tenth time Alec Bedser's bowling analysis in a certain match against Sussex – 20 overs, 9 maidens, 48 runs, 7 wickets ... it had been a satisfying sort of rhythm ... he could see the stalwart figure taking long strides up to the wicket, that final little leap before the ball was released, the smooth follow-through ... he might almost be at the Oval on a drowsy summer afternoon, with the heat hanging in shimmering waves around the gasometer ... He began drawing a lazy analogy between cricket and crime ... some matches were quite straightforward affairs, like an open and shut case ... others were tricky ... you never knew which way they were going to turn, like this Rossiter job.

His reflections were suddenly cut short by the shrill ringing of the telephone. Lathom sighed, rose with some effort and went to answer it.

'Oh, it's you, Wyatt,' he said in a voice that betrayed no pleasure.

'Sorry to disturb you on your afternoon off, Inspector,' Wyatt sounded like a Public Relations Officer dealing with a particularly awkward customer.

'Was it anything urgent?' demanded Lathom, blinking the sleep out of his eyes.

'Well, yes, it is in a way ...'

'Something happened in the "Rossiter" affair?'

'Yes, again in a way. As a matter of fact, Inspector, I want to invite you to a party.'

'Did you say a party?' queried Lathom testily.

'Not the usual sort of party,' Wyatt hastily assured him. 'I'm expecting a very distinguished guest, as a matter of fact.'

'Now, look here, Wyatt, I spent most of the war guarding VIPs. They don't cut much ice with me!'

'Perhaps I should have described him as "notorious", rather than "distinguished".'

'That's worse!' sniffed the inspector. 'Nothing more overrated than notoriety.' He stifled a yawn and wished Wyatt would ring off, so that he could resume his reading.

Then, quite suddenly, he blinked.

'What was that you said?' he asked in an astonished voice.

'I said I rather thought you would be interested to meet "Mr Rossiter".'

'Are you joking?'

'Certainly not. You come to the party – tomorrow night at eight o'clock at the Madrid, and you'll meet the gentleman in person.'

'But – but – how do you know he'll be there?' stammered Lathom.

'Because I shall invite him,' replied Wyatt smoothly. 'Don't forget, Inspector ... Room 34, Madrid Club, eight o'clock sharp.'

Wyatt rang off. Lathom eyed the receiver a trifle dubiously, as if he doubted whether he had been hearing correctly, then replaced it.

Wyatt experienced some little difficulty in persuading Perivale to withhold his warrant for the arrest of Linder, and it was only by giving his definite promise that 'Mr Rossiter' would be unmasked at the Madrid the following evening that Wyatt finally succeeded, for Sir James was still being subjected to a certain amount of discreet pressure from the Home Office.

While he was at the Yard Wyatt asked for a photo of Luigi, but there was apparently none in the records.

'I'd like Royston to make quite certain that it was Luigi who was concerned in the abduction of Marjorie Faber,' he said.

'Yes, it would be advisable to check on that,' agreed Perivale. 'The poor girl was in no condition to recognize anybody by the time Luigi took over.'

'How is she, by the way?'

'Her father telephoned this morning to say she's still a bit shaky – it's chiefly shock, of course. Anyhow, he's very thankful to have her back.'

'Well, what are we going to do about Royston?'

'He'll have to be arrested, of course – on a charge of being a party to the abduction. However, as he gave us a certain amount of evidence, I can probably get him let off fairly lightly,' said Perivale. 'The problem is whether to arrest him while "Mr Rossiter" is still at large. He might try to contact Royston, and that would give us a pretty good line.'

Wyatt paced thoughtfully across the room and stood looking out of the window at the traffic along the Embankment.

'I'll get a picture of Luigi from the Madrid,' he decided at last, 'and go round to Royston's flat and have a talk to him. Is that all right with you?'

Perivale nodded.

'D'you want anyone with you?'

Wyatt shook his head.

'No, I'd sooner talk to him alone. I'll go along to the Madrid and get that picture now.'

He strolled over to the door.

'And don't forget our little party there tonight,' he added.

Perivale nodded rather glumly.

'I must say you choose some peculiar times to throw parties, Wyatt.'

'I don't see why not,' smiled Wyatt. 'Publishers throw parties to launch a new book; film producers uncork the champagne when they show a new picture. Why shouldn't I introduce "Mr Rossiter" in a nice, friendly atmosphere?'

'Have it your own way,' grunted Perivale. 'If I really thought you were going to introduce us to him, I'd attend fifty parties.'

'See you later,' smiled Wyatt, picking up his stick, and closing the door after him.

He was able to get a picture of Luigi without much difficulty, and, armed with this, he made his way to the flat in Long Acre which was the address given him by the manager of the Palais. It was turned midday, but Royston opened the door to him still wearing a dressing-gown over his pyjamas.

'Oh, it's you,' he said in a surly tone. 'What is it this time?'

'May I come in?'

Royston hesitated a moment and looked round uneasily.

'All right,' he said at last, leading the way into a large, untidy room.

'Sorry if I broke into your first sleep,' said Wyatt pleasantly. Royston glared at him.

'I didn't get to bed till four. I reckon I got a right to sleep sometime,' he snapped. 'What was it you wanted?'

Wyatt produced the photograph.

'Was this the man who took over from you in that case we were discussing?' he asked.

Royston studied the picture.

'It's like him,' he said at last. 'Of course, it was dark at the time, and I didn't get a good look at him close to.'

Wyatt nodded and replaced the photo in its envelope.

'I don't think it will be necessary for you to identify him at the mortuary,' he said.

'You mean he's dead?'

223

'Don't you read the papers?'

'I don't get time for that stuff,' said Royston impatiently. 'Are you trying to tell me that this man Luigi was "Mr Rossiter"?'

'I'm not telling you anything of the sort. That's one reason I came here – to warn you to watch your step, Royston.'

'What d'you mean?'

'Well, if "Mr Rossiter" happened to hear that you'd given information to the police, there might be a little unpleasantness.'

Royston shifted uncomfortably from one foot to the other.

'I don't know anything about this "Mr Rossiter",' he said at last. 'I always thought it was Luigi.'

'So did several other people. Luigi just happened to be one of his agents. But you may depend upon his being well informed about the Marjorie Faber affair.'

'Who is this guy, anyway?'

'It wouldn't help very much if I told you. For one thing, you probably don't know him, and for another he might use one of his lackeys to make things uncomfortable for you. He's got a hold on quite a number of people, and he doesn't scruple to use it, so I'm giving you fair warning. If anything looks at all suspicious to you, don't hesitate to telephone the Yard at once.'

Royston laughed harshly.

'Me phone the Yard! That's a good one! Don't you worry, mister, I can take care of myself.'

'That savours of "famous last words",' said Wyatt, as he stubbed out his cigarette. He was standing by the half-open door when a door across the hall snapped open and a sulky voice called out: 'Georgie! How much longer are you ...' The voice trailed away and the door slammed.

Wyatt looked at Royston and shrugged.

He had had plenty of time to recognize the sullen profile and tousled blonde hair of Lauren Beaumont.

The private rooms at the Madrid Club were one of its main attractions. They were tastefully furnished, and each had a small replica of the cocktail bar downstairs in a corner near the door, so that guests could be given drinks as soon as they entered. There were half a dozen very comfortable chairs and two spacious settees. A large electric fire glowed pleasantly in the centre of one wall.

Perivale and Lathom arrived at five minutes to eight, to find Wyatt and Sally busily preparing cocktails and setting out various bottles and glasses on the bar. Lathom looked vaguely uncomfortable, as if he resented being invited to a party, and begrudged the valuable time ... he might have spent at home sitting in front of a large fire buried in *Wisden*. However, he accepted a tankard of beer and wandered off to a chair while Sir James leaned against the bar and chatted with Wyatt and Sally as he sipped a double whisky.

Maurice Knight was the next arrival. He wore evening dress, and informed them that he was going on to a European film première at a cinema in the Haymarket. Sally watched him shrewdly as he sipped a cocktail. She could easily imagine him pictured in the glossy weeklies as a typical man-about-town.

By way of contrast, when he arrived with Doctor Fraser, Hugo Linder looked a trifle pale and ill at ease. It was noticeable that he avoided Perivale and Lathom and he and his fiancée took their glasses into a corner remote from the rest of the guests.

Sir Donald Angus was obviously in a bad temper. He was still wearing his overcoat, and refused to take it off, saying he did not propose to stay long. He seemed quite determined to be unpleasant, and began by refusing a drink. He looked round the assembled guests and grunted: 'Didn't expect to find you here, Inspector.'

However, Lathom could be equally churlish if provoked.

'If it comes to that, I didn't expect to see you either, Sir Donald.'

Wyatt interposed by introducing Sir Donald to Maurice Knight. Angus acknowledged this with a curt nod, then turned to Wyatt.

'Now, Mr Wyatt, perhaps you'll tell us what all this is in aid of. You've practically got me here under duress, and I dare say the same applies to one or two of the others. What's it all about; that's what I want to know?'

Sally looked across at him and smiled.

'It's quite simple, Sir Donald,' she said. 'My husband has had the bright idea of collecting together all the suspects in the "Rossiter" affair under one roof. Have you any objection? We thought that as you had been so closely connected with the affair you would take a lively interest in its conclusion.'

'This is interesting,' said Knight quietly. 'Might I have another cocktail, Mrs Wyatt?'

Sally poured the drink and handed it to him.

'As my wife has so loyally inferred,' went on Wyatt, 'I hope very shortly to have the pleasure of introducing you to "Mr Rossiter".'

There was a murmur of surprise as he made this announcement; the guests looked at each other questioningly.

'Are you serious, Wyatt?' said Knight at last.

'Do you mean to tell me that you're seriously suggesting that "Mr Rossiter" is here in this room?' stammered Angus.

226

'That's what Mr Wyatt said, Sir Donald,' put in Lathom sardonically.

Knight selected a cigarette from a box on a side table.

'You'll forgive my saying so, Wyatt, but don't you think you owe us some explanation?'

'Of course I owe you an explanation,' agreed Wyatt, who had now taken the centre of the floor. 'I want you all to listen carefully, even though you're not concerned with every aspect of the case. Are you sure you won't have a drink, Sir Donald?'

'Aye, maybe I will change my mind after all – make it a Scotch if ye don't mind.'

'That's fine. Well now, yesterday morning Mr Linder and Doctor Fraser called on me to tell me exactly how they became involved in the Rossiter affair. In the course of his story, Mr Linder omitted one rather important fact.'

'What was that?' demanded Linder, half-rising from his chair.

'You forgot to tell me why you went up to Shorecombe, Mr Linder, and why you made a particular point of getting on friendly terms with Bill Tyson, the fisherman.'

'I can explain every—' Linder was beginning, but Wyatt waved him aside.

'I want to leave that for the time being and talk about Luigi. When "Mr Rossiter" began his activities, his line of business was not abduction, but simply blackmail. Now, so far as blackmail was concerned, Luigi was in rather a unique position. The sort of people who frequent the Madrid are not exactly the souls of discretion, and Luigi had plenty of opportunities for securing information. After a little time, however "Mr Rossiter" became ambitious; he decided to relegate the blackmailing business to the background and concentrate on abduction. Which brings us to Coral Salter, a dance hostess who had no scruples when it came to blackmailing her clients, but she drew the line quite emphatically at the prospect of being mixed up with abduction.'

'H'm, that's fairly obvious,' grunted Perivale. 'She must have decided to double-cross "Rossiter", so she was murdered.'

'And taken to my flat,' put in Linder. 'It must have been part of a plot to throw suspicion on me.'

'But, look here, Wyatt,' interposed Angus. 'Are you trying to tell us that Luigi was "Mr Rossiter"?'

'No, of course not. He was his right-hand man. When "Rossiter" switched over to the abduction racket, Luigi realized he was turning over big money, so he tried to double-cross "Rossiter". And "Mr Rossiter" retaliated by throwing suspicion for at least one murder on to Luigi. It all helped to confuse the issue and distract suspicion from himself. "Mr Rossiter" had a knack of designing his murders quite neatly.'

'That was why he did the same with me then?' queried Doctor Fraser.

'You're making out this "Mr Rossiter" to be a pretty shrewd bird,' commented Knight. 'Are you trying to tell us that he was throwing suspicion on to three people simultaneously?'

'That's what I'm telling you, Mr Knight,' replied Wyatt steadily. He turned to Sir Donald Angus.

'Sir Donald, would you care to tell us why you went to the Palais at Rammerford the other evening?'

Angus scowled.

'I don't see that it's any of your business,' he replied uneasily. 'It has nothing to do with this case.'

'I wouldn't be too sure about that. If you don't want any

more unpleasant publicity, Sir Donald, I think you'd better tell us,' said Perivale in a tone that was mildly threatening.

Angus set down his glass.

'Very well, then, if you must know. I went because Lauren Beaumont had started blackmailing me. She'd been there the night before and told the whole story to that little swine of a band-boy, and he put her up to it. I had to go down there to hand over the money – it was in my coat pocket when you saw me, Wyatt.'

'All right, Sir Donald,' nodded Perivale. 'I'll be pulling in Royston on the abduction charge tomorrow, so that'll square your account I dare say ... unless you'd like to make a charge yourself?'

'No, no, I've had enough publicity of that sort to last me the rest of my life,' growled Angus. 'I wish I'd never set eyes on that girl.'

'I don't suppose you'll see her again, Sir Donald,' smiled Wyatt. 'She's gone back to Royston.'

'Let's get back to the "Rossiter" case,' interrupted Lathom impatiently. 'You were going to tell us why Linder went up to Shorecombe.'

'He went for two reasons. First, because he suspected that "Mr Rossiter" had taken Barbara Willis there, and second to make certain inquiries concerning "Mr Rossiter" himself.'

'Why at Shorecombe?' queried Lathom doubtfully.

'Because,' said Wyatt deliberately, '"Mr Rossiter" happens to have been born there.'

This caused a minor sensation. Wyatt allowed it to subside, and finished his drink.

'You seem very certain of that, Wyatt,' said Knight.

'I don't see why you should be so surprised,' replied Wyatt.

'After all, you interviewed his father – the old fisherman named Bill Tyson!'

There was a moment's silence. Then Lathom said in a tense voice:

'I don't believe it!'

Linder leapt to his feet and glared at the inspector.

'He's right, you fool!' he declared emphatically. 'You ought to have guessed it the day Tyson committed suicide.'

He subsided into his chair again, and they waited for Wyatt to continue.

'Doctor Fraser was being blackmailed by "Mr Rossiter",' he went on evenly. 'Hugo Linder knew this, and he went to Shorecombe to try to persuade Tyson to influence "Rossiter" to return certain letters to the doctor. Tyson knew, of course, that his son was a waster, but he never in his wildest dreams suspected that he was the notorious "Mr Rossiter". When Tyson and Linder found the body of Barbara Willis, there was a note on it which said: "With the compliments of Mr Rossiter".

'Tyson took that note and confronted his son with it. From that moment, he knew that Linder had told the truth. The old man was almost out of his mind with anxiety and shame. I dare say he studied that note a thousand times. He'd been looking at it again that morning when we found him ...'

'It's an interesting theory, Wyatt,' said Lathom with the merest trace of sarcasm.

'It's more than a theory!' retorted Wyatt. 'Don't you remember what happened the night Sally and I tried to interview Tyson? We were quite deliberately forced off the road.'

'That's right!' put in Knight eagerly. '"Mr Rossiter" was determined to prevent you from seeing Tyson – just as he tried to stop me.'

'Did he really try to stop you, Mr Knight?' asked Wyatt quietly.

'What do you mean?' said Knight, looking genuinely bewildered. 'I told you I traced the car number to Luigi and—'

'Yes, it was a very neat little story,' agreed Wyatt. 'It fitted in quite nicely with several of your plans I should imagine. You came to see Mrs Wyatt and myself the morning after the accident to discover if you'd been recognized the night before. Also, to tell us the story about the number plate and throw suspicion on Luigi, and finally to cover up any damage which might have been done to your car when you deliberately forced us over the bridge.'

'Are you suggesting that Knight is "Mr Rossiter"?' asked Lathom in some surprise.

'Or that "Mr Rossiter" is Maurice Knight. Put it which way you like,' replied Wyatt, never taking his eyes off Knight.

'I knew it!' said Sally almost to herself.

Knight leaned back in his chair and laughed.

'You're letting your imagination run away with you, and ignoring the facts, Wyatt,' he said. 'May I remind you that "Mr Rossiter" has tried to murder me several times?'

'On every occasion, Knight, there were never any witnesses to the attempt. We've only your word for it that any such attempt took place.'

'Then what about the time when you were in my car, and there was a bomb thrown from that van?'

'If we'd seen the man inside,' replied Wyatt confidently. 'I think we should have recognized Charles Luigi, who had been released on bail an hour earlier, and was intent only on wiping out old scores. He'd realized that you were the cause of his being arrested.'

'And I suppose it was Luigi who tried to kill me the night before last?' queried Knight sarcastically. 'Two hours after you'd picked him out of the river.'

'No one tried to murder you the night before last,' said Wyatt calmly. 'Royston tipped you off that we were going to that warehouse, and you tried to get Doctor Fraser down there. But that little plan didn't quite work out, and instead we had the pleasure of meeting Mr Linder. So you had to switch the suspicion on to him – hence the penknife which you posted off to me. It was a knife that Linder had lent to your father.'

Knight began to show some signs of weakening.

'It's a lie! A pack of lies!' he cried. 'You're trying to fake a case against me!'

Sir James, who had not spoken for some little time said:

'On the contrary, Mr Knight, I think you've built up a pretty strong case against yourself. I must ask you to come back to the Yard and—'

Before he could finish his sentence, Knight had moved quickly towards the door.

'Stay where you are – everybody!' he ordered. They could see he was holding a small revolver which he had snatched from an inside pocket.

'Put that gun down!' snapped Wyatt, gripping his walking-stick.

Knight ignored him and backed another pace.

Lathom's hand closed over the syphon on the side-table near him. But Knight noticed the movement.

'Leave it alone, Inspector!' he cried, but Lathom had already lifted the syphon as if to throw it.

The report of the revolver sounded like a small cannon, and Lathom dropped the syphon and clutched his wrist.

In the resulting confusion, Knight grabbed hold of Sally and held her in front of him as he faced the others.

'That'll prove I'm not fooling,' he said grimly. 'Now, Mrs Wyatt, move back to the door – and if anybody tries to stop me I shall shoot first at Mrs Wyatt.'

He was about a yard from the door when it opened abruptly and Fred Porter's head appeared.

'They said at the Yard I'd find you here—' he began, then suddenly appreciated the situation. Before Knight could turn his head, a hefty right uppercut had lifted him a couple of inches off the floor. The revolver discharged itself into the ceiling, and Sally had already ducked out of the line of fire.

Knight was half stunned by the blow, and it was a matter of seconds before Lathom and Wyatt had overpowered him.

The person most concerned about the whole business was Fred later.

'I hope I did right, Sir James,' he said anxiously. 'Blimey, the last time I let loose that uppercut, it half killed a pal o' mine in the Police Boxing Championships.'

'You certainly came in at just the right moment, Fred,' said Wyatt a trifle breathlessly. 'Are you all right, Sally?'

'Yes, I'm fine. But the inspector's wrist is bleeding.'

'I'll see to it,' said Doctor Fraser at once, and began to examine the flesh wound.

After the guests had gone, Wyatt turned to Fred and said gratefully:

'Well, we weren't expecting you, Fred, but it was lucky you dropped in just then.' Fred rubbed his bruised knuckles and said:

'I've been trying all day to get you on the phone, but you were out. We've been having a bit of trouble down on the farm.'

'Oh, dear,' said Sally. 'What is it?'

'It's been our unlucky week, you might say,' sighed Fred. 'Hodgetts' bullocks got in the orchard Sunday, and chewed up half the new trees, and the rain has played the devil with the raspberries.'

Wyatt looked across at Sally.

'I'm glad you found us, Fred,' he said quietly, 'it's time we came home. As soon as I've written my report on this case we'll be there.'

Two hours later, Wyatt, Sally and Sir James Perivale sat in the Wyatts' temporary flat. After accompanying Lathom and Maurice Knight to the Yard, Sir James had returned, on their invitation, for a 'nightcap' and a last discussion on the 'Rossiter' affair.

The room was lighted only by a small table lamp, and the fireglow flickered cheerfully on the small group. While he was waiting for Perivale, Wyatt had completed his notes on the case, and he still had the neat blue file on the arm of his chair. He would dictate the full report to a stenographer at the Yard first thing in the morning and they would be home by lunch-time, he planned.

'I don't know what we'd have done without you on this case, Wyatt,' said Sir James generously. He paused and looked across at Sally. 'I suppose there's no chance of you both coming back here permanently?' he added hesitantly.

Sally smiled and shook her head.

'We're both too fond of the country now,' she replied, looking across at her husband, and receiving a confirmatory nod. 'And there's Lionel's health to be considered.'

Wyatt leaned over and patted his wife's hand.

'It's been nice to come back, Sir James,' he admitted,

'but I'm afraid it's a case of back to the land for Sally and me.'

'How I envy you,' said Perivale, yawning and stretching his arms. 'Well, I'm no end grateful for all you've done. And now I really should be making a move.'

'Oh, no, Sir James,' said Sally. 'It's only half-past eleven. I've got lots of things I want to ask you and Lionel about this case.'

'Have you indeed?' murmured Perivale, with a slight lift of his bushy grey eyebrows. 'Well, I can't guarantee that I'll be able to give you all the answers. In fact I'd be quite interested to hear some of your husband's explanations of the various side issues. I'm looking forward to seeing his full report.'

Sally settled more comfortably in her chair, and Wyatt put another log on the fire.

'Question number one,' began Sally. 'Why did Maurice Knight want to throw suspicion on Luigi, who was a useful member of the organization?'

'I think I know the answer to that,' said Perivale. 'Knight knew that Luigi had ideas of his own about running the organization. He was convinced that Luigi wouldn't be so anxious to do that if the police were after him.'

Sally looked far from convinced.

'Are you sure that Luigi wanted to take over?' she asked.

'No doubt about it,' replied Wyatt. 'Even when he thought the police were suspicious, he was still game. Knight greatly underestimated his man there. I'm inclined to think we did, too!'

'He'd certainly got an ace or two up his sleeve,' conceded Perivale. 'I could never quite weigh up that business with the young waiter fellow.'

'You mean the impersonator – Carver? Well, Luigi managed to get it out of Carver that Knight had bribed him to do that impersonation on the telephone to Sir Donald Angus. But Luigi covered himself very neatly by making Carver confess that he received his instructions from Doctor Fraser.'

'What was the point of that?' asked Sally, looking somewhat puzzled.

'Because Luigi thought that once he had eliminated Knight then it would be a nice cover for him if we went on suspecting Doctor Fraser.'

Perivale nodded thoughtfully as Wyatt rammed home a charge of tobacco in his cherrywood pipe. 'I can't say that had occurred to me before, Wyatt,' he admitted. 'That fellow Luigi had his wits about him. Look how he coolly produced those two fellows to go bail for him; then as soon as he's free he immediately goes after Knight. He'd got a nerve all right!'

There was silence for some seconds while Sally digested this and Wyatt sucked energetically at his pipe.

Wyatt opened the file on the arm of his chair and began thoughtfully turning over his notes.

'It rather mystifies me,' went on Sally, 'why Knight walked in on us that night in Coster Row. He seemed to be quite anxious to draw attention to himself on that occasion.'

'Of course he did!' nodded Wyatt. 'He went down there to collect the money from Reed, suddenly realized that the Professor was in no condition to be trusted, and immediately decided to get rid of him. Under those circumstances, he had to draw attention to himself. He simply daren't take the risk of being spotted.'

'You see, Sally,' explained Perivale, leaning towards her

on the arm of his chair, 'Knight was playing the part of the amateur detective, and you expect the amateur detective to pop up in unexpected places and poke his nose into things that don't concern him.'

'Exactly, Sir James,' agreed Wyatt.

'I suppose it was Luigi who killed the taxi driver, Vic Taylor,' she asked.

'Naturally. It would have put Luigi in a difficult spot if Taylor had identified him as the man who bribed him to kidnap you.'

Perivale lay back and lighted a cigarette.

'When did you first suspect that Knight was "Mr Rossiter"?' he asked. 'Was it that night you bumped into him at the Madrid?'

'That's a pretty smart guess, Sir James. It was that night, as a matter of fact. When I told Knight about Tyson's death he was considerably taken aback. I couldn't quite see why he should be so affected by the news; after all, he was only supposed to have met Tyson once in his life. That was the time he interviewed him down at Shorecombe.'

'I noticed that, too,' said Sally. 'But it never occurred to me to suspect any closer link between them.'

Perivale flicked the ash from his cigarette.

'Well, quite frankly, I suspected Angus,' he confessed, 'and Lathom spent days hob-nobbing with Linder, quite certain he was our man.'

'Even Sally knew better,' smiled Wyatt in some amusement. 'Her hunch turned out to be a pretty good one. I really think you should get her to give some lectures at Hendon, Sir James!'

'I was never one to say: "I told you so",' said Sally, the merest trace of a self-satisfied smile playing round her lips.

As Sir James rose to leave he said to Wyatt:

'If ever you should change your mind about coming back, I can promise you'll be next in line for the first Chief Inspector vacancy.'

'I'll keep it in mind,' promised Wyatt as he saw his guest to the door.

When he returned to the lounge Sally was collecting the glasses and generally tidying up the room.

'Well, that's the end of Ariman, alias "Mr Rossiter",' she murmured. 'Are you satisfied, Inspector Wyatt, or does the idea of being promoted to Chief Inspector interest you?'

He squeezed her shoulder.

'I'd sooner be plain Farmer Wyatt, of Green Orchard, Lusham,' he replied. 'What about you?'

She smiled provokingly and playfully ruffled his hair.

'If it's all the same to you,' she said, 'I'll just go on being plain Mrs Wyatt of the same address.'

Paul Temple's
White Christmas

This complete short story was specially written by Francis Durbridge for the Christmas 1946 edition of *Radio Times*, following the original broadcast of *Paul Temple and the Gregory Affair*, whose final episode had aired on Thursday 19 December.

Steve stopped talking about Switzerland, tore up the Winter Sports brochure, and went out shopping. She said that she would meet Temple at the Penguin Club at a quarter past four. 'I shan't be a minute later than four-fifteen,' she said gaily.

That was two hours ago.

It was now precisely twenty-seven-and-a-half minutes past five and Temple was still waiting. He sat with his back to the bar staring out at the rain and drinking a dry martini. Cecil, the bar-tender, was talking about *The Gregory Affair*. He'd been talking about *The Gregory Affair* for thirty-seven minutes. Temple was tired. He was tired of waiting, of the Club, of Cecil, of hearing about *The Gregory Affair*, and – most of all – he was tired of the rain. He was almost beginning to wish that he'd taken Steve's advice about Switzerland.

It had just gone half-past five when Steve arrived. She put her parcels down on the high stool and smiled at Cecil. 'It's filthy weather, Paul – don't you wish we'd gone to Switzerland?'

Temple brought his wristlet watch dangerously near her veil. He said: 'It's five-thirty, you're just an hour and a quarter late, Steve!'

'Yes. I bumped into Freda Gwenn and she never stopped talking. The poor dear's wildly excited.'

'Why is she excited?'

'She's going to Switzerland for Christmas and ...'

Temple took Steve by the arm, said goodbye to Cecil, and picked up the parcels.

They stood for a moment in the doorway looking out at the rain. 'If there's anything I like better than a good old English winter,' said Steve, 'it's a good old English summer.'

Temple said: 'What do you expect at this time of the year?'

'I know what I'd like! I'd like ...'

'You'd like to slide on your posterior all day,' said Temple, 'and dance your feet off all night.'

Steve said: 'You *are* in a pleasant mood, darling! What you need is plenty of fresh air and exercise.' She was thinking of St Moritz and the Palace Hotel skating rink.

Temple nodded. 'It's a good idea, we'll walk back to the flat.'

It was still raining but they walked.

When they got back to the flat there was a note from Charlie. It was on the small table in the hall and like most of Charlie's notes it was brief and to the point. '*Off to the Palais de Danse. Sir Graham rang up – he's ringing again. Be good. Charlie.*'

Temple didn't care very much for the 'be good' touch, but it was typical of Charlie. It was an hour later when Sir Graham telephoned. Steve was in the bathroom.

'You remember that Luxembourg counterfeit business you

helped us with last year?' the Commissioner said. Temple remembered it only too well. For one thing the leader of the organisation – a man called Howell – had mysteriously disappeared.

'Yes. I remember it, Sir Graham. Don't tell me you've caught up with the elusive Mr Howell?'

'We haven't, but it rather looks as if the Swiss people have. They arrested a man they believe to be Howell just over twenty-four hours ago.'

'What happened?'

'Apparently this fellow had managed to get some sort of an organisation together and was ready to start work at Grindelwald. By a sheer stroke of genius the Swiss authorities caught up with him.'

'Did they get the rest of the organisation?'

'No, I'm afraid they didn't.' Forbes laughed. 'As a matter of fact they're not absolutely certain that they've got Howell.'

'What do you mean?'

Forbes said: 'Well, the Swiss people seem to think that while Howell was lying low after the Luxembourg business he had a fairly drastic facial operation: you know the sort of thing – plastic surgery.'

Temple could hear Steve splashing about in the bathroom. He said in a low voice: 'Do I come into this, Sir Graham?'

'I'm rather afraid you do, Temple,' said Sir Graham. 'The Swiss authorities want somebody to go out there and identify Howell. Preferably somebody who worked on the Luxembourg business.'

'Where is Howell?'

'He was arrested at Grindelwald but they've taken him to Interlaken. I rather gather the police are a little frightened that the rest of the gang might try to rescue him.'

Temple said: 'When do you expect us to leave?'

He heard Forbes chuckling at the other end of the wire.

'I thought Steve would have to come into the picture!' he said. 'You leave tomorrow morning on the eleven o'clock 'plane. You'll land at Berne and go on to Interlaken by train.'

Temple said goodbye, put down the receiver, lit a cigarette, and sat watching the bathroom door. After a little while the door opened and Steve appeared. She was wearing a grey negligée. Temple had always thought it was a very nice negligée.

Temple said: 'I've got a surprise for you. I'll give you three guesses.'

Steve said: 'It's stopped raining.'

'No.'

'MGM have bought your last novel?'

'No.'

Steve brushed her hair with the towel. 'My intuition isn't working tonight. I give up.'

Temple said: 'It looks like being a White Christmas after all. We leave for Berne tomorrow morning.'

The 'plane landed at the airport and Temple and Steve made their way towards the Customs. Temple took one look at the weather. It was raining. 'If there's one thing I like better than a good old Swiss winter,' he said, 'it's a good old Swiss summer.'

Steve laughed and took him by the arm. There was a man waiting for them at the barrier. A tall, clean-shaven, rather distinguished looking man in a dark brown overcoat.

He touched his hat to Steve and addressed Temple:

'Mr Paul Temple?'

'Yes?'

'My name is Velquez, sir. Inspector Velquez. I've been asked by the authorities to drive you into Berne.'

Temple eyed him cautiously, and said: 'Why Berne, Inspector?'

The man smiled. 'We've taken Howell to Berne, sir. We thought it might save time. My car is at your disposal.'

Temple said: 'Well, Inspector, my instructions are to proceed by train to Interlaken. I think I ought to get this change of programme confirmed by your superior.'

Velquez smiled. He had quite a pleasant smile. 'Then I advise you to telephone through to headquarters,' he said, 'you'll find the telephone in the waiting room and the number is Interlaken 9–8974. Ask for M. Dumas.'

Steve stayed with Velquez while Temple telephoned.

It was apparently M. Dumas himself who answered the telephone. He was extremely affable and rather amused by the precaution Paul Temple had taken.

'Velquez is certainly one of our men,' he said, 'he'll have you here within twenty minutes.'

'How do you know he's your man?' said Temple, 'he might be an impostor!'

'Describe him!' snapped Dumas, and there was no mistaking the note of asperity in his voice.

Paul Temple described Velquez.

Dumas said: 'You've nothing to worry about, Mr Temple – that's Velquez all right.'

Temple put down the receiver, walked out of the telephone booth, and went back to Velquez. Velquez was holding his umbrella over Steve and they appeared to be getting along famously together.

He smiled when he saw Temple approaching.

'Well,' said Velquez, 'I take it I'm to have the pleasure of your company?'

Temple nodded, grinned, and put his hand in his inside pocket. Both Velquez and Steve expected him to take out

245

his cigarette case: they were not unnaturally surprised when they saw the revolver he was holding. It must be recorded in fact that Velquez was surprised, nervous, agitated, and not a little frightened.

He had good reason to be – the revolver was pointing directly at him.

Paul Temple and Steve had left the electric train and were making their way towards the start of the snow run. It was Christmas Eve.

As she started to fasten her skis, Steve said:

'I suppose Velquez – the man who met us at the airport – was a friend of Howell's?'

'A very close friend,' said Temple. 'The idea, apparently, was to abduct us and hold us as hostages until Howell was released.'

'And what about the telephone call? Did you get through to that number Velquez gave you?'

Temple nodded. 'I got through all right and the old boy at the other end – a confederate of Velquez's – confirmed that Velquez was a member of the Police.'

'Then what made you suspicious?'

Temple smiled. 'I described Velquez to his friend as a tall, rather distinguished looking man with spectacles.'

'But he didn't wear spectacles!'

'Of course he didn't,' said Temple, 'but his friend was just a trifle too anxious to be obliging *and immediately jumped to the conclusion that Velquez had disguised himself for the occasion!*'

Steve looked puzzled for a split second, then she began to laugh. She was still laughing when she began her downward swoop with far less caution than her lack of practice warranted. At the first difficult turn she capsized in a smother of white foam, and Temple, barely ten yards behind, was unable to avoid her.

They sat regarding each other for a moment, then Temple managed to regain his feet and went over to give her a hand.

As they brushed the snow off their clothes Paul Temple looked at his wife and grinned.

'We're certainly having a White Christmas!' he said.

BY THE SAME AUTHOR

Beware of Johnny Washington

When a gang of desperate criminals begins leaving calling cards inscribed '*With the Compliments of Johnny Washington*', the real Johnny Washington is encouraged by an attractive newspaper columnist to throw in his lot with the police. Johnny, an American 'gentleman of leisure' who has settled at a quiet country house in Kent to enjoy the fishing, soon finds himself involved with the mysterious Horatio Quince, a retired schoolmaster who is on the trail of the gang's unscrupulous leader, the elusive 'Grey Moose'.

Best known for creating *Paul Temple* for BBC radio in 1938, Francis Durbridge's prolific output of crime and mystery stories, encompassing plays, radio, television, films and books, made him a household name for more than 50 years. A new radio character, *Johnny Washington Esquire*, hit the airwaves in 1949, leading to the publication of this one-off novel in 1951.

This Detective Club classic is introduced by writer and bibliographer Melvyn Barnes, author of *Francis Durbridge: A Centenary Appreciation*, who reveals how Johnny Washington's only literary outing was actually a reworking of Durbridge's own *Send for Paul Temple*.